Advance praise for DOWN FOR WHATEVER

"Frederick Smith's *Down for Whatever* is proudly about life in Los Angeles, about how we all live; trying to find love, trying to make sense of our lives, but few of us write more honestly or so entertainingly about that struggle."

Jervey Tervalon, author of *Understand This*

"Finally, the boyz come out of the hood. Fresh, funny and real. Queer Latino and African American male characters living, loving and telling it like it is in present day L.A. Playful with serious insight. Bravo Mr. Smith on your first novel and certainly not your last."

Monica Palacios, Writer/Performer,
"The Original Sufer Chola"

"In *Down for Whatever*, Frederick Smith brings us an utterly unique, singular and strong new voice that is smart, sexy, hip, painfully honest and wickedly funny. Smith's debut novel fearlessly mixes it up, crossing borders of race, class and culture as he takes us inside the world of young black and brown gay L.A. men looking for love. An exhilarating debut. More please!"

Denise Hamilton, author of the bestselling
"Eve Diamond" series

"With his wonderfully wicked sense of humor on every page, Frederick Smith's *Down for Whatever* is a fabulous romp of colliding egos and cultures, longing and lust, and most of all, friendship. An absolute delight to read."

Kerry Madden, author of *Gentle's Holler*

"A stupendous debut novel, *Down for Whatever* is a must read! Unapologetically black and unabashedly gay Smith is a great writer akin to the luminaries of the Harlem Renaissance and James Baldwin. His seductive and wonderfully vivid literary style offers the reader layered complex portraits of four L.A. African American and Latino gay men searching for love devoid of stereotypes and clichéd sentimentalities."

Rev. Irene Monroe, religion columnist,
The Religion Thang

DOWN FOR WHATEVER

FREDERICK SMITH

KENSINGTON BOOKS
http://www.kensingtonbooks.com

Author's Note: This is a work of fiction. It is inspired by my emotions and personal responses to issues that have arisen among friends, colleagues, family, family of friends, and society at large. Some of the issues and scenes take place at real places and locations. Neither the characters portrayed here nor any of the events that happen in the novel should be construed or understood or implied as real, regardless if they take place in real or fictional locations. They are all a product and result of my imagination.

KENSINGTON BOOKS are published by

Kensington Publishing Corp.
850 Third Avenue
New York, NY 10022

All Kensington titles, imprints and distributed lines are available at special quantity discounts for bulk purchases for sales promotion, premiums, fund-raising, educational or institutional use.

Special book excerpts or customized printings can also be created to fit specific needs. For details, write or phone the office of the Kensington Special Sales Manager: Kensington Publishing Corp., 850 Third Avenue, New York, NY 10022. Attn. Special Sales Department. Phone: 1-800-221-2647.

Kensington and the K logo Reg. U.S. Pat & TM Off

ISBN: 0-7582-0979-7

First Kensington Trade Paperback Printing: July 2005
10 9 8 7 6 5 4 3 2 1

Printed in the United States of America

Acknowledgments

I am grateful to many people for their support and encouragement. First to my parents and sister, Fred, Sandra, and Monica Smith. Thanks to my extended family: the Davis, Lytle, Thomas, Franklin, Neal, Burks, Watkins, Vernon, and Herrera families.

Thanks to my teachers and writing mentors who encouraged my writing from childhood, teachers like Mary Ramsey, Thelma Dinwiddie, Dana Payne, Ben Johnson, and Susan Watson.

Thanks to the authors who mentored and encouraged me to pursue my writing seriously: Kerry Madden-Lunsford, Denise Hamilton, Jervey Tervalon, Tayari Jones, Dana Johnson, Keith Boykin, Helen Zia, and Reverend Irene Monroe. I appreciate the support and critiques by my writing workshops: International Black Writers and Artists Los Angeles (especially Nancy Hayes and Randy Ross), Silver Lake Advanced Writing Group (Larry, Stephanie, Lori, Slade, Matthew, Elaine, Catherine), and VONA Voices Novel Workshop (Diem, Kira, Lea, Gail, Sara, Rhonda, Jeanne, Laura, Meeta, Ida, Melanie, Amy).

Thanks to my first readers for their feedback: Crystal Irby, Daniel Dejene, Oskar Ayon, and Manuel Cruz. For their support, encouragement, and approving my timeoff requests to do my fiction thing: Daria Yudacufski, Connie Martinez and the Cross Cultural Centers/University-Student Union staff at Cal State L.A.

For their ability to drag me away from my computer long enough to have drinks and dinner: David Herrera, Belinda and Javier Vazquez, Howard Perez, Eddie Guillen, Daryl

Garcia, Matt Rees, Colleen McLaughlin, Faith Kazmi, Daniel Choi, Sarah Figueroa, Joel Torrez, Jr., Rhonda Mitchell, Sabrina Feeley, Patrick Bailey, Bryant Alexander, Bitta Farahmaud and Kenrick Ali.

Thank you Ibarionex for the cool photos, and Ted and Monica for the cool website design.

Thanks to my literary agent, Nicholas Roman Lewis, whose feedback, humor, confidence and ability to keep it real have been most appreciated.

Finally, a big BIG thanks to my editor, John Scognamiglio, who, along with the team at Kensington, has been supportive, encouraging and most fun to work with during my first book process. Anyone who I may have forgotten, fill in your name here _____, and know that I thank you too!☺

Chapter 1

KEITH

If you blink, you'd miss finding Tempo.

Tucked away in a strip mall with inexpensive family eateries, hair salons, currency exchanges and prepaid cell phone stores, the allure of blending in is why Tempo attracts such an eclectic mix of men. It's low key and wouldn't attract attention from an unsuspecting girlfriend or passerby on the street. Especially those who think men who like men only hang out further west on Santa Monica Boulevard.

Something about Wrangler jeans, Tony Lama boots, Stetson *tejanas* (cowboy hats) and Panhandle Slim fitted shirts make men look extra macho while they're standing out front smoking cigarettes, catching up on the latest *chisme* with each other. The occasional *cholo* and *veterano*, Salvadoreño and black and out-of-place West Hollywood boy speckle the line, which has grown past the El Pollo Loco restaurant and onto the sidewalk. They're all beautiful—in a blue-collar sort of way. Definitely not a fetish. Just something attractive. You know?

What you don't know is I'm breaking my annual New Year's resolution, renewed just six weeks ago: No more late nights out, no more hangovers, and definitely no more looking for love in all the wrong places.

But here I am once again at the Sunday *tardeada*, an afternoon party, at Club Tempo in Hollywood, which hosts a who's who of L.A.'s closeted, married and butch Latino men and their fans. I'm with my on again/off again, much younger and much better built friend Rafael. That was another one of my New Year's resolutions: Be nice to Rafael. That's another story, as you'll find out soon enough.

Another thing you don't know is I don't do the waiting-in-line thing. So I give the valet a healthy tip to let Rafael and me breeze through security and to the ticket window. I pay both our cover charges—I can't believe Rafael only brought twenty dollars with him—and get our numbered tickets, which serve as our passports to the different floors in the club.

The live band, which consists of accordions, drums and male singers singing in the popular off-key *norteña* style, is in the *vaquero* room on my right, the reggaeton and hip-hop music is blasting to my left, and I get excited about the night. I feel at home. Weird, I know. I'm black. And standing in a room full of hard-core, full-blooded Mexican men. It's a packed house and the energy feels positive, even on a chilly, sixty-degree evening in February. So far, I'm in a good mood, not feeling guilty about breaking my New Year's resolution, and I just want to find our favorite Tempo waiter and get a pitcher of beer for Rafael and me. Not my normal choice of drink, but when in Rome . . .

Well, there *was* a Rafael and me like five minutes ago, but Rafael has gone off to the bathroom and disappeared. This is Rafael's little game. He gets "lost." Says he can't find you. You end up partying alone. Some party and friend, huh?

So I down one beer very quickly and pour another one right away. I have to look occupied. *Keep your head up, smile, watch all the happy couples pass you by. Like you're part of the furniture here. Like you're invisible.* I thought the days of being invisible were over when I stopped trying to fit in with white boys at white bars. *It's okay. Pretend you're a pageant contestant and smile at everyone, whether you know them or not.*

I told myself I was through hanging out with Rafael after his hookup with the boy I wanted last night—the black personal trainer from our gym. Yeah, I broke the New Year's resolution last night too. Kinda went like this: Arena is a huge warehouse club. Where Tempo is laid back and leisurely, Arena is fast and frenetic. Shell out fifty dollars in less than five minutes for cover charge, coat check, a shot of Cazadores tequila and a weak cocktail. Walk through the dance floor crowd like you're Toni Braxton in the video for "He Wasn't Man Enough for Me," and you and your boys sip on your drinks, smile and, in tandem, casually rotate and dance your circle of friends around so you can get a 360-degree view of the crowd dancing around your circle. No sweating allowed, so after ten minutes of dancing, decide to go upstairs. Take the side ramp, so that the three thousand club guests who didn't see you on the dance floor can see you and your boys work the forty-five-degree angled runway. Pray you don't slip on your slick-bottomed shoes or miss a beat of the synchronized steps you and your boys have perfected like you're cast members of the male brown-and-black version of *Sex and the City* or the Spanish-language soap *Soñadoras*. While smoking a Dunhill, not a run-of-the-mill domestic, eye some guys across the patio, see a few closet cases from the gym and pick out one you'd like to hook up with. You've seen him out and about for three years since moving to L.A., made eye contact and smiled before, but never actually talked to each other. It's so third grade, but you hope this one likes you back for a change. He doesn't. He likes your friend Rafael instead. As usual, I'm the odd man out. Rafael gets the man he wants. Marco Antonio, my best friend, has his actor boyfriend, Alex.

Tommie, my condo mate, has his college basketball player, Tyrell. Love, or at least a cheap one-night-stand, is for everyone else. Not for me.

Maybe things will be different tonight at Tempo. Maybe not.

Tonight, I'm more like Rafael's taxi driver and errand boy. I have his cigarettes, keys and funky little twenty-dollar bill. He waltzes over with some cute Mexican cowboy in cinnamon-colored leather chaps, drops off their drinks by me, and they head out to the dance floor. I swear I overhear Rafael say I'm like his old-maid chaperone. My Spanish is a lot better than he thinks. Screw him. Let him have his fun. I don't want him around anyway. My good mood is gone. I'm ready to go.

I never should have broken my New Year's resolution to come out. Sundays are always too crowded at Tempo anyway, with *chicos* looking for cheap *cerveza* and *carne asada*. And even as I complain about my broken resolution, I'm in awe of the blue-collar boys here and this mini-culture of the gay world that most people don't realize exists. I never imagined I, the preacher's son and church boy from Detroit, would hang out in a place filled with cowboy hats, boots and *vaqueros*. Latino men who work with their hands. Who work the earth and in factories and restaurants for hourly wages and no benefits. Who marry women but have sex with men. Who look like they could be someone's father, *primo*, *tío* or the next-door neighbor who played soccer and baseball with your older brother. Latinos who like the sounds of their old countries, like *quebraditas*, *rancheras* and *cumbias*, but enjoy life in the new country. But I am here now and taking in the scene. I know they must look at me and wonder what the hell I'm doing here. I can only imagine their thoughts: *Why isn't he over at Catch One or one of the Ivan Daniel First Fridayz L.A. events?* I wish I could make an announcement: *I'm a fan. I appreciate the culture. I'm not just here to exoticize. I'm not looking for a mail-order partner or a Latino houseboy. And I do like black men, by the way, thank you.*

So I'm sitting on a wooden barstool on the side of the dance floor. The pitcher of beer I was sharing with Rafael is warm now and losing its bite. I don't want any more, but I don't want to just sit here by myself and look bored. I pour a little from the pitcher, and it foams up to the top of my plastic cup. Great. Warm fuzz. I feel like Charlie Brown minus the bag of rocks.

I feel a tap on my shoulder. To my relief, it's my friend Chris Aquino, linked arm-in-arm with two young *muchachos* and without his partner, Jake.

"¿*Qué pasa*, Keith?" Chris asks and air kisses around the side of my face. "Are you here alone, or with Marco and Tommie?"

"Rafael's out there dancing. Marco's with the actor boyfriend. Tommie's at home."

"Cool. Cool. Good to hear it. Guys, this is my good friend from Stanford—Keith."

We do the customary handshakes and cocktail toast. We're an odd bunch. A thirty-something Filipino who has botoxed himself back to twenty. An almost-thirty black. And two post-pubescent Latinos. They're obviously models on Chris's partner's X-rated Web site, based on how much crème brûlée-colored abs and biceps they're showing in the middle of winter in L.A. The two pretty-boys look brainless, like they couldn't care less about me being in their mix, so I ask if they want refills on their Cosmopolitans. They decline. They have to meet with some other friends on the second floor. So urgent, I'm sure. Air kisses. Good-bye.

But I look around the club anyway, and through the crowd I see Rafael dancing chest-to-chest with yet another new boy. We saw this one waiting in line when we pulled into the parking lot. Two boys in ten minutes. What a slut. I turn away quickly so Rafael can't see me watching him, and I'm staring into the chest and then eyes and face of a really, really handsome man standing to my right. He's like a taller version of that Mexican American singer I like, Rogelio Martínez, complete with goatee, beautiful dark brown eyes with long lashes surrounding them and golden bronze skin. He smiles, nods and leans closer to me, the brim of his *tejana* bumping the top of my head,

"*Hola, guapo. ¿Como estas?*" he asks and smiles.

"*Bien, gracias. Pero, no hablo mucho español.*"

"Well, I speak English too." He flashes his beautiful white teeth again. Nice lips, too. "*¿Como te llamas?* What's your name?"

"Keith. What's yours?" I shout above the music, but then the DJ stops and I'm shouting in the semiquiet room. I'm embarrassed.

"Cesar."

"*Con mucho gusto,* Cesar."

"Good to meet you, too, Keith."

I don't know what to say next, because Cesar's so good-looking and I can't get past it. He's really talking to me?

"I like your shirt, Keith. Red's a good color for your skin tone. A gift from your Valentine?"

"I'm single, but thanks for the compliment. You look nice, too."

"Thanks," he says and smiles. The DJ has started a new song, and Cesar leans down against my ear again so I can hear. "I'm not with anyone either. It's always the finest boys who're single. And don't worry, I won't ask you why you don't have a boyfriend."

"You're funny, Cesar."

"You're very handsome, Keith. *¿Eres Dominicano? ¿Cubano? ¿Boriqua?*"

"Who? Me?"

"Who am I with?" He smiles, winks and puts his arm around my shoulder. I smile back, thinking about how I love physically looking up at a man for a change. And his gold-colored sweater shimmers and matches his skin perfectly. I just pray he doesn't slide his hand down any farther, or else he'll be feeling a little bit of love handle.

"*Soy de Michoacán.*"

"What?" He looks confused over my comment that I'm from the Mexican state of Michoacán. It doesn't register.

"Got you!" I say and laugh. "I'm African American. Black. Don't know much more than that about my background. History."

"Tell me about it. So much history robbed and erased," Cesar says.

"Whoa. You're getting real activist. I like it."

"I know. Don't trip, Keith. I'm like that sometimes, usually not in clubs."

They obviously forgot to turn on the air conditioner, and with all these grown men dancing up a storm—now playing: Ana Bárbara's "Bandido"—it's like a downtown L.A. sweatshop. I dab myself with my handkerchief, and Cesar does the same with his. And we haven't even danced yet. We decide to walk outside to the smoking patio to talk more without competing with the music.

"You look nice in the natural light, Keith."

"Thanks. You're no 'Monet' either," I say, referring to boys who look cute in club lighting, but less than cute when the lights go up. "So what do you do, Cesar?"

"I teach at Pasadena City College and Santa Monica College. Chicano studies and history classes, mostly."

"Really? So you *are* an activist? You look too young to be a professor." He looks barely twenty-one.

"I'm twenty-nine. What about you?" Cesar asks.

"I'm twenty-nine, too."

"Let me guess what you do, Keith. Model?"

Boy, Cesar's trying to flatter me. "Nope."

"Hairstylist?"

Funny. "Think again."

"Retail queen?"

"Wrong again, Cesar. One more guess or you'll have to pay the price."

"Hmmm. I think I wanna pay the price, Keith." Cesar pats my butt.

"Come on."

"Let me see," Cesar says and breaks away from me. He spins me around. "A professional dancer? '*La Negra Tiene Tumbao*'? Celia Cruz wrote that for you, huh? I've seen your moves before."

We both laugh. I'm far from a great dancer, and though I've got rhythm, sometimes I end up looking like a dancer stuck on repeat—same arm, leg and hip movements over and over on the dance floor.

"No, Cesar. I do consulting. Diversity training." I hand him my business card.

"So you're kind of an activist, too. That's cool. Very needed here in L.A."

"It's fun and frustrating at the same time. L.A.'s got issues," I say.

"You must not be from here, dogging my city like that."

"Michigan," I say and put my hand up, as any true Midwesterner would, and point to the bottom right where my hometown is. "Get it now . . . about being from Michoacán?"

"Keith's got jokes, I see. I did my grad work in Ann Arbor. I'm A.B.D."

Hmmm, not bad. A Ph.D in the making; just needs to write the dissertation.

"I did undergrad and grad at Stanford, but I grew up in Detroit."

"We probably crossed paths in Metro Airport at holiday breaks. Wouldn't that be funny?"

"Yeah. I think about weird stuff like that all the time."

"My family's from Sinaloa in Mexico, but we moved here when I was two."

"That's cool. I've never been there, but went to Jalisco once to visit Guadalajara and Puerto Vallarta for spring break when I was a student. Part community service, but mostly fun."

"It's nice over there, but you have to come see my town and my family one day," he says. "See, there's the kind of guy you take home, and the kind of guy you take home to the family. I can tell you're the second kind."

I know I didn't just hear Cesar making an invitation for the future. To meet the family? Cool.

"So, Cesar, your family knows about you? Being with men, that is?"

"My traditional Mexican family? No way."

"So how do you get around the dating issue? They must ask about it."

"I'd have to tell them you're a colleague or something," he says. "What about yours?"

"They know, but not because I told them," I say. "They found a letter I wrote to the first guy I dated, someone from Stanford, when I was home on a holiday break, and they said I should never bring that part of me home. My dad's a minister, so it's total 'don't ask, don't tell' in our house. So we don't talk about it. It's cool. I respect their house, you know?"

"That's deep," Cesar says. "A sinner on Saturday and an angel on Sunday."

"I'm a good boy."

We both laugh and say, "Yeah, right," at the same time.

"I'm talked out, Keith. ¿*Quieres bailar*? Wanna dance?"

"Sure. Why not?"

Besides, I like the song the DJ just put on—Celia Cruz's *"La Negra Tiene Tumbao"*—and dancing with Cesar will give me a chance to one-up Rafael. Especially when he sees Cesar is at least six-foot-three, looks quite muscular in his tight ribbed sweater, and is very much a gentleman as he leads me through the crowded dance floor. His fingers and hands feel strong and very soft, like he's not afraid of a good manicure. Cesar doesn't notice, or pretends not to notice, that everyone's eyeing him up and down. I notice the looks, though. But for the moment it feels good having him grab my hand and give it a little reassuring squeeze.

"Is this okay?" Cesar asks referring to a spot in the middle of the dance floor.

"It's fine. Just fine," I say, and position myself so Rafael can see my face and the back of Cesar's head.

I'm feeling comfortable and smile. Cesar pulls me closer and my head leans on his chest. I breathe in his masculine scent, a natural spicy fragrance. I wonder, am I dreaming? Is this man actually here, holding me, allowing me to lean against him? Is he enjoying this as much as I am? Am I boring him? Am I good-looking enough for him? Do I feel fat to him? Does he care that people are staring at us, this interracial dance couple? Can he feel my nervous heartbeat against his body? I think about the long dry spell I've been through the past couple of years and feel optimistic Cesar could be the one to end it. Oh, God, please let this work out. No games. No drama. Please let the drought be over. Please let me find a real boyfriend before I'm thirty.

The music stops as the DJ steps aside for another live band to start playing, and Cesar and I separate and move to the side of the floor.

"Keith . . ."

"Cesar . . ."

"You first."

"No. You."

I look up at him and he is looking down into my eyes, and I swear he's pursing his full lips as if he's ready to kiss me.

"You have nice lips, Keith."

"Thanks. You do too."

"This feels nice, Keith." Cesar rubs my back and smiles.

"I was gonna say the same thing," I say, and then think about the next big question on my mind. I have to know if this is real. "It's not a problem or an issue that I'm black, is it?"

"You are? Black?" Cesar asks and backs away to inspect my face. "When I see you, I don't see black. I just see a human."

"You're so full of it, Cesar."

"Of course it's a joke, Keith. And just so you know, I only date men of color, so if they're black, brown, red, or yellow, citizens or illegals, *chunties* or professionals, it's all right with me. I just haven't gone white."

"You're not into being objectified? It's like soooooo twenty-first century," I say in my best L.A. Valley Girl impersonation.

He joins in the joking. "I can't wait to get my little Latino houseboy, so he can cook and clean and *chupa mi pinga* every night."

"Groovy, Cesar. Where do I sign up?"

"Silly boy," Cesar says.

"I can't believe you're actually smart, and funny, and in a club," I hear myself saying to Cesar. I pinch myself. Don't want to appear desperate or clingy. And I want to make sure this isn't a dream. I know there's got to be a catch. There always is.

"So what are we going to do about it, Keith?"

"Let's just see what happens."

"I'm cool with that," he says and hugs me tight against him. By now he's felt the ten extra pounds on me, but so far, no reaction.

"You know what? I need to take a bathroom break," I say.

"No problem," Cesar says. "I need to find my friends. I'll be standing over where we met."

"Cool."

"Maybe we can exchange numbers, Keith? I'd love to meet for coffee or dinner."

"Sure."

"Don't be long."

I find a private stall and give myself my own pageant-winner performance. Full smile. High five. I jump up and down. Hug myself. Cesar is what you'd call a twelve on a scale from one to ten, and he's actually into me. Of all the fine men out tonight, Cesar's feeling me. I can't believe it, especially since he's initiating everything—the approach, the dancing, the conversation. If this works out, I can kiss the club scene good-bye and live happily ever after at the magical age of thirty—every gay man's self-proclaimed age for giving up club life. Maybe breaking my New Year's resolution this weekend was worth it. They always say God works in mysterious ways.

After I wash and dry my hands, I head back out into the crowded club to look for Cesar. I don't have to look too long to know everything that glitters isn't gold. There's always a catch. Cesar's talking and laughing up a storm with Rafael. They're both drinking fresh cold bottled beers. As usual, Rafael's wasting no time doing what he does best—seducing men. I'm not giving up on this one, though.

"Hey, Cesar, I'm back. What's up?"

"Oh, this guy just sent me a beer," Cesar says. "Rafael, this is Keith."

I cut my eyes at Rafael. "We know each other already. We're friends. I'm his ride tonight."

"Small world," Cesar says and puts his arm around my waist. "Let me get you something to drink, Keith."

Cesar goes to the bar, and Rafael smiles. I don't.

"You sent him a beer? With what money? I've got your money, remember?"

"Oh, don't cause a scene, bitch," Rafael says. "Cesar paid for it when I couldn't find your ass."

"Rafael, you can have anyone you want. Please don't mess this up for me."

"Bitch, I'm just clinching the deal for you. Besides, I got two other men I'm workin' up in here tonight."

"Then work them and leave Cesar alone!"

Cesar returns with a drink for me and hands Rafael a business card. "Call me if you're interested in taking some classes, Rafael. East L.A. College might be closer to where you live, and I'll hook you up with my friends in admissions."

Well, isn't this just grand? Rafael's suddenly into academics? And why the heck is Cesar handing his card to Rafael? Is he that bold?

"Thanks," Rafael says and shakes Cesar's hand. It lingers a little too long, as far as I'm concerned. "See you boys later."

Cesar smiles and puts his free arm around me again. If Cesar likes me, it's difficult to tell. Especially with the flirt action going on between him and Rafael. It's too early to be suspicious, right?

"Look, if you want to go and talk to my friend, go ahead. It's not the first time."

"Are you jealous, *moreno*?" Cesar asks and squeezes my side. "Don't trip. You'll get my home, my cell, and my work numbers before the night is over. You'll have me on serious lock-down."

"I'm not jealous. I just know how Rafael works."

"But you don't know how I work."

Cesar purses his lips again and nods his head. I know he wants to give me a kiss. Been in this scene with a thousand different cast members. I want to kiss him, but not in a bar full of people. Especially in front of other men who will suddenly find Cesar even more irresistible and an easy target once they see us together. Plus I don't want other people thinking I'm easy or loose by kissing up on a stranger in public. I wish I were a fourth of the slut Rafael is and could live life as pornography like he does, but being a PK—preacher's kid—keeps me confined to an invisible morality code even when the Hemmings family isn't around. When what I really want to do is give one last pitch of my worthiness: a negative HIV, a positive credit record, good family lineage (a PK and Howard University legacy at that!), a shiny import in my driveway, more stocks than one person deserves, undergrad and graduate degrees from Stanford and connections that could help Cesar's career. But instead, I say nothing.

"Fine, Keith. We'll just talk later. I'll be upstairs."

And though he's not my man, for a few short minutes I'd like to feel Cesar is on his way to being mine. If he gets sucked into Rafael's web, then so be it. But it's a chance worth taking, because sometimes a man has to go through all the riffraff to find the true jewel he's meant to have. And at least for the moment, I know that jewel is me.

Chapter 2

MARCO ANTONIO

Alex, my up-and-coming actor extraordinaire, should be here in less than ten minutes, and I'm a nervous wreck.

I give my apartment a final glance. Everything looks set for a romantic and intimate evening. Living room—just the right touch of cozy ambience with vanilla candles, flower arrangements in the right places, and a low fire in the fireplace. Music selection—Alejandro Fernandez, Rocio Dúrcal, Pepe Aguilar. They're Alex's favorite singers. Final check of the dining room. Everything's in place. The kitchen smells delicious, like a good Mexican restaurant, and should appeal to Alex's love of home cooking. I'm setting the scene. It's about time we take things to another level—the bedroom, like other normal couples. Except that Alex is working out of town so much that we never see each other. And when we do see each other, it's a quick hello or good-bye outside the airport, or a quick call from a studio set. He never seems to have time to physically see me, but somehow we've got this connection going for the past year. But like I said, tonight is going to be our first time. I definitely want to. And once he gets a taste of what I've got cooking, he'll want to make love too.

But before we can go there, I have to make a confession to him. I outed him today at Sunday dinner. My family is Oprah Winfrey, Barbara Walters and Teré *La Secretaría* from the Mexican gossip show *La Oreja* all rolled into one.

"College boy, *cuentame de tu nuevo novio*," my *tía* Florinda smiles, with her red-shellacked lips and big blond hair, obviously a store dye kit, that's too long for a woman pushing fifty. But whatever. It's family day. And Florinda's my aunt and I have to give my respect.

We're sitting, very cramped, mind you, in a vinyl booth at one of those all-you-can-eat buffet restaurants. This is so *tía* Florinda—unlimited calories and lots of fat—but the rest of the family doesn't object, so here we are. As a kid, these places were fun. It was all I knew of the U.S. when we moved here from Mexico. Restaurants with so much food to eat you could make yourself sick. It was new, exciting, and the first thing I associated with my family's new life in a new country. Now, I cope and deal as a good son would. This is the Sunday family ritual, even though most days I wouldn't be caught dead in a place like this. The seats are red, noisy and very sticky. And I'm stuck right in the middle—my cousin Lalo, *tío* Jose Luis, *mi abuela*, and *tía* Florinda on my left; my mother and father, my teenage sister, Chloe, her white boyfriend, Ryan, and my six-year-old brother, Ross, on my right. We are the Vega family in full glory.

They all sink their forks into two- and three-thousand-calorie plates of food and pretend to sip on their *horchatas* or Kern's Nectar drinks. I wish I were back in Father Ken's Mass at St. Agatha, listening to his homily on the gospel of Luke. Because if I could go back just an hour, I would have opted out of this embarrassment.

It's not that my parents hate the fact that I date men, but they don't exactly jump for joy. It's not a Mexican thing, my dad says. They want grandkids, my mom says. I respond, I can and will adopt two Mexican kids one day. It causes my mom to go ballistic and pray to all sorts of saints, even when I tell her there's hope in Chloe and Ross to provide genetic grandkids if they choose to have kids. Even taking them to a support group for other Latino parents of gays and lesbians couldn't convince them to see my life, and theirs, as a reality.

On the other hand, my *abuela* is cool, which surprises me. I wish some of her personality had rubbed off on *mi madre,* her daughter. She says I'm dual-spirited like the Aztec god Ometeo, who encompasses a balance of both masculine and feminine energy. Nothing like the either/or Western and European views of sexuality, which my parents have bought into as they seek their own version of the American Dream.

I could go on and on about their attempts to assimilate over the years. I mean, how many people of Mexican descent name their kids Chloe or Ross? Or try to force their kids to not speak Spanish, even though they still speak their native tongue? I'm lucky I kept a working knowledge of our language, but Chloe and Ross might as well be little white kids growing up on the west side of L.A., because they know nothing of our culture. I wish they'd had the same experience I did of being born and growing up in Mexico as a child.

Anyway, I cut my eyes at *tía* Florinda and continue eating. I'm sure she's loving this scene. She lives and breathes drama—on screen and real life. *Tía* Florinda's had this life-long rivalry with her sister—my mom—and she's jealous that my mom produced the smartest kids and the first college graduate in the family. She branded me the "arrogant one" and "college boy" because I chose a private school, Stanford, instead of going to a local standby like Cal State L.A. or East

L.A. College. She thinks her son Lalo is all that—despite the fact that he's notoriously known for not being able to keep a wife, a job or an apartment in his own name. And he didn't even finish his Cal State L.A. degree, and I've heard it's the easiest school to get into and graduate from. My *tía* Florinda's also jealous, or more like ashamed, that she and her family got the indigenous genes, while ours picked up most of the Spanish and European ones. It's no big deal to me, having light skin and light eyes, but it's part of their sibling rivalry. So of course my sexuality is the trump card in her competition with my mom.

"I really don't want to take the spotlight. Let's not spoil dinner just talking about me."

"Go on and tell us, Marco Antonio. I know my handsome nephew's dating someone, right?"

I can't believe she's pressing on with this. Yes, I'm dating someone, but he's a public figure who doesn't want to be out of the closet, and I definitely don't want to confide in *tía* Florinda or the rest of my extended family. Besides, my parents don't exactly want to hear that their oldest child is not only a dual-spirited man, but is a practicing one at that—even though Alex and I haven't slept together in the months we've known each other.

Not exactly family conversation, but if it'll get the spotlight off me, I'll whet her gossip-seeking little appetite. Besides, on the acting scene, Alex is barely B-list in Mexico, rising C-list in the U.S. Who really knows him?

"Well, you're right, *tía*. I am dating someone."

"*Yo se*," she says and holds up her glass to toast herself in an all-knowing, congratulatory manner. "*¿Quien es?*"

"He's an actor. Remember that *novela* that was out last year, *Los Tres Hombres de Hortensia Valencia*? He was *hombre* number two."

"The evil one who framed Hortencia for murdering *el padre de la iglesia*?" Florinda asks with heightened interest. Alex's role was the juiciest one on the show, besides Hortensia Valencia. Everyone is glued to this new revelation like it's a *Dynasty* cliffhanger. "Alejandro de la Torre?"

"Yeah. That one."

"Alejandro de la Torre's one of . . . *them*?"

"One of *them* meaning gay? Sí, *tía*."

"But he's such a . . . a . . . man! *No es posible que él es un maricón*. He was in *People en Español* with that new singer from Colombia, La Princesa, and they were . . . kissing."

"Publicity," I say flippantly and take a sip of my *horchata*. "Actually, Alex and that singer can't stand each other. The pictures were just to get the press off their backs for still being single and not married at their ages."

"You mean she's one of them, too?!?" Florinda's eyes bulge and she fans herself. "¡*Dios mío*!"

"¡*Claro*! Oh, and how about not using that word—*maricón*—anymore. It's nasty."

"Sorry, you're the college boy. I don't always know the correct words," she says. "I thought you were dating that black man you're always with. That's a relief!"

"I am not dating Keith. And what if I was with a black person?"

Florinda is silent and everyone looks down at half-eaten meals, pretending again to be out of the conversation of my love life, which has clearly dominated this Sunday's family dinner.

My father clears his throat and enters the conversation.

"¿*Estas enamorado con un actor*?" He wants to know if we're in love.

"*Sí, Papá.*"

"¿*Estas contento*?" Are we happy?

"*Sí, estamos muy contentos.* He's just very busy. He just finished filming this movie in Tijuana about the drug industry. This weekend, he's in San Francisco finishing up an episode of some new medical drama."

My father smiles, shakes his head and starts eating his *flan,* a custard-like dessert. He gives me the thumbs-up sign and gives Florinda the keep-your-mouth-shut look. Florinda looks sick.

"Well, I guess you all got more info than you wanted. Like I said, I didn't want to take the spotlight. *Tía* Florinda insisted. Don't repeat any of this. It's not really public knowledge."

My sister giggles. "I think it's cool."

"Bring him to Sunday dinner," my dad says in Spanish. "I've never met an actor before. And I can't wait to tell the guys at the factory that Alejandro de la Torre's part of the family."

"Not yet," I say. "We're still testing the waters. Besides, we're both so busy with our careers. And you can't reveal anything about Alex's secret to anyone. It's not public."

"Don't let your career get in the way of being with a famous actor," Chloe says, as if her seventeen-year-old self knows anything about relationships, except for her high school crush, Ryan. "Life is short. Time goes by too fast."

Check the clock. Great—8:24. Alex should be here in exactly six minutes. That gives me time to check myself out again in the mirror. This French Connection outfit Rafael picked out for me looks great. Hair—strategically spiked, but not too boy-band looking.

Dingdong. Dingdong.

Alex is five minutes early. I love an on-time man. I look

out the peephole and scan Alex adjusting his monochromatic
shirt and tie combination—cirrus blue, my favorite color—
and notice he now has facial hair and sideburns. Looks good
against his light brown skin. He's added a few blond high-
lights to his dark brown hair. I open the door and we greet
each other with a long hug and a short peck on the mouth.

"*Hola, mi'jo.*"

"*Hola,* Alex. Come in. Let me take your jacket."

He takes out a small gift-wrapped package before handing me his black leather jacket. "It's just a little something I
picked up for you in San Francisco. Open it now."

I tear the silver paper and a small jewelry box is in my
hand. I open it. A chain and pendant—a cross.

"It's white gold, *mi'jo.* Let me put it on."

Alex turns me around and places the jewelry around my
neck. He hugs me from behind. It feels good. Especially
when he kisses the back of my neck.

"You like, Marco?"

"Of course. You didn't need to buy this. Thank you."

I turn around and kiss him, and he leads me away from
the front door through the hall corridor. I love the way his
arms feel hugging me from behind.

"It's good to be back in L.A. I should be here for a while,
hopefully."

"I missed you a lot."

"You look good. You been working out? You feel tight."
He pats my chest and my stomach.

"I'll leave that up to your imagination, babe," I say, and
grab his hands. "Maybe you'll get another chance to touch
later."

I escort Alex into the living room, where I serve him an
appetizer of stuffed mushroom caps and a glass of red wine, a
nice vintage Keith bought for me when he visited Spain last

summer. Alex shares the ins and outs of his latest shoot, a pilot
for a new medical drama set in San Francisco, which he says
might get picked up for the fall season. He also tells me he's
auditioning for a new character on an American soap opera,
The Bold and the Beautiful. If the soap job comes through, he
says he'll be in L.A. on a permanent basis and making some
decent money. Good for him and good for us. I'm proud of
my Alex.

"So how's work at *Casa Raza, mi'jo?*"

"Same. Lots of families in crisis. Women whose husbands
leave them. Broken hearts. Low self-esteem. Normal counseling stuff. Nothing to write home about."

"We could use someone like you while we're filming a
project. This show biz thing attracts some crazy people."

"I hear. Look at you." I smile at Alex.

"Come here, *mi'jo.*" He leans in to kiss me. "We need to
talk. But let's eat first."

"I have something I want to talk to you about, Alex."

"An evening of suspense and drama. How appropriate for
a couple of Mexican queens, huh?" Alex hugs me tight.

"You're making me nervous."

"Don't worry about it," Alex says. "Let's eat."

Time for dinner. I lead Alex into the dining room. The
table looks perfect—I borrowed my mother's best settings. I
don't feel perfect. I feel like I'm about to get the biggest let-
down of my life—that he doesn't want me anymore. And,
well, Alex is not going to be too happy with the fact I shared
his sexuality secret with the biggest mouths north of the border.

"*Mi'jo,* come on. Stop moping. *Esta bien.*"

I bring him appetizers: tequila shrimp and avocado salad.
*Why go through all this trouble fixing fancy foods for a man who's
about to let me go?* I don't even know what I find so special

about Alex, except for the shallow things I normally don't fall for—marquee good looks, an excellent body and a career in show business. Well, I like the fact that we share the same *cultura* and that he appreciates my career helping people in crisis. And despite the good looks, Alex can carry on a decent conversation that doesn't center on himself all the time. Not bad for an actor.

In the meantime, Alex says he enjoys the food so far.

Next is my main course: chicken enchiladas (my mother's recipe), Spanish rice, corn, tortillas, and a pitcher of Cazadores tequila mixed with Squirt and lemon juice.

In the midst of all this, Alex tells me he hates that he's had to be out of town so much in the beginning of our relationship. He says he appreciates me for putting up with his crazy schedule, that most people dating or married to actor types can't deal with the long periods of separation. I reach across the table and grab his hand, tell him counselors are supposed to be able to handle anything. Alex says he's full and happy, with the meal and with me. We're both buzzed from the drinks.

After dinner, we wash dishes together, laugh and flirt with each other. I lead him into the living room where we can lounge on the sofa. He still hasn't brought up what he wants to talk about, nor have I brought up outing him, but at this point I just want to enjoy quiet, laid-back after-dinner conversation. Pepe Aguilar is singing perfectly to us. Alex loosens his belt and tie to get a little more comfortable. I massage his shoulders and arms. He feels bigger. He says he needed to bulk up for some stunts on the San Francisco shoot. After sneaking in a few kisses, I tell Alex the night isn't over yet in terms of food. I bring him dessert: strawberries dipped in chocolate sauce. And champagne.

Everything is perfect. I am happy and at peace. Not worried one bit about what Alex wants to talk about. A perfect Sunday night . . . a perfect dinner . . . a perfect date. We lie, relaxed and buzzed, on the floor.

Holding onto Alex and just enjoying the moment, I remember I need to tell him how I revealed his secret life to my family. Just as I tell Alex I need to talk to him about something, he says the exact same thing. I let him go first.

"So what exactly are your expectations?" Alex asks.

I've heard this line before. It's the nice way of easing into the I-think-you're-into-this-more-than-I-am conversation. Most times, to save face, I back down. But not tonight.

"I want to continue getting to know you, I guess," I say. "I mean, with our work schedules, we've hardly spent time together."

"That's why I hope I can get the job with the soap opera, so I can be here in L.A."

"That would be cool."

"Because?" Alex asks.

"Because I like you, Alex," I say. "I want to make this turn into something a little more permanent."

"Are you serious?"

"What do you mean 'am I serious'? Why do you think I put up with the separation all these weeks while you're out working? Just for kicks?"

"I'm glad to hear you say that," Alex says and hugs me. "I want to be with you, too. You understand me better than any other man I've tried to get close to."

"You had me worried you had some bad news. All this time you wanted us to be together?"

He stands up and walks over to the patio door, where another bottle of champagne is chilling. He opens it and pours himself a glass.

"Well, Marco, there is one little thing I have to tell you."

"What's that?"

"First of all, it wasn't my idea," Alex says and sips from his glass. "It was my manager's."

"Okay. What's up?"

"I got married about a week ago."

"Married?"

"Married."

"What are you talking about? You just told me about how you wanted to be with me."

"It's no big deal. You know the singer from Colombia, La Princesa? It's a career move."

"This is crazy," I say, and take a healthy swallow of champagne. "I don't believe this, Alex."

"Come on, *mi'jo*. It's just in name only. But I wanted to tell you before you heard about it on TV tomorrow. Someone leaked it to the press."

Alex pulls out a small gold ring and a picture of him, his bride and the wedding party. Lots of well-known Latina and Latino actors, singers and performers from the U.S. and Central and South America standing in a church courtyard. All I can do is shake my head slowly back and forth. And wonder why I've been putting my life on hold for this man for all these months. He tells me it's all for the studio. That his career and La Princesa's singing career are on the verge of something big in the United States. That neither can have sexuality rumors circulating about them. That I knew what I was in for when we met at the HIV Research fundraiser party last year and he told me he was in the closet. That this is all part of the Hollywood game. That he still wants us to be together, even though he has a wife. A *wife*. This, despite the fact he hasn't made love to me, or made any gestures thereof, in all these months of being together. Not even a quickie, and I know the man gets horny with all his phone sex and dirty talk to me. Helloooo, Marco Antonio Vega. Time for you to pick up the clue phone: Alex must be getting it from someone else and sees you as the stable, secure one to come home to. Even with the busy schedule, Alex could make time for sex.

I stare at him for what seems like hours, though it's just a few seconds, and say nothing. What can I say? It's not like he came and consulted me with this decision, like should happen in any normal, healthy relationship. But then again, how normal and healthy is this? Fewer than five dates and a few hundred phone calls don't necessarily make a relationship. And let's not talk about the lack of a sex life between us. I wouldn't doubt that someone like Alex, with his gorgeous face and body, is sleeping with someone else while he's away from me. I wouldn't be surprised if he tells me that he and La Princesa are having a baby just for the sake of their reputations and careers. What a fool I've been, and am about to be.

The front door creaks open. Damn, why is Rafael home so early? I don't want him to see any of this tension between Alex and me. He and Keith are already skeptical of this long-distance thing with Alex, and Rafael's always telling me "*Amor de lejos, amor de pendejos.*" Long distance love is stupid love.

"*Mi'jo*, we were just exercising and wanted to drop by to see if you needed anything for tonight," yells my mother, as she, *tía* Florinda and my *abuelita* march into the apartment with their Rockport walking shoes on. "Oh, my God, he's already here!"

The three of them gawk and smile and stand in awe of a real live actor standing before them.

"It's really you," *tía* Florinda gushes and wraps her arms around one of Alex's. "Alejandro de la Torre. *Soy* Florinda Avila, *la tía de* Marco Antonio. I thought College Boy was lying about you."

Alex puts on his award-winning smile and kisses each of their hands. "*Con mucho gusto, mujeres*. You've raised a good son and nephew, and he's far from a liar."

"Mom, what are you guys doing here?" I ask and do a quick check of myself to see if my zipper or any buttons are undone. I can't disrespect my family by looking like a whore in front of them, though Alex and I have barely gotten to first base.

"Marco, *cariño*," Alex interrupts. "Don't be rude to your family. You guys have to excuse Marco. He's been a little testy tonight."

"Probably because he's stressing himself over having the perfect evening," my mom says and touches my forehead. "*Mi'jo*, you don't look so good. Are you feeling okay?"

"Not really."

Alex grabs my hand and rubs it. *Tía* Florinda notices Alex's gesture, sighs one of those this-is-so-romantic sighs, and snaps a picture with one of those cheap disposable cameras she just happens to have in her purse.

"Come here, *Tía* Florinda. Let me pose for you," Alex says and puts his arm around me. Then he poses for a shot with my mother, then my mother and grandmother, and then a shot of him and my aunt. And he's worried about publicity? He doesn't know he's posing for pictures with the biggest gossip of the San Gabriel Valley, my aunt, who will surely make copies for all her friends and family.

"Mom. *Tía*. Go. We're having a date!"

"Well, it was nice meeting all three of you. Mrs. Vega, your enchilada recipe reminds me of my mother's."

"*Gracias. ¿De donde eres*, Alejandro?"

"Mexico City."

"We're from Guadalajara."

"We'll have to get together and share stories one day,"

Alex says. "I apologize for Marco's attitude. He and I have had a little bit to drink tonight."

"I've been dealing with the attitude since he was born," my mom says. "You might as well get used to it."

"Hellooooo! I'm standing here," I say. "Wait until I leave if you want to talk about me, would you?"

"Hey, Alejandro, I'm hosting Sunday dinner at my place next week. Why don't you and Marco Antonio stop by? You don't have to mention any of the 'you know what' stuff," *tía* Florinda says and points back and forth from Alex to me and back to him. "Just come by and meet the rest of the family."

"I'd be honored. We'll definitely be there."

"We'll see. I might have to work," I say and give Alex a pinch on his arm. "Actually, Keith and I have plans."

"On Sunday? Family day?" *Tía* Florinda asks and rolls her eyes. "You and Alejandro better be there."

"*Mi'jo*, give me some sugar. We're leaving. It looks like everything is okay over here."

I kiss my mom, aunt and grandmother good-bye. Alex does, too, as if this is getting him out of the doghouse with me.

"See you at dinner, Alejandro!"

After the door closes behind them, I turn to Alex and say, "When hell freezes over."

"Such a bad boy, *mi'jo*," he says and tries to put his arms around my waist. I pull away at each attempt. "Your family loves me."

"My family loves a liar."

"*Mi'jo, estas enojado conmigo?*"

"Yes, I'm angry with you. You made me look like a little bitch to my family, and they think you're all that because you're a fucking actor and charmed their panties off."

"I'd like to get into your pants tonight," Alex says and

manages to get a small kiss to reach my cheek. "If you'll let me, *cariño*."

"You've forgotten one thing, Alex."

"What's that?"

"La Princesa. Your wife. Remember?"

"I told you it's all just for the media. This *chorizo* is all yours, baby," he says, and presses his groin against my leg.

"Alex, all I have to say is if you choose to be with her, or anyone else, you're choosing not to be with me."

"You and I are not over. You're the one I want."

I blow out the candles on the table, go to my bedroom and lock the door behind me. I don't care where Alex goes— the living room, back to his house in Silver Lake, or cruising the streets of Hollywood. But he's not going with me, and he's not making a bigger fool of me than he already has.

Chapter 3

RAFAEL

"How can I make you smile?"

This brotha's whispering the best six words I heard tonight, brushing my ear with his LL Cool J lips. How I ended up pressed in this private corner area in Tempo with Keith's crush from the gym is a mystery to me. I met him last night at Arena and ain't even know he was coming to Tempo tonight. And how was I to know Cesar and Keith were even talking or getting to know each other? Don't blame me 'cause I got what it takes to get and keep a man. It ain't the first time, and probably won't be the last, that Keith falls for dudes who're outta his league. The fine ones, the A-list boys, always want me. I'm young, beautiful, built and, most of all, Latino, even with my dark skin, and I have to get it while the getting is good. Don't want all my good years to slip away. I don't even really want this nig—this brotha, but if Keith keep up the attitude, I'll give him something to get jealous about. I'll get the brotha *and* Cesar.

Besides, I don't know why Keith standing there all alone like a *gorda* at a *quinceañera* and staring at me, 'cause it ain't like we're leaving the club anytime soon. Keith thinks the world turns on his time frame, and when he bored with a scene he think everyone else should be too. It don't work that way. Keith drove his own damn car and can leave if he wants to pull this kinda shit tonight—he the one always showing off his bling bling with his new car updates every year and tossing his plastic out to pay the bill every time we go out. So now he over there with that sulky, pouty, impatient look like he ready to go. *Pendejo* needs to chill and find Cesar. And not get so hot and bothered by a little flirting.

It ain't my fault that he ain't get no love tonight. He had his chance, but in typical Keith style he probably ruined it. See, Keith is real smart, an overachiever I guess is the word they say. I say "nerd." But he get too deep too fast. Hell, men don't wanna know about how many degrees you got, stocks you own, vacations you took or books you read. At least not in the club. And especially not in the first five minutes of conversation. Save that shit for later, like when a man trying to get serious and settle down. Besides, most of the men up in here, including yours truly, workin' a nine-to-five *and* a six-to-ten (French Connection in the daytime, Macy's at night), and don't know the difference between a Ph.D and an M.D., don't know what a P.E. ratio is, can't understand the concept of a timeshare and ain't read nothing beside the want ads or sports pages in recent memory. How I got stuck with two dorks for friends—that rich bitch Keith and my goody-two-shoes roommate, Marco Antonio—who don't know nothing about men is a mystery to me. I'll tell you how. Marco Antonio calls himself "saving me" from my life on the streets and let me move in. Keith's his tag-along college friend.

See, Latinos don't want someone making them feel less than a man—that damn *machismo* thing is a bitch. I keep telling Keith to get with the program if he trying to hang with *la raza*, especially the ones straight from Mexico. But he old and stuck in his ways, and still learning about how L.A. and us

Mexicanos work. Keith can have a tendency to be a little ob-
noxious about his "life achievements," and think he know
everything, so you can bet that's what drove Cesar away. And
that's why he standing there all alone. He could be out there
dancing. But it ain't my problem to worry about.

The only thing I need to be thinking about is this: Am I
getting some dick from this gym trainer tonight? Or tomorrow night? Because regardless of the answer, this boy is turning me the fuck on and, if it were legal, I'd go down on him
right now in this corner. If we find an empty bathroom stall,
I just might. Because the way this brotha is working this spot
on the left side of my neck, I'd probably do anything for him.
Now I don't normally do brothas, though I lived around a lot
of them in South L.A. It's where I got this crazy Spanglish/
street slang way of talking, which got people thinking I'm all
East Coast Latino. I'm straight-up West Coast, born and
raised in L.A., and got family from Colima and Guerrero. I
got lots of love for my fellow *Mexicanos*, but I know they all
staring at me like I'm crazy for hooking up with this brotha.
I mean, Mexicans only hook up with other Mexicans. It's one
of those things we know but don't talk about. Anyone's fair
game to me. And the way this boy got me feeling right now,
I can see why you'd never want to go back.

Jermaine. That's his name, I think. Shit, I'm making out
with the trainer from our gym and I can't remember his damn
name. I should know it. Because Keith and I go there a few times
a week—Monday, Wednesday, Friday between six and eight
in the morning—and we see him working there. And now I
got him, my back against the wall, and this six-foot-two brotha
with cornrows, who could almost pass for that fine-ass singer
D'Angelo, is letting me have it! I hope he look as good as
D'Angelo did in that "How Does It Feel?" video, where he was
all greased up and butt naked, singing to the camera. Right

now, gym trainer's twelve-nooner is pressed up against me through his Sean John's and his thick-ass lips feel so good.

"Boy, I axed you a question. How can I make you smile?"

"You could do a lot. But you gotta work to find out."

"So a nigga gotta beg?"

Hello!?!? He's talking to Rafael Dominguez. I don't mind hooking a brotha up, but he needs to come correct before I give it to him. And I am definitely giving Jermaine some tonight.

"I know you got game. Tell me why you wanna make me smile."

"Because you fine, you got flava and you tight." Jermaine palms my butt and squeezes. "And I wanna tear that up. Bare."

"I'm down for whatever, but I don't know about that."

"Trust. I'll get you to take it bare."

"I can't wait to see you try." I suck on his neck a little and slip my fingers into the open zipper of his jeans. "Can you bat a thousand tonight, Jermaine?"

"Damn, you making a brotha smile right now."

"I can make you feel good all night."

Suddenly, Jermaine and I are drowning in more lights than J. Lo at a movie premiere. What the fuck?

"Yeah, officer," Keith says and points his fingers in our direction in the corner. "I think my wallet fell on the floor over here. It's so dark and hard to see."

I know Keith ain't lost nothing but his mind.

Instead of focusing on a supposed lost wallet, the security guards focus their attention on my hand and Jermaine's dick.

There are no criminal charges. No handcuffs. But thanks to Keith, Jermaine and I are escorted out and banned from Tempo for two weeks. Big whoop. It ain't stopping me from getting what I deserve tonight. But Keith better watch his back, because he will get what he deserves as well, once I'm done with Jermaine.

Chapter 4

TOMMIE

If it ain't one thing, it's another.

Just as me and my new partner, Tyrell, are making some good Monday morning three-day weekend love, and this close to the point of no return, the phone rings and the answering machine clicks on.

"Tommie Jordan, get yo' ass out of bed and buzz me up," yells my trifling older sister, Sylvia, through the speaker. "I know you up there 'cause I see that sharp-ass Escalade you just bought."

She laughs. I don't.

"Fuck, Sylvia," I pick up the receiver and do my best I'm-sleeping-and-you-just-woke-me-voice. "Give a brotha some slack. It's a day off for everyone."

"What black person you know celebrate Presidents' Day? It's almost eight o'clock, Tommie. I gots bizness to take care of, so let us up."

"Us?"

"Oh, right. Just me and a friend, that's all."

"Give me ten minutes and I'll meet you down at the gate."

"Why you being so shady, Negro . . ." I hear her shrill as I hang up.

Damn. Sylvia always be stopping by at the most inconvenient times. And it's hard to keep the mood going with your older sister waiting downstairs at the condo entrance. Sylvia act like she don't have the sense God gave a goat, but I definitely don't want her running into my Tyrell up in my room. She'll put it all together, I know.

I tell my Tyrell he needs to lay low. Nobody except my roommate and a few other punks know about me, and I ain't putting my business out there in the streets—especially not to Sylvia. Discreet is my style, and I ain't throwing my reputation away for some twenty-two-year-old college ball player from UCLA. It ain't a major reputation, but when you're the former lead singer of the new-jack-swing singing group, Renaissance Phoenix, you don't want people knowing things about you. Even though I ain't singing, just running my own record shop, I like my private life private. I ain't getting punked out over Tyrell Kincaid.

Before I make it to the living room, I hear Sylvia's loud-ass voice. She's banging on the front door like she a damn piggy for the LAPD. This early morning visit can only mean one thing: Sylvia wants money. Because weeks can go by without me hearing from her. Not even a "hello" or an "I don't really give a shit to call you except when I want something" message.

I do a quick once-over of the living room and realize I gotta get rid of my roommate Keith's gay-ass *Adelante* and *QV* magazines on the coffee table. Why he like them Mexicans in those magazines is a mystery to me. His little crew is all Mexican, and they always trying to get me to go to they little gay-ass salsa clubs. They was begging me to go out to Arena and Tempo this weekend, but I was kicking it with my Tyrell the whole time. Keith wasn't into all this multicultural we-are-the-world bullshit when we was growing up in Detroit. That Stanford crowd changed him. Fuck them Mexicans, is what I say. All I need 'em for is to wash my truck, take care of the pool and grass outside Keith's and my condo, and ask if I want my fries supersized. ¡No más!

So am I surprised to see Sylvia standing at my door, head full of black and pink plastic rollers, dirty slippers, and acid-washed jeans, with some Mexican man old enough to be our daddy. I knew the drugs messed up her head somewhat, but I ain't think she'd stoop that low for some dick.

" 'Sup, Tommie. Give your old sis some sugar." Sylvia plants a sloppy kiss on my cheek. I pull away quickly, wondering if her lips been on that old man this morning. "You smell like sex, little bro. This my man Gustavo."

I stand there and stare as Sylvia and Gustavo breeze by me. She sets him in front of the TV and puts on a Spanish channel. ¡Qué bueno! as they say. She motions me over to the kitchen.

"What is it this time, Sylvia?" I fold my arms and keep my head down, waiting for the big announcement or excuse to come.

"I know you got some girl over, so I'll make it quick. You know my baby 'bout to turn six years old now, right?"

"I know. I visit Keesha and her father from time to time."

"Well, she down in Gustavo's car now. I'm taking her back to her daddy's. Anyway, next time I get her for a weekend it's her birthday, and I wanna do something cute for her, right? The last thing I need is her daddy talking shit, right?"

"Are you asking me or telling me?" I ask. "Anyway, Dennis got good reason."

I wish Sylvia would get to the damn point, or maybe I should, so I can get back to my Tyrell. I was *this* close, and my

thirty-one-year-old body don't work like it used to. I mean it
works, but every once in a while the runway gotta be a little
bit longer for the takeoff, if you know what I mean.

"Well, I wanna throw Keesha a party at Chuck-E-Cheese
or somewhere like that," Sylvia says. "I think it'll be a couple
hundred dollars at least."

"Last time I loaned you money, I never saw it."

"Look. I'm working now. I ain't smoking that shit no
more. I just wanna do something nice for my baby girl."

"What about him?" I say and point over to Gustavo. He's
sitting on the new sand-colored leather sofa Keith bought,
and his dirt-covered work boots are kicked up on the glass
coffee table. "Your new man can't help you out? I don't mean
to put Mr. Mexico 1950 on blast or nothing, but hey."

"He got his own wife and kids to take care of. Come on,
cut me some slack, Tommie."

I think about my Tyrell back in the room as I try and figure out how to handle this. I want Sylvia gone. She wants
money once again.

"Fuck me over again, huh? Let me get my fuckin' checkbook."

My Tyrell is laying naked over my goose-down com-
forter, his twists sprawled over his face like spider legs. I whisper, "I'll be rid of her in a minute."

I go back to the kitchen and sit at the small table. My
checkbook registry tells me I shouldn't be loaning any
money, because it'll mean another late payment to American
Express. And I'm barely making my truck payments. Maybe
I'll get another extension on my loan from moneybags Keith.
I gotta get Sylvia off my back so I can get back to my Tyrell.

"I hope this'll do you for a while." I hand her a three-
hundred-dollar check.

She snatches it, smacks her lips, and sighs. "I guess it'll do. Gustavo, *vamanos!*"

"A thank-you will do."

"Yeah . . . uh, right. I'll get back at'cha little bro." She play-punches my shoulder.

"Don't I even get to see Keesha?"

"Gotta run," she says. "We'll be by later."

And just like that, Sylvia and her Mexican man toy out the door. I can't believe she ain't even offer to bring my niece up to see me sometime soon. Figures. Probably be another three months before I hear from Sylvia again. That's cool. Because my well-deserved reward, my Tyrell, is in my room and hopefully ready for another round this morning before I have to take him back to campus.

Chapter 5

RAFAEL

Slavery over, ain't it? The way Jermaine been working my shit all night long *and* this morning, I feel like I'm his little Mexican slave boy. So much for emancipation.

"Get on your knees."

"Lie on your stomach."

"Scream my name when you come, boy."

"Don't kiss me on the mouth."

"Put that rubber in the trash."

Of course I oblige and am feeling sore everywhere on my body. I needed this, for real. I'm surprised Jermaine even came over after the scene Keith caused last night at Tempo. Gotta hand it to Keith, he got me good. Can't wait to get him back. Revenge is a bitch. And I'm good at being a bitch when I need to.

Before Jermaine, it'd been two weeks since I got some good dick. I mean, there's been some mediocre dick and some get-me-by-in-the-meantime dick, but I ain't had it this good since that hookup with the 7-Eleven worker, Enrique, who supposedly plays football for Garfield High School. It's a shame to have skills like that at only seventeen.

Anyway, I'm glad Jermaine in the shower now, so I can

rest up a bit before another round—what is it now? *Cinco*?
Or *seis*? Well, anyway, I can't wait to tell Marco Antonio about
it, but I know he probably spending part of the day with his
family. Maybe Keith. He'll call me to apologize about last
night, I know. They both gonna get a kick outta this *chisme*.

I'm gonna get a little *chisme* myself and just sneak a peak
in this nigga's wallet. Not to take nothing. Just to see what he
all about, especially since he was all talk about how he want
to see me again. About how he seen me over at the gym before. About how he love my tight ass and body. About how I
seem more black than Mexican and that's cool with him.
About how he ain't been with nobody as uninhibited and
free in bed as me. About how much he like a dude to be
straight acting if he plan on kickin' it. I ain't told him yet, but
Rafael Dominguez don't kick it with nobody. Especially if
they trying to get serious after a one-night stand. And most
especially if they ain't putting no cash into my flow.

Hmmm . . . let's see . . . California ID . . . real name is
Jermaine LaDon Ross, cute name . . . born in 1969 . . . '69?!?
The sixties? Shiiit. I thought he was born in the early eighties
like me. A nigga look all young and shit. And why does he
work all the way in Montebello, which is on the east side, but
his address say Inglewood? Oh, well, ain't my business. I just
hope he don't want no ride. Inglewood too far to be driving
all the way from Montebello, plus I gotta put my little Tercel
in the shop for some way-overdue work. Oh, good! He got
the MTA bus pass here. All the way with MTA, coolio! OK . . .
a Target credit card, employee ID from the gym, an instant
lottery ticket—hmm, a $5 winner . . . T.A.N.F. card—Temporary
Aid for Needy Families? What's that about? Everybody knows
you need kids to get that kind of card. Oh, shit, that's because
he got a family portrait tucked in the back. Cute little black
boy and brown girl. Greasy faces, though. A diva-looking baby

mama. Could lose the Kool Aid red streaks in her braids. Let's see what's on the back. "Thanks for making us a family. Love, your wife Quiana, Jermaine junior—age six, and Jermonda—age three."

Well, I'll be damned! This nigga married. That's why he put it on me so good in bed. It's always the closet cases and married men who make the best lovers. That makes at least five in the past two months alone, and I don't even try to get them. They step to me—when I'm working in Macy's or French Connection, every other day at the gym, anytime I go out clubbing, even at stop lights when I'm cruising in my old-ass Toyota. Marco Antonio always telling me I'm setting myself up for some serious trouble messing around with closeted and married men, but it ain't my fault. Can't help it that I'm so beautiful. And if they don't come clean with the info before we start messing around, who am I to judge? I guess Jermaine is just one more notch on my belt. Sorry.

Well, while I'm sitting here trippin' on this earth-shattering information, I guess I forgot to listen for the shower to turn off, because next thing I know, Jermaine's standing in front of me and catches me with his family picture. He starts calling me all sorts of "punk-ass bitch" and "stupid wetback faggot" names and looking like he ready to fight, which I don't want to because his six-foot-two, seven-percent-body-fat ass would definitely kick my ass. Then he says some ignorant shit like, "You lucky I'm a Christian and it's Sunday," before he snatches his pleather wallet out of my hands.

"It's Monday," I say. "Holiday weekend, stupid."

"Don't even think about calling my wife or showing your faggot ass up at my gym anymore. Same for your friend who got us kicked out the club last night."

"Look, I said I'm sorry."

"Don't forget. I know where you live muthafucka."

I stare, cock my face, and in my best don't-make-me-move-my-neck head move, I tell him, "Don't forget. I know where *you* live, Mr. Ross."

Silence.

Then he goes, "Ain't no faggot gonna kill my game. I'll kill a bitch first before—"

And Jermaine punches me hard in the chest, and I fall back onto the dirty sheets and towels we used to clean up after sex. That hurt! Then he knocks my cologne bottles and face products off the dresser on his way out. Shit, that's expensive Issey Miyake and Clinique products spilling all over my carpet. I almost yell for help from Marco Antonio, but then remember he's with his family.

Jermaine shouts from the living room, "Don't fuck with me, faggot!"

I hear the front door of the apartment slam. I peep out the window and see Jermaine walking down the street, looping his belt in his baggy-ass jeans and straightening out his T-shirt. Thank God this crazy nigga gone, and I don't have to drive his ass back to Inglewood. I got thirty minutes before I gotta put on my happy face for the Presidents' Day sale at Macy's. Big whoop. At least I can tell Keith he better off without Jermaine the trainer.

I don't usually call home too much, but today's run-in with Jermaine got me thinking about my ma and what it was like growing up in an apartment full of hard men who like to fight. Man after man running through our place and our mother, each one trying to be a stepfather to me, my older half-brothers Memo and Manny, and younger half-brother Rolando, but never making it official by offering to get married and making us a real family. Memo, Manny, Rolando and

I share our mother, but each of us got different fathers we
have no memory of or relationship with.

The last "stepfather" who lived with us before I moved
out found me messing around with a neighborhood *cholo* in
the kitchen one hot summer night and beat the shit outta
me. Then Memo beat the shit outta me for not being a
"Dominguez man" and standing up to the last stepfather.
That was when I was fourteen. The next year didn't get any
better—more teasing, more names, more making fun of my
skin being the darkest in the family. And even when Ma tried
to defend me, Memo and Manny would just shut her down
like she was a lady in the streets.

So with us not having a lot in common anymore, and me
not having a death wish in my own home, I jetted from
Boyle Heights. Hit the streets and pretty much raised myself.
Did what I do best. Worked Santa Monica Boulevard for a
bit. Lived off a few sugar daddies, until I realized I'm too
young and beautiful to be an old man's property. Did a short
stint in South Central. Hooked up with a party crew and
started throwing parties, and when those bitches turned on
me and kicked me out the crew, I found Marco Antonio. Or
rather, that bitch found me at my lowest, most embarrassing
moment and took me in. Probably the best thing to happen
to me—meeting Marco Antonio and, I guess, Keith too. I was
lucky to survive five years out there, 'cause some of my other
boys didn't make it. Or they still out there trying to do party
crews or Santa Monica work. And even though I see Marco
Antonio and Keith as my new family, I know I still got folks
over in Boyle Heights, which is just a few minutes from our
place in Montebello, but whatever. As long as my two grown-
ass brothers still living with Ma and Rolando, I won't be
stopping by any time soon.

"Ma, *como estas?*"

"Hola, mi negrito. Long time no see."

"I'm busy with work. I got two jobs now."

"Next time you get a chance, you should come over," Ma says. "Your brother Rolando would love to see you."

There she goes pulling out the violins. Rolando and Ma would be the only family I'd want to see: Ma, just to see that she's doing fine; Rolando, to make sure he's not getting pulled into street activity like Memo and Manny. I hear he's got a lot going for him, that he's kinda nerdy like Keith, is ju-nior class president and thinking about going to Loyola or Santa Clara for college.

"Ma," I say. "I just called to see how you are. Wanted to hear your voice."

"Is something wrong?"

"Naw, it's cool," I say. "What about you? How's money for you and Rolando?"

"I got a job over at the dollar store and Rolando's tutor-ing for the next-door neighbors in the afternoons."

"Good for you, ma. Tell Rolando I said hi and to stay in school."

"I will," she sighs. "I just wish I had a man to take care of me and help me out. Life is hard."

"Well, I've seen the men you've been with. I don't think they're worth it."

"Well, how's *your* love life, *negrito*? Since you seem to have all the answers."

Ma can change tones and get crazy on you like that, but I'm not in the mood to trip on her back. Not with dealing with crazy-ass Jermaine earlier today.

"Not much to report. I wish."

"Well, one day we'll have to double-date. Imagine that, you and your old lady out on the town with a couple of fine, rich fellas."

"Crazy. Imagine that. Well, I gotta run to work. Glad to hear you're well."

"Next time, instead of calling, why don't you stop by? Everyone asks about you all the time. When I tell them you stay over in Montebello, they all think you're rich or something."

"That's a joke," I say and laugh. "But I'll stop in one of these days. Promise."

But the thing is, I know I won't be heading home anytime soon. My life is with my boys—Marco Antonio and Keith. Because enough time has gone by to make me forget what used to be important, and to make me realize I don't want to live the way I used to.

Except, of course, sex with gorgeous people, wherever I want, whenever I want. I am Rafael Dominguez, after all. ¡*Claro*!

Chapter 6

KEITH

I'm lying in my new and very comfortable sleigh bed, hoping that my prayers can be heard above the loud banging of Tommie's bed against the wall. For the price I paid for this less-than-five-year-old condo in Pasadena, you'd swear the walls would be soundproof against your roommate's morning lovemaking. Lord, hear my prayer:

God, all I want is a love to call my own. I have been blessed with an abundant life. Loving parents. Intelligence. Wicked and sarcastic sense of humor. Good looks. I can pay my bills on time. I have food, shelter, a nice car and excellent health. What more should I ask for?

I have so much I want to share with another human being. I thank You for using me as a vessel through which to share Your vision to enlighten others. I thank You for surrounding me with good friends, good people and positive thinking—even when I'm crazy and judgmental with them.

I know that You have a purpose for me and that Your vision will manifest as You see fit. God, I hope that having a life partner, someone special to share my life and special qualities with, is part of that vision. I want someone who has intelligence, charm, integrity and a sense of responsibility. I want someone who wants to share in my love for You, Heavenly Father, and has a higher vision for himself and what he wants out of life. He can be good-looking, too. That wouldn't hurt.

Lord, I want to be more than just the reliable, faithful companion to my friends. I want to be more than someone who's seen as the "nice one" who gives good advice, kind words and is always there in times of need. I want the kind of excitement and passion my friends Marco Antonio, Tommie or even Rafael, for that matter, have. I want to have something interesting to talk about besides my work, my stocks or being the son of a preacher.

God, all I want is a romantic partner to call my own. I want to be happy. I want a man. I want my parents' understanding. Help me stay strong and secure. In Jesus' name I pray. Amen.

It takes just a few minutes for an answer to my prayer. It's Cesar. I'm surprised, considering how we left things last night.

"Let's drive over to the beach," Cesar says.

"It's too cold," I say.

"Stop whining, *moreno*, and pack some sweats and maybe a change of clothes for later."

"Okay. If you insist."

"I do. I'm leaving in ten minutes. I'll see you in half an hour."

And we're off, leaving the urban sanctuary of my Pasadena condo for the lazy seaside life of Newport Beach. With no morning rush-hour traffic to compete with because of the holiday, we make it to the beachfront cottage of Cesar's colleague in just under an hour. The fog is still thick, but doesn't choke away the aroma of fresh morning air. We're both hungry, but decide to explore the beach before it gets too crowded with other city dwellers enjoying the three-day weekend.

"I hope this meets your approval, Keith," Cesar says. "It's not city glamour, but I wanted you to see the real me. Sweats, T-shirt, no hair gel, bags under my eyes . . . You got some bags, too."

"Ha. Very funny, Cesar."

"So what time did you leave Tempo last night?"

"Too late, waiting for Rafael and his hookup. That's another story."

"He's a cute kid," Cesar says. "Kinda immature, but cute."

"Yeah, yeah, yeah. Everybody loves Rafael." I roll my eyes.

"But I want me some *moreno*." Cesar flashes his pearly whites.

"Oh yeah?"

"Oh yeah." He grabs my hand and pulls me to the side of a lifeguard station. "I wanted to do this last night, but you were so stubborn . . . and all jealous."

He lifts my chin and bends to meet my lips. It's short and tasteful for a first kiss. His breath still smells like toothpaste.

"You kiss good, Cesar."

"Thanks. You too, sexy boy."

"You really like me? Why?"

"Don't be such a dork, Keith. Let's go make breakfast and see what else I've got planned for today."

He starts to lead me away, but I pause.

"Cesar, we just kissed and I don't even know your full name."

"Cesar Luís Reyes."

"Darren Keith Hemmings. I've been using my middle name ever since I was a kid."

"What else?" Cesar asks.

"I don't know. It just seems a little weird that we're on a date and don't really know each other."

"I'm an open book, Keith. Whatever you want to know, I'll tell. But first, how about some breakfast?"

And this is what's got me so leery about Cesar. He is too nice, too handsome and too willing to talk about himself— not that he's done it yet, but he's not closed off to sharing— and I don't get a psycho vibe either.

"Cool then. Let's eat."

With next to nothing to work with, Cesar's got a feast prepared for us: fried potatoes with onions, scrambled eggs with tomatoes and jalapeño peppers, flour tortillas and fresh orange juice. We spend the morning laughing and reminiscing about growing up in the seventies and eighties, while reruns of *Good Times*, *The Jeffersons* and *Gimme a Break* broadcast on cable.

"Ready for more questions, Keith?" Cesar asks while we're drying and putting the breakfast dishes away.

"Sure. You ask first."

"I wanna know *como sabes tanto español? ¿De clases o tus novios?*"

"Definitely not from boyfriends," I say. "I learned in high school and college. Of course, living in California, I can't help but use my skills."

"So you got skills, huh?"

"You better recognize." I snap the dish towel at his thigh.

"You betta rec-a-nize." Cesar rolls his eyes and neck around, briefly jumping out of his manly exterior. "Come here, boo."

He hugs me and kisses the top of my hair. He rubs his body against mine.

"Love me some thick *moreno*."

"Cesar, please. Next question." I pull away a bit.

"When was your last boyfriend? Date? Whatever you call it, Keith?"

"Promise not to laugh?" I can't believe I'm about to make this confession.

"Promise."

"Almost ten years. When I was at Stanford, believe it or not."

"Ten years? Damn. That's a long time to go without."

"Ten years without a boyfriend," I say. "There've been dates. Just nothing beyond the first or second. Maybe a third date. What about you?"

"When's the last time you had sex?" Cesar asks.

"Too much information. When was *your* last boyfriend?"

"I got out of a situation about a year ago. We were together for two years."

"Black boy?" I ask.

"Mixed. Lat-chino. Mexican and Korean."

"That's definitely a California thing. You don't see that combo in Michigan."

"We met when I moved back to L.A. after grad school," Cesar says. "But I don't want to talk about him. No drama, but it's over."

"That's cool."

"And your one ex?"

"Black. Med student at Stanford. Lost touch."

"Good catch. I see you choose well. You're not a slum dater."

"I don't hang with *gente corriente*," I say.

"Oh you don't?" He pretends to take two puffs on a long cigarette. "Such a snob, Keith. *Gente corriente*? What are you doing with me then?"

"Hopefully getting to know you."

"So tell me about Darren Keith Hemmings, boy from the Detroit hood." Cesar flashes gang signs at me in a joking way.

"I'm not from the hood. But I am from Detroit."

"So what was it like growing up there?" Cesar asks.

So I tell him about Hemmings House, where I grew up, which sits at the rear part of a secluded subdivision in northwest Detroit called Palmer Woods. Red-brick mini-mansions and White House replicas, plantation-sized front yards and winding streets and driveways are and were the norm for Detroit's elite, like us, Reverend Hemmings' family, who were privileged enough to live there. In the twenties and thirties, when many of the homes were built, auto executives, politicians and steel magnates called Palmer Woods home. After the riots in the sixties, when most of those white executives no longer felt safe living in the city among the burgeoning black middle class and under rule of Detroit's first black mayor, Coleman Young, most of them moved out and made way for the black talented tenth to move in. The first generation to benefit from Brown vs. Board of Education and other civil rights legislation, the black middle class bought up the homes being abandoned by their white counterparts and university classmates at cheap prices. Reverend and Mrs. Hemmings purchased our family's four-level, six-bedroom English tudor, nicknamed Hemmings House, in the late sixties. Children of black politicians, newscasters, school board members, auto engineers, doctors and some of the leftover Motown singers who hadn't abandoned Detroit for L.A. were our neighbors and friends.

I also share the pitch I was going to make last night: negative HIV, positive credit record, good family (a preacher's son and Howard University legacy at that!), new import in the driveway, more stocks than a single person deserves, undergrad and grad degrees from Stanford. But I add that I'm the youngest of three successful kids whose parents are still married, and that my family thinks my coming out to California for college was the downfall of my life and the embarrassing moment of the Hemmings family legacy. I should have followed the three generations of Hemmings men who graduated from Howard University, pledged black and gold, and went back to lead our church members and community. But for me, Stanford and California have been the most liberating and educational experiences of my life. I can't imagine my life without warm weather, without import cars, without beautiful people who have style, and without diversity of people and experiences. One thing my daddy seems to forget is if I hadn't moved to California, gone to Stanford and met those computer whizzes around Palo Alto, I never would have risked my little savings nest egg on buying stocks in upstart Internet and dot-com companies back in the early and mid-nineties before they went public. Thanks to my smart investments, Reverend Hemmings now has the largest and most beautiful new church in Detroit, complete with all the trimmings a man of his prestige could ever brag about. They have certainly benefited from my so-called liberal California life. And even though Reverend Hemmings has never uttered a homophobic sermon, never even allows such words in his pulpit, and doesn't accept faith-based government money, I just can't bring attention to my whole liberal California self when I'm back at the church or with them. It's like inviting Michael Moore to a slumber party with conservative politicians and business CEOs. Could be a lot of fun, and a chance for real learning, but why bother even going there when you know what the same tired arguments and resistance would be?

"Just shows that everyone's got a story," Cesar says. "I've been checking you out for a while, believe it or not, and I never would have guessed what your life is like."

"Well, at least you listened. Most men don't take the time of day to get past clothing or shoe labels."

"You'll find I'm not most men, Keith."

We move to the living room and explore the bookshelf with hundreds of best-sellers and a dozen board games stacked on the bottom. I beat Cesar at Scrabble, and he wins dominoes in the afternoon. I pick up lunch from a small seafood restaurant within walking distance of the beach cottage. At sunset, Cesar lights a few candles on the porch, and we watch the Pacific Ocean put the sun to rest for the night. We lean our heads together and enjoy the quietness around us, with just an occasional crashing wave interrupting the silence.

"I don't want to go back, Cesar."

"Let's stay," Cesar says. "I don't teach until tomorrow evening, and you're your own boss. Play hooky."

"I didn't want to let you go last night, either. I just didn't know the deal with Rafael."

"We're not talking about him anymore. It's about the preacher's kid and the gardener's kid now." He turns to me and kisses the tip of my nose.

"No catch? No surprises?"

"I could make some up if you want."

"No thanks," I say, and rub the side of his face. "You're so fine."

"So are you, *moreno*," he says. "I had my eye on you for a long time. But you and your friends have attitude and don't hang with *gente corriente*."

"Oh yeah? So you've seen us out?"

"You, Rafael and who's the other one?"

"Marco Antonio. My best friend from Stanford. And my roommate is Tommie."

"I see you guys runway in the clubs like you're working

for Donatella Versace. *Por favor, moreno.* You act different when you're around your peeps, like when I've seen you over at First Fridayz."

"You've seen me there?"

"Yeah, when it was over in Hollywood, and you were trying to act all hard with the brothas," Cesar says. "I mean, you're no flamer, but please *moreno*."

"Whatever."

"It's all good. Either way, you appear confident and attitudinal. Maybe that's why you haven't had someone steady in almost ten years."

"Don't analyze me, Cesar."

"Just telling it like I see it."

"Then take me back to Pasadena." I stand and open the screen door.

"You're not getting away that fast, Keith," he says and scoops me up, which isn't the easiest task. He tosses me onto the sofa and slides next to me, nuzzling up to my neck. "Sexy *moreno* boy."

"Let's not get too carried away. We just met last night."

"Why not? You know I like you."

I sit up a little. "Just to make sure we really like each other and it's not just about sex, I'll stay here in the living room. You can take the bedroom, since it's your friend's house and all."

"Boo, no fair," Cesar pounds his fists in the air and pouts his mouth. "That's okay. I don't need the temptation anyway."

"Thanks for understanding," I say.

"But one day, I'm gonna let you have it."

"Really? Ooh, I'm scared. I'm gonna get ravaged by a hot Latin lover."

"I'm the one who should be scared," Cesar pauses and

laughs. "You're the one with ten years of buildup. You're gonna be a freaking fire extinguisher when you finally release."

We kiss good night, and he stays in the other room as promised. It's no dream. I think I'm on my way to a life with Cesar.

Chapter 7

TOMMIE

After taking Tyrell back to UCLA and hitting the gym, I'm back in Pasadena. There's no sign of Keith anywhere. I'm home alone, restless, and missing my Tyrell like crazy. He got a ten-page paper to finish up and barely started it, so he can't swing back by like he promised 'til later tonight. I ain't mad at him, it's just always something last minute coming up in our plans—basketball practice, a paper, an exam, press interviews, or his government-official daddy flying into town from D.C. surprising Tyrell's ass all the time. I got a predictable schedule. All I got is the record store to look after and home. I was looking forward to spending time with my Tyrell. I should just get a porn out my bedroom closet and finish myself off, and that's just what I'ma do right now before I end up hitting the streets and getting myself into some trouble.

Just as I get myself worked up enough, I whip out Tommie junior and start to imagine what he'd feel like inside my Tyrell again, then—I don't know why—Keith's friend Rafael pops into my head, and all of a sudden Rafael's riding on Tommie junior, while Tyrell's sucking on my neck . . . then somewhere in all this excitement and madness, just as

I'm about to reach the point of no return, I hear the answering machine click on. I forgot I turned the ringer off.

It's my little niece, and she's crying. She say she been at Gustavo's apartment all day, ain't seen Sylvia, and gotta get back to her daddy's tonight so she can go to school in the morning. Gustavo's teenage girls or their mother won't drive her. I don't think they can even communicate with Keesha. Talk about a way to bring a brotha down in a major way.

Luckily, Keesha is a smart girl for an almost six year old, and know the address to where she been this three-day weekend. She stuck in East L.A. with Gustavo's family, and since none of them speak any English, they can't help Keesha at all. I could kill Sylvia, especially when Gustavo's wife pulls out a coffee-stained map and points to Las Vegas and charades playing a slot machine. So Sylvia and her old man went off gambling with my money. Keesha's so-called birthday party.

Instead of going off like I want to, I take Keesha over to the closest McDonald's in East L.A. for a little dinner and fact-gathering mission.

"You shouldn't be sad, Uncle Tommie, because you're eating a Happy Meal with me," Keesha smiles, showing all her gums and missing teeth. She definitely got her chocolate skin from our side of the family. Them green eyes are definitely from Dennis's side. "Are you having fun?"

"Of course. You're my favorite niece."

"So don't be mad at Mommy. She's having fun with her friend, *Señor* Ramirez."

"Does Mommy always take you to his house when she gets you from your daddy?"

"Most of the time, but it's fun because I have friends over there," Keesha says. "We play, and they teach me to say Spanish words, and his wife cooks orange rice and soft tacos for me."

"Do they treat you good?"

"They're nice, Uncle Tommie, but we can't talk to each other a lot because I don't know that much Spanish. It's okay. I'm learning in school, and one day I can teach you!"

"Silly girl. Do you like living with your daddy or your mommy more?"

"I like them both," she say and look down at her little Happy Meal toy. "I wish they liked each other. Mommy's always yelling at Daddy when she comes to pick me up."

I'm no head doctor, but I know I'm supposed to find out about her feelings. So I ask, "How does that make you feel?"

"Sad. But I know not everyone is supposed to be friends with everyone. Did I tell you I'm getting the promotion in the fall? Mrs. Chao told me I'm the smartest girl she's ever taught in kindergarten."

"That's great. You are a smart girl, Keesha. You will make a good college girl one day."

"That's when I'm old like you, Uncle Tommie," she giggles and starts squirming around in her seat. "I'm ready to go home now."

"You barely touched your fries, girl."

"I just wanted the toy, and besides, I don't wanna get fat."

"You too young to be thinking about getting fat, Keesha. Eat your food, and then we can go."

I better get some advice from Keith on how to deal with Keesha and food. I don't think she supposed to be thinking about getting fat at her age.

"You're cool, Uncle Tommie. How come you don't have any kids yet?"

"One day I might."

"When you get a wife?"

"Maybe."

"You could adopt me . . . psych!" She laughs and stuffs a handful of fries in her mouth.

I couldn't imagine settling down with kids and a dude. It just don't seem right, but I see it on them news shows every now and then. My two-way buzzes, and I look down at it to read the message. It's my Tyrell sending a greeting. He apologizing, but say he'll swing by after midnight. That's cool. And I think, well maybe if it's with the right dude, someone with a level head on his shoulders, I could settle down and raise a family.

Chapter 8

KEITH

When Cesar drops me off in the morning, I turn on a CeCe Winans CD and plop onto my bed. Cesar Luís Reyes likes me, I like him back, and I can't wait to tell Marco Antonio, Rafael and Tommie that my relationship recession is over. Maybe once I get cleaned up and rested. It's nice having nothing to do, and all day to do it.

It's turning me on just listening to Tommie's bed creaking this morning, and imagining him and his boy, Tyrell, together. It's not like I want to sleep with my roommate—that would be like incest or something. He's like my brother. But maybe ten years ago or so, when he was in that Renaissance Phoenix singing group, or fifteen years ago when he was singing lead in the junior choir at my daddy's church in Detroit, I would have done just about anything for Tommie Jordan. I had the biggest crush on him, with him being two years older, dark brown like hot chocolate and taller than most of the other teenage boys around our church. But Tommie's like family, and probably my closest friend outside of Marco Antonio, who's my Stanford buddy.

As for Rafael, well, I can tolerate him for just so long until he starts in on this whole "I'm beautiful, I'm young, I'm what everybody wants" kick. I know everyone wonders why I hang out with Rafael. To be honest, he's fun to hang out with, and I can soak up a bit of popularity when we're together. Even when he's whoring around. Like at Tempo the other day. I can't believe how Rafael picked up a black man—I mean a fine brotha—because Rafael never talked about wanting to be with a black man since Marco Antonio brought him into the fold a few years ago. Never. What's up with that the sudden change of heart? Maybe it shouldn't surprise me. Rafael sometimes seems more black, more African, more African American than me.

In the meantime, I can't even get a black man to look my way in L.A., and I'm a way better catch than some of the trailer-white-trash-blue-collar-blues-just-moved-north-of-the-border-retarded-and-gold-diggerish men who end up with the black men I'd want to get with. I don't want to rehash all my ethnic studies and psychology classes, but we are in L.A. after all, which seems to be the headquarters for self-hating, internally oppressed men of color. They appear confident, content and together, but allow themselves to be treated like trophies or commodities when it comes to dating—whether it's with a man or a woman. Too bad my peeps can't get it together in the head. Look at me—I'm getting negative again, and I just had the best first date I've had in years. My moods change so fast, you know?

Anyway, my stereo must be loud enough for Tommie to know I'm up. He knocks on my door and opens it.

"'Sup, Keith. Welcome back. I'm 'bout to bounce."

"Where are you going?"

"Taking my boy back to UCLA, then heading over to the record store. You?"

"Not much," I say. "I had a date. We spent yesterday and the night at Newport Beach."

"No shit?" Tommie asks. "That's cool. Oh, you missed another episode with my crazy sister."

"Really? What miracle brought Sylvia all the way to Pasadena?"

My phone rings. I wonder who this could be. Maybe Cesar?

"Money, what else?" Tommie says. "Anyway, I'm out. Talk at'cha later. Oh, I left a CD sampler on the kitchen table for you. It's got some Anita Baker, Rachelle Ferrell, and Teena Marie live stuff on it. You and your date can play it while you get busy."

"Whatever, Tommie. Thanks."

Tommie turns around to leave. He's got a nice butt in those sweatpants. Hmmm . . . maybe if he was single, and I was single . . . nope, not even gonna go there.

"See you later. Bye, Tyrell," I yell into the hall before picking up my phone on the nightstand.

"Bitch, what you doing? Where you been these past days?"

I swear Rafael sounds more black than I do.

"Cesar and I had a date," I say. "We spent all day together down at this . . ."

"Well, you ain't gon' believe how that nigga turned me out."

"That what?"

"That nigga," Rafael says and pauses. "Oh, I mean Jermaine. You so damn politically correct. That is what they call it, right?"

"I told you before that people with class and education, like me, don't use the 'N' word."

"Okay. Dang. Chill. I just wanted to tell you about my trick."

"And people only use the word 'politically correct' to make fun of people's desire for equality."

"Yeah. Right. Whatever. So you wanna know or not, Keith?"

I roll my eyes and yawn. Thank God, Rafael can't see me. It's the same script with him. Rafael calls me this same time every morning, usually after a trick has left, and before he leaves for his first job. And he shares all the nasty details: how big it was, how long it lasted, and how many times and ways it was done. I don't know if the Guinness Book has a category for "it," but Rafael would be in the running for recognition. So I humor the kid.

"So tell me."

"Oh, *Dios mío*, Keith. It was sooooo good. He had the best body and let me have it twelve-play style. Okaaaaay! And I guess what they say about nig—I mean black men is true 'cause it was sooooo thick and long, and made that beautiful thud sound against his stomach when I played with it. And—"

"So, Rafael, you and Jermaine going to see each other again? I mean besides seeing him at the gym?"

I'm feeling just a tad upset, or jealous, or I don't know what I'm feeling, because Rafael got with a black man, and I'm black and can't seem to get a black man to do the things to or with me they'll easily do with someone not black. Just breathe, Keith. This is Rafael, not your master's thesis, not your business or investments portfolio. It's not important in the grand scheme of things. It's just a meaningless fling.

"Oh, hell naw. Can't get attached to a trick. And besides, he's married with children, *comprende*?"

"No way!"

"Way," Rafael says. "And he almost kicked my ass, too, but that's another story. One worth telling over an apple martini at The Abbey. Wanna go? I'll drive."

"I'll drive," I say. "My car's better, anyway. And maybe I'll invite Cesar."

"Fuck Cesar. What's he gonna do for you anyway? Marco and I are your boys. We come first."

"I'll ignore that. I'll pick you and Marco up at nine-thirty."

I turn on my laptop and set my food aside, some Korean takeout I had delivered. I need to check my schedule for the week to see if or where I'm working. Lucky me, there's just the Pasadena City College session in a couple of weeks. Cesar's school ☺. They want me to facilitate a diversity training session for new faculty. It's like preaching to the choir as far as I'm concerned, because it's usually the newer and younger college faculty who are most open-minded. It's those old and tenured ones, those who've been around since the turn of the last century, who need training the most. Anyway, I can't believe PCC is paying me as much as they are for a three-part workshop. I'd do this work for free, but I know I can't live off my investments and savings forever, and besides, I need to do something to keep my brain working. I am not about to become one of those complacent people with a little bit of money who do nothing but shop and eat at fancy restaurants every day. Speaking of eating out, I need to find a place for Marco Antonio and me to meet this week. He wants me to lead a new group he's starting at *Casa Raza* on ethnic relations and sexism in the gay community. Sounds fascinating. I'll do that work for free. It's a good cause.

So now that I know it's a relatively easy workweek, I sign in to check my e-mail. Let's see: junk investment schemes, two inquiries about my diversity training workshops—one from a hospital, the other from a friend who directs the Black Culture House at Stanford—and a note from my sister, Stephanie, checking in to see how I'm doing. I'm sure she's either at church or at Hemmings House, so I decide to call her house and leave a message. Don't really feel like talking to her. Surprise—Stephanie answers.

"What are you doing home?" I say, and start munching on *kimchee* wrapped around a slice of Korean barbequed beef. "I thought you'd be over at the church."

"I'm at home resting. Doctor's orders. I think the twins are coming early."

"I hope Julian's helping you out."

"Yeah, he's cool. He's good to your big sister. How's life in L.A. these days?"

"Same old script, different cast," I say. I know she wouldn't want to hear about Cesar. "Did you get those clothes and toys I sent Little Julian?"

She giggles. "Yeah, but you could have kept the little boy and girl dolls," she says. "I'm not trying to raise a politically correct son. Not yet, anyway. But the Afrocentric children's books were nice, though. We read those every night. I don't know about the Hispanic ones, though. I want him to speak English."

"They're called Latinos, not Hispanics, and if you're smart, you'll put Little Julian in a Spanish class today."

And then I realize I really don't have much to say to my sister, except for trying to correct her misguided thinking. It's been that way pretty much since I left for Stanford. As with most of the Hemmings, Steph'll change the subject when challenged to think in a different way than she's used to.

"So you know your friend Quincy is working at Channel Four News now? You should send him a note. He rejoined our church after he moved back to Detroit."

Quincy is the only man my parents and family would remotely tolerate in my life as more than a friend, since he and his family have always been active members of our church.

The only redeeming quality I could possibly see in him now is that he grew up out of his nerdiness and is this major heart-throb newscaster. But other than that, it's a no-brainer. I'm not interested. I've got Cesar now.

"Thanks, but no thanks, Steph. Besides, I'm not really looking for long-distance romance."

"Well, don't be surprised if he calls or visits you out in L.A. You know how Mother is with giving out our phone numbers to old friends."

"Yeah, I know. Bad habits are hard to break. But please do not encourage Quincy."

"I'll try," Steph says. "Well, I have to run. Julian's hosting a men's prayer group here tonight, and I'm playing the hostess."

I'd swear she's living in the 1950s rather than the 2000s, but I decide to bite my tongue and not comment. At least I got her to keep her own last name rather than take on her husband's.

"Be careful, Steph, you're pregnant. Besides, your husband can take care of himself and his prayer group."

"You'll change your independent nature when you find someone. Solomon's changed."

Solomon, the main player up in Daddy's church, and also my older brother by a year, is now engaged and settling down with a deacon's daughter. "Hmmm, don't think so. But anyway, I can take care of myself."

"Well, Julian and I hired someone to help around the house until the twins arrive," Stephanie says. "You should call home more often. Everyone worries about you out there in crazy California."

"I'm cool, Steph. You take care now. Bye."

She just has to throw all the good news of the Hemmings family in my face, knowing that in the long run, it just makes me look like the rebellious kid son who's off living this wild and immoral life in L.A. If only they knew how basic and simple things are for me. I work. I dance. I drink. I volunteer. I try to be a good person. Some would call it boring. Most would say I'm just being a normal preacher's kid.

Just a normal preacher's kid who's hooked up with a gardener's kid.

Chapter 9

MARCO ANTONIO

I just made a date with someone new. Well, the guy's not new. But I might be seeing him in a new light. Maybe. Not sure yet. We're meeting up with Keith and Rafael later tonight for drinks and dancing.

Julio Centeno is sweet and has all the qualities someone would look for in a partner—he's well-read, well-adjusted and, well . . . just plain fine. Salvadoreño. Tall. Educated. Works at the University of Southern California, doing cultural events and programs. Julio volunteered for the HIV-prevention fund-raiser that my agency, *Casa Raza*, gave last year. After that, we maintained communication. I've gone to a couple of his soft-ball games—he plays for the Mayan Warriors, a gay softball team that's part of The Wall-*Las Memorias* agency—and he's invited me to some of the team gatherings and parties as his date. It's all friendship. I'm with, well, used to be with, Alex. I go not just for Julio, but because I know other guys on the team. It's important for us Latinos to support each other and stick together, whether we're Mexican, Salvadoreño, Rican, Dominican, Cuban, South American, mixed, whatever. And running into Julio last night at the gym reminded me how much of a support he has been for me. He's been my movie, dance and dinner partner for the past year or so, but has also been my shoulder and confidante during the lonely months of enduring Alex's busy filming schedule. If I could describe Julio in one word, it would be "comfortable." So we're going out, and I'm thinking maybe Julio could be the one.

Rafael doesn't approve. He thinks he knows me better than I know myself and that I'm making a big mistake settling for an everyday guy like Julio, instead of the glamour and excitement Alex offers. Of course, all Rafael thinks about is blinging and banging in bed. And he seems to have forgotten that before Alex, all there was were regular, everyday guys—bank tellers, law students, more than my share of teachers, and a fireman or police officer here or there. Just your average, everyday Latino men in L.A.

"Bitch, you in denial," he says. He's picked up on a little of my counseling vernacular and now thinks he's the next Dr. Isabel or something. "Didn't you learn anything up at Stanford about marrying well?"

"Whatever."

"You need someone with Benjamins. I wouldn't give a flying fuck if he married or not. It's not a *real* marriage."

"Believe me, Rafael, we all know you wouldn't."

Too many of us boys who like boys thrive on the thrill of the chase, drama and heartache, but honestly it doesn't do a thing for me. I'm not one of those drama queens just searching for anything, like Rafael is. As far as I'm concerned, less is more. Keep it simple. No conflict. I'd rather have peace than be right all the time.

"Married men. Men with girlfriends. Men with boyfriends. They all make the best fuck buddies. No strings. Keep it on the down low."

"Not for me."

"Then I'll take Alex," Rafael says and finishes the protein smoothie he's been sipping on. "Just kidding."

"*Pues.*"

"Well, I'm out. Gym. Work."

"You gonna see your gym buddy from last weekend?"

"The black boy?" Rafael says. "Please, bitch. So over it."

I've never known Rafael to date or sleep with someone not Mexican. His type is always young, built, Latino, and looks like a model or stripper. They're always fair-skinned and look like *güeros*. I think it has to do with him growing up poor and thinking a white-looking Mexican rather than a more indigenous-looking one raises his status. The African American gym trainer was a surprise, and I'm sure brought out all of Keith's deep shadow beliefs about looks, weight, ethnicity, age and the club scene. We'll connect if I can get him away from Cesar one of these days.

"*Pues.* I'll see you later."

My cell rings.

"*Qué haces, mi'jo?*"

It's Alex.

"Nothing. Getting ready to go visit my family."

"We're still on for Sunday dinner?"

"Unfortunately."

"I love your *tía* Florinda," Alex says. "What a character."

"I know. She's crazy."

"I wanted to see you today. I'm going to a movie premiere and thought you'd love to walk the red carpet with me."

"La Princesa's not available?"

"She's in Miami making a music video this weekend."

"Like I told you before—if you choose to be with her, you're choosing not to be with me."

"You're being hard on me," he says. "I know you still have feelings for me."

"I have to go. Bye, Alex."

"The limo will pick you up at seven."

"I won't be here. I've got plans."

"Then I know you'll be aching to see me Sunday for our big coming-out party at Florinda's."

He laughs and hangs up.

Pinche cabrón. He thinks he's getting the last word on our relationship. Alex better think again. I'll be out with Julio.

Chapter 10

RAFAEL

"Hey, is Mr. Man working this afternoon?"

I'm calling my homegirl Roneshia, who works with me on weekends at Macy's. She and I got this deal going that if we know our boss Mr. Monroe ain't coming in, we'll take turns clocking in and out for each other. Today is my turn to play hooky.

"No, he's not on the schedule. So I guess that means you're not either, huh?" She laughs and goes on, "Who you got a date with today, baby boy?"

"I'm thinking about going out to Arena. Haaaaaaay!"

"You ain't never lied, Rafael," Roneshia says. "I could use a drink right now. These little suburban moms with their wannabe Eminem sons are getting on my last nerve today, ordering me around like my name is Aunt Sadie or Lulabell. I wish they sold this hip-hop gear out in Malibu, Monrovia or wherever the hell white people live in L.A."

"You one *loca* bitch, girl."

"Yeah. Well, I can't wait until we close. It's no fun without my baby boy here to make me laugh. I'll clock you in. What's your ID number again?"

I give her the information, and she tells me to hold for a

second. While waiting, I start going through an envelope stuffed with phone numbers and names scribbled on cocktail napkins from the clubs. Jorge . . . Ricardo . . . Gabriel . . . Jose Luís . . . Misael . . . Armando. Half these homies I don't even remember. But there's one in particular I want to find, 'cause I think I need a maintenance check: Enrique, the 7-Eleven Garfield High School boy. I'm getting horny just thinking about him.

"I'm back," Roneshia announces. "That nosy bitch from the Misses department, Wanda Hooker, was taking her break in the clock-in room—and it's not even noon yet—asking all kinds of questions about my weekend. Anyway, I should get off the phone soon. The little N-Sync wanna-be boys are starting to circle around this section, and you know they find ways to lift merchandise quicker than you can say 'Winona Rider.'"

"Okaaaaay," I reply, more to finding Enrique's number than to Roneshia's statement. "Hey, I got something to tell you right quick, girl, and then I'll let you go."

"Hmmm, let me guess? You got dick. Big surprise. Save some for us women, okay?" She laughs.

"It was a brotha. He was fine, too. Looked like D'Angelo, with cornrows and everything. And before you ask, yes, it was absolutely fantabulous! We met last weekend."

"I ain't mad at you, Rafael! But I can't believe you went out and didn't tell me. I'm dying to see what a gay club is like."

"I'll take you to Circus next time I go. You'll love it. Trust."

I want to go out tonight, but I spent my check buying two new outfits. So I pull out the credit cards I think I can still use and check the balances. If I can at least get a twenty-dollar bill, I'm hitting someone's club tonight. I'm almost afraid to check my balances, in case a customer service rep interrupts and asks for a payment. But just my luck, the old reliable plastic comes through again.

Before heading off to the ATM, I dial up Enrique's cell. Poor boy's hooked on Rafael. He picks up on the first ring.

"Hold on, okay," Enrique says, and I hear a door slam. Now all I hear is a bunch of traffic in the background. "Wassup, Rafael?"

"Nothing much, Enrique. *¿Qué haces?*"

"Man, my girl's here for the afternoon. That's why I had to come outside to the porch. I've been thinking about hooking up again."

"Oh yeah?" I'm sure his seventeen-year-old dick is hard as a rock right now. Last time, he came in his pants before I even touched the merchandise, and I had to get him up again about ten minutes later, which wasn't a problem. How lucky for his girlfriend. "The big, bad tight end wants another piece of Rafael, huh?"

"*Verdad, verdad, cariño.* I was hoping you'd call me again. I haven't seen you at the 7-Eleven anymore."

"Well, you're busy now with your girl. *Te llamaré mañana.*"

"No!" he shouts. "I mean, I can get rid of her if you want, Rafael."

"That's okay, Enrique. I promise I'll call tomorrow and maybe you can come over after school . . . before I go to my other job."

What I really want is for the boy to come over right now, but it ain't happening. I hope his girlfriend, who looks like she should be called "Chola Spice," based on the picture he showed me, takes care of Enrique's horny ass today. Because if I find out she doesn't, she may just get replaced by yours truly on a permanent basis.

"*Bueno.* I better get back inside," Enrique says. "My

mom's making *menudo*. I'll bring you some tomorrow,
Rafael."

"Sure, *papi,*" I say. "Whatever you want."

I hear some fumbling and yelling, and then some girl's
shouting into the phone, "Who the fuck is this? Why you
talking to my man like that?"

The phone goes dead, which is alright with me. I ain't got
time waiting for no high-school fool. I grab my keys and
head out the door to get my little money from the ATM. If I
play my cards right, getting this twenty-dollar cash advance
will pay off with a good lay tonight.

Chapter 11

TOMMIE

I just lit two incense sticks, made a Hpnotiq and Hennessy and got my *Kings of Comedy* DVD on. I need this downtime. Me and my boys played ball for a coupla hours over at Balboa Park, over in the valley, and that took a lot out of me. I hate to admit it, but I ain't in the same shape I was just a few years ago. I still got my six-pack and biceps that won't quit, but my stamina ain't the same. Can't run as fast with the young boys.

But my Tyrell ain't complained once about me being ten years older. We give and take, go with the ebb and flow, so to speak. It's been that way since we met at that benefit game a coupla months back, with college ballers, old-school celebs and the staff from that hip-hop radio station. I seen him checking my shit out in the locker room, and I was kinda checking his out too. I'm all, whassup? I mean, who could resist my chocolate brown self? Who could resist his dreads and dimples? He said we should work out at the gym sometime. I slipped him my digits—my real ones, not the fakes I give out to them fags who be trying so much crap to get close to me. Tyrell called that night after his mandatory study hall.

And here we are. Or here I am, sprung on this college kid. And that's a big surprise for someone like me, who didn't think nothing about this man-to-man action until I moved out to California for my music group, Renaissance Phoenix. I seen so much crazy mess here in L.A. Stuff I ain't never seen growing up in Michigan. The men be all obvious and up-front. Kinda like how I used to be with the honeys back in the day. Shiiit, I almost got married twice, but things just fell through. Women ain't stupid.

Keith, my condo mate, say it's a cop-out, an excuse, and that moving to California didn't turn me this way. That peo-ple don't just wake up and change their sexual preference. I guess it kinda make sense, because all that time I was with the ladies, I was having private thoughts about men. When Keith let me move in after my music group faded, I couldn't hide my curiosity anymore. Talking to him and reading some of his books and magazines just opened a door for me. Made it so easy to go out and experience the best kinda closeness and sex I ever had. And it's been a lot. But them days of sex with no feelings are over for me, thanks to my Tyrell, and it's not all just about sex between us, either.

Sometimes I wonder what my Tyrell see in me and my sorry ass. I look good and all, but I got baggage that no twenty-two-year-old would want in a relationship. Like being in my early thirties with no real skills except for play-ing ball and singing. Like having people kinda recognize you, but not know exactly from where or what. Like having a sis-ter who drains the fuck out of my finances and my patience. Like having a niece who being raised by two tore-down par-ents—my crazy sister and my former singing partner, Dennis. Like owning a record shop, but knowing that it's really in your roommate's name and knowing you have to repay him for his initial investment. Like having to keep asking Keith for a little slack each month on rent at the condo, even though he got more than enough cash and don't really need to charge me anything. Like being on the down low with the fellas. That last one ain't much of a problem for us, though. That's how we like it.

My Tyrell got a bright future ahead of him whether he does professional ball or something with his UCLA political science degree. I peaked ten years ago, when Tyrell was like twelve or thirteen. I wish I hadda done things different when I was part of Renaissance Phoenix. Like saved money. Hired better managers. Negotiated better contracts. Took credit for songs I wrote instead of letting producers get all the attention. Maybe even gone solo when I had a chance. But when you're young and naïve, you don't think of nothing but new clothes, getting laid and paid, and living in the present. The paid part might be a little overstated, 'cause all the big bucks gone and now that I really look at the situation, we really wasn't all that paid. I get a check every six months for a coupla thousand. That's it.

All I know is if my Tyrell feeling me as much as I'm feeling him, I'ma need to make some changes in my life. Do something more productive than owning and managing a record store. If I was him, I wouldn't want no uneducated, thirty-something music industry has-been. Not in L.A., anyway. But until the day he leaves me . . .

Shiiit, I'm supposed to be in chill mood. This Hpnotiq got me buzzing and thinking too much. One of "The Kings" is talking about receiving "special treatment" in the bedroom, which ain't good for me to be hearing about now. I'm horny and my Tyrell ain't done with practice and study hall yet. I need a hookup. I could call up someone . . . hmmm, my ex-girl Adrianne? Tonya? Jermaine? Nah, he married now. Be good, Tommie. Be good. Just take matters into your own hands and take care of it yourself. As soon as Keith leaves, I can do just that.

Speaking of Keith, he going out again with them Mexican boys he hang with. I guess when your job ain't nothing
but to go and do presentations once or twice a week, you can
spend your time out all weekend like Keith do. I shouldn't
put him on blast like that, though, because it's his investments
and savings that got me in my business and living in this phat
condo for next to nothing. I just don't see what he see in
having all those color-of-the-rainbow friends. I may be in
L.A. now, but one thing you don't ever have to worry about
me doing is dating outside my race, like a lot of the brothas
out here. I like my men and women dark and sexy like me.

Someone's knocking at the front door, which gets my
mind off my Tyrell. It's Keith's friend Rafael, and he just walks
on in like he owns the place.

"Whassup, Tommie?" He slaps my hand hard as a brotha
would.

"Chillin'," I say. "You walk in someone's house in the
wrong hood like that, you gonna get shot."

"I know, and I'm sorry. Me, Keith and Marco got it like
that," he says and smiles. "I see Keith ain't ready yet. That figures."

"He back there with Cesar."

"This supposed to be boys' night out, not ball-and-chain
night," Rafael says.

I watch Rafael walk across the room wearing one of
those tight wife-beater T-shirts, vintage-looking jeans and a
cowboy belt buckle with sparkles all over it. He filling them
jeans out nice, though, almost as nice as a brotha would. Yee
haw! I need to keep my mind on my Tyrell, though.

"You want a drink, Rafael?"

"Sure. What you got?"

"Hpnotiq."

He smiles. "My favorite. Pass it over, bro."

I laugh. He puts the bottle to his lips and looks at me. A long time. A little longer than normal. He nods. I look away and back at the comedians on TV.

Rafael keeps talking. "I like Bernie Mac, but Steve Harvey's the man. I know you listen to him on 100.3 The Beat, right?"

Rafael hands the Hpnotiq back.

"They both cool with me," I say.

"I know that's right."

There Rafael goes looking at me again like that. I ain't really down for no Mexicans anyway, so he betta not think he gonna get something up in here. I turn up the volume.

"Why you so quiet, Tommie? What you thinking about?"

"Nothing. Don't worry 'bout it."

"I'm psychic," Rafael says. "Let me guess."

"It's probably more like Keith flapping his lips to you. But take a guess if you must."

Why Rafael moving next to me on the sofa is a mystery to me. I don't see how his circulation ain't cutting off, seeing how those jeans cling to his legs.

"Your little college man hitting the books tonight, as usual, and you'd rather him be here with you, right?"

"Something like that," I say and grin. "Don't worry about what I'm going through, Kenny Chesney look-alike."

"You got jokes. I'm laughing. Ha. Ha."

"So whassup with the country gear?"

"It's urban cowboy, thank you," Rafael says. "Just changing up the look for the *vatos*. You should go with us tonight. The men would eat your cnocolate ass right up."

"I don't think so. No offense, but I don't fuck around with Hispanics, Mexicans, whatever y'all call yourselves."

"Don't hate," Rafael says, and grabs the Hpnotiq bottle. "I fucked around with a nigga last weekend."

He keep looking at me, a little bit longer than I'm comfortable with, and his tight jeans are turning me on a bit.
Rafael gets up and stares at himself again in the full-length
mirror. One thing, Rafael got a body on him. Not tall, long
and lean like the ballers I usually like, but in a meaty soccer or
baseball player kinda way. I ain't about to fuck up things with
my Tyrell, though, so I better end these thoughts. I'm buzzed,
anyway.

"You can finish it. I'm done," I say.

"Sure you don't want to come tonight, Tommie?"

"Not with you, that's for sure."

"Well, enjoy your video and your solo night. How innocent."

Rafael kisses his hand and blows it across to me. He kinda
cool, but he ain't got a thing over my Tyrell, no matter how
much he try to flirt. Besides, Keith done told me about how
much sleeping around Rafael does, and I ain't about bringing
no diseases up in my shit.

"Rafael," Keith yells, and I hear his bedroom door open.
"Sorry I'm late."

"You need to check your little friend, Keith," I yell as
Keith and Cesar walk into the living room. I can't believe
Keith dressed up like one of them urban cowboys, too, except
his is more Hugo Boss-meets-Oprah-dressed-in-black cow-
boy than a Wal-Mart version. I feel like I'm watching Country
Music Television live in my own place.

"What's going on in here?" Keith asks.

"Not much. Waiting on you, bitch. Sharing a taste of
Tommie's cock . . . tail." Rafael struts across the room and
puts the empty glass on the kitchen counter. "I didn't know
Cesar-the-Keith-pleaser was coming too."

Keith looks at me in the living room, and then at Rafael
in the kitchen, and then at me again. I hope he don't start his

little *Murder, She Wrote* Jessica Fletcher detective routine. He rolls his eyes and huffs.

"You ready to go, Rafael?"

"Yeah, *vamanos*," Rafael says. "Tommie, we'll pick up where we left off next time. I'll stop by your store one day while I'm on break."

Rafael and Cesar walk out the front door. Keith turns to me and whispers, "Remember, you have Tyrell. Don't be stupid."

Believe me, I know what I got, and I'm not about to mess it up.

Chapter 12

KEITH

It's the same tired routine every weekend. Skip dinner to avoid a bloated stomach. Take a quick nap. Do a quick modified workout of crunches, push-ups and squats to firm and tighten up. Smear a pale green mud mask over your face. Sip on a strong cocktail while waiting for the mask to dry. Sort through all the clothes in your closet, complain to your roommate Tommie—the closet case—that you have nothing to wear, and finally settle on the trusted black sweater, black pants and black urban cowboy hat combination. Shave, shower and shimmy around to your favorite CD—could be Britney, Faith Evans or Whitney, depending on your mood. Wait for the boys, Marco Antonio and Rafael, to pick you up, because it's their turn to drive. But tonight, you've got a surprise for them. They get to spend time with Cesar. He's coming out with the group for the first time.

Marco Antonio and Rafael corner Cesar and me outside on the smoking balcony at Arena and waste no time conducting the gay resume check and interview:

- How old? (They approve that he's within the plus or minus five-year range.)

- What does he do? (A job requiring a college degree is preferred, and being a college professor definitely qualifies.)
- Where did he go to school? (Salesian High School for Boys, UCLA undergrad, University of Michigan masters and doctoral work get two thumbs up.)
- Is he with someone? ("Keith, who else?" Gets laughs.)
- Is he dating someone? (There is a difference between this and the previous question, and they had to ask, to which he promptly answers "No one but Keith.")
- Does he only date black men? (No.)
- Does he date other Latinos? (Yes.)
- Does he own a car? (Yes, and it's made in the new millennium.)
- Live at home or in his own place? (L.A.-raised boys are notorious for staying in their parents' homes well into their mid to late twenties, but he's in a townhouse that he's buying.)
- What part of L.A.? (Tells a lot: a new-monied westsider, a puff-puff Pasadena boy, a family-oriented boy from Downey, or a down-to-earth East L.A. type? His townhouse is in Glendale, a suburb north of L.A., that has tons of Armenians, young professionals and families.)
- Where did he grow up? (Born in Mexico—Sinaloa—raised in L.A. since a baby.)
- And the important question: What are his intentions? (To be happy and to make Keith happy.)

Everything checks out for the moment, and Cesar smiles, offers up a cigarette to Marco Antonio and Rafael, which they decline, telling you they're going downstairs to watch the drag queen show, so you can be alone with Cesar. You're sure they'll do their own analysis and share their findings with you later.

You and Cesar continue to make small talk and laugh at all the straight people below waiting in line for the hetero club next door. He compliments your caramel-colored skin, razor-lined haircut and sexy lips. You compliment his Brown Pride style of dress tonight and willingness to put up with Marco Antonio and Rafael's line of questions. You both give each other the eye and that little head nod that says "Let's get to know each other a little better tonight." Cigarettes done. Drinks empty. You give him an Altoid. He buys you a drink in the hip-hop dance room and you "Shake It Fast, Pass the Courvoisier," and "Back That Thang Up" for so long that you forget your boys are downstairs, but now that the drag queen show is over it will be next to impossible to find them in the sea of *cholos*, homies, *fresas* and pretty-boys shaking their bodies to the latest Paulina Rubio, Shakira and Enrique Iglesias dance mix.

Cesar slips his hands into your back pants pocket and kisses you in the middle of the hip-hop dance floor. Little do you know that your Dreamlover's ex-Dreamlover, the Lat-chino, is watching you the whole time from the other side of the hip-hop room, and is pissed off, on probation and proba-bly about to go postal on you, which he proceeds to do. Long Island Ice Tea belongs in a glass—not on your favorite Banana Republic black sweater, nor drenched on your Kenneth Cole boots, nor in your face.

Cesar and ex-Dreamlover yell at each other about stuff you're clueless to.

"How could you cheat on me like this?"

"Who left who first?"

"You still have my leather jacket!"

"Where's my DVD player?"

"You fucked up my life!"

"You fucked up my credit!"

"*Chinga tu madre.*"

"¡*Chinga* tu *madre!*"

"Tell your nigga to stop mad dogging."

"Quit showing up at random places acting crazy."

Now what's really crazy is this: The crowd continues dancing, drinking and doing their own thing as if this is just a basic, everyday conversation in the suburbs. You'd think someone would care to stop the insanity, but they don't. You realize that Cesar is embroiled in his own real-life miniseries, and you've unwillingly auditioned for a supporting role in this south-of-the-border *novela*. And you remember this is just one of a thousand similar scenes and men you've encountered since moving to L.A.

So you leave Cesar to handle his business with Lat-chino, clean yourself off in the downstairs bathroom and look for your boys. One—the innocent-acting Marco Antonio—is dancing with Julio, the boy from the Mayan Warriors softball team he's been flirting with for months (you realize you've never met Marco Antonio's so-called actor boyfriend yet). Your other boy—the one like a loose and malfunctioning slot in Vegas, Rafael—is making sweet talk against the wall with someone new, someone really fine as usual, another black boy. This one looks like the light-skinned reggae singer Sean Paul. You're a little upset about the Cesar/Lat-chino ex situation, and hate that you promised your best friend, Marco Antonio, you'd do your best to get along with Rafael, his former social work client and current roommate and friend.

What bugs you most is that Rafael's trick is another black boy. This one appears mixed black and something else, and you have an "a-ha" moment of sadness. Black boys don't talk to each other in the gay L.A. scene, or any other gay scene, when they're in the presence of non-black boys. Why's that? Better get Oprah on the case. Your paranoid side tells you black men aren't en vogue anymore, with any ethnicity, in the gay scene. Everybody loves Latinos. And mixed boys. And anything watered down with white-boy features. Just not all black. And while your own education may have taught you that exploitation, divide and conquer, and treating ethnic boys as objects are nothing new in the gay community, you feel bad that many men of color get trapped in the web and don't know it. The fact that you're a black boy in a gay world shaped by white privilege negates all your good qualities and makes you feel like cigarette ashes on a barroom floor. Especially when you can't seem to find a date for almost ten years, unless you're willing to settle for someone as old as Santa Claus, into power and dominance and who just talks about themselves all night, thinking you'll be submissive and laugh at all their tired stories. All you know is you've had a nonexistent dating life in L.A. until now with Cesar. And that you're pushing thirty and haven't had a real boyfriend since you were twenty and a college undergrad. Where is Shawn Bentley? He'd be a doctor by now. Could have been good together. Anyway.

So what's a boy to do when you've just been pulled into a nighttime melodrama, had liquor poured all over you and been yelled at by Cesar's ex? Just stand on the side of the dance floor, wait for Rafael and Marco Antonio to finish what they've started at the club and wonder how those leftover greens, macaroni and cheese and catfish will taste when you finally get home at four-thirty in the morning. Because you sure are hungry, horny and a little bit buzzed.

You hope your roommate, Tommie, and his partner, Tyrell, are already asleep, so you won't have to see them cuddled up on the new living room furniture you bought and won't have to retell the same made-up story about your night: "Yeah, it was cool! Met lots of cool people! Had fun!

Got a couple of numbers! Cesar's great!" Cool. Awesome. Great. Dandy.

You know tonight was a mistake and you should have kept your butt at home like you planned, but nooooooo! You worried too much about who and what you would be missing out on if you didn't head out to the club tonight. Heck, you're twenty-nine years old and know your lifelong Dreamlover's not going to be found in a place like this, even when Dreamlover—er, Cesar—walks your way to apologize and to ask for another chance.

"What? You want me to crawl on rice?" he asks.

"No," you respond. "Rice and broken glass."

"Fine." Cesar turns around and walks away. Just like the rest of them.

You realize he doesn't get your sarcasm or understand that you would gladly give him another chance. Good luck finding him tonight—one of three thousand brown and black men in smoky club lighting—and you doubt he'll return your call if you leave a message. You hope you can make things right. You hope he'll be as interested in you as he was before the crazy ex showed up. You hope you're not chasing another slum date—a boy who's not at your level. But knowing the dating pool is lacking, you know you should go and find Cesar. And then you wonder what's crazier: Cesar's ex causing a scene on the dance floor? Or you wanting to make things right with Cesar when he apparently doesn't have things right in his own life?

Cesar's ex. Naturally.

But in the meantime, the New Year is just two months young and you can still keep your resolution to not go clubbing so much. But for now, it's the same old arena, same script, same cast, and same Saturday night scene you hate and love at the same time.

Chapter 13

MARCO ANTONIO

I'm waking up with Julio, but it's not what it looks like. We're just friends, though Keith and Rafael think he's the perfect replacement for Alex. Whatever. Julio is a friend, and honestly I wouldn't consider being with him as more than a friend. We talk. We listen. We share problems. We laugh. He got me through the long months of Alex being away on a movie set or making a video. Well, that's something I don't have to worry about any longer, especially once this afternoon's Sunday dinner is over.

I make a little breakfast before I have to put on my acting face for the day. Going to morning Mass with my family is something I can deal with, but going to the family party with Alex will take all the strength I can muster up. It's such a façade, the whole deal with Alex. When I told Keith, Rafael and Julio all about it last night, they just laughed at me.

Julio's still laughing about it as I pour a glass of orange juice and fix him a plate of *chorizo* and eggs, with several jalapeños on the side to help fight his hangover. He couldn't drive last night after he, Keith, Rafael and I came back from another Saturday night of dancing and heavy drinking, so he stayed over. It was all innocent. Nothing happened. And he's promised to help me with the chores around the apartment after breakfast, even with the hangover. If Alex were half the man Julio is, he and I would have a chance. But as long as he's got that wife, no matter if it's just for the cameras or not, I'm not taking Alex back. All I have to do is make it through the family dinner my *tía* insisted on hosting for Alex, and everything will be all right.

"You feeling alright, Julio?"

"Yeah. I just drank too much," he says while putting on the black T-shirt he wore last night. He's just wearing boxers and the middle buttons are loose, exposing his goods. "Why'd you let me drink so many Kamikazes?"

"It's cool. We all took care of you."

"I didn't do anything crazy, did I?"

"Well, it's nothing big," I say. "Don't worry."

"No, tell me."

"You just told me how much you love me over and over once we got here."

"How embarrassing," Julio says. "I'm sorry, Marco."

"It was cute," I say and sit down across from him at the dining room table.

"Cute?"

"Yeah."

"Just cute?"

I can tell Julio is a little disappointed with my response. I wish I could give him more than that, but as long as I've got this Alex situation . . . What am I saying? It'll be over in just a few hours. *Stop tripping, Marco Antonio.*

I hear Rafael's bedroom door open, and he and some young kid dressed in blue sweatpants and a hooded sweatshirt come into the kitchen. It's not the Sean Paul lookalike he was making with last night at the club.

"Whassup, bitches?" Rafael says. "This is Enrique."

"Enrique?" I say.

"I'm about to drop him off and then head to Macy's. You hungry, Papa? Can he have some of your food?"

"*No tengo hambre,*" Enrique says. "My mother should have breakfast ready when I get home."

I give Rafael a strange look, and he throws his car keys to Enrique.

"Papa, go start up my car, *por favor.*"

Enrique leaps out the door on Rafael's request.

"How old is that boy, Rafael?"

"Bitch, as long as there's grass on the field, I'm playing the game."

"You don't need any trouble messing with minors," I say. "I'm supposed to report stuff like that."

"Bitch, I ain't your client anymore. I'm your friend and roommate. And he's just four years younger than me. Chill."

"Just be careful, Rafael. You don't want any accusations out there."

"Homeboy's closeted and neither his mama or his girl-friend know he into *chorizo.* In other words, he a willing participant and ain't telling nobody about us fucking around."

"Alright. I'm just saying."

"Thanks, Mom," he says, and picks some eggs off my plate. "Bye, Julio. Bye, Marco."

Rafael leaves, and Julio and I continue eating our breakfast. I've got just a few minutes before I have to leave for Mass.

"So anyway, Julio, you wouldn't want to come to a party this afternoon?"

"I'll let you handle that one," Julio says. "Besides, I've got a softball team meeting today. But call me later and maybe we can do something. That's if you're not offended by what happened last night."

"I'm not offended. I think it's cute."

"I'd hope you'd see it as more than cute. I knew everything I was doing last night, and I meant everything."

I had a feeling Julio wasn't kidding, but I'm just not in the
position to make more than a joke out of the situation right
now.

Tía Florinda looks like she spent her last dime on her Ross
dress-for-less outfit, the decorations and the food at this little
fiesta she put together. What's usually a weekly family dinner
for around ten has exploded to almost seventy people in the
backyard of her small Huntington Park home. It's a good
thing we're having sunny weather this March afternoon, or
else we'd be cramped inside. She's got three six-foot tables
loaded with family favorites: enchiladas, tamales, grilled *carne
asada* and *lengua* (steak and tongue) for tacos, *birria* (specially
prepared goat meat), fresh Mexican cheese, *pastel de tres leches*
(cake of three milks), and all the sides the Vega family would
ever want to eat. And as with all Mexican family gatherings,
there's a bottle of El Jimador tequila at every table and some
hidden by the chair legs of the elders. Dozens of plastic chairs
line the gray cinderblock fence containing the backyard. There's
even one of the on-air personalities from 97.9 *La Raza* DJ'ing
for the gathering and a portable dance floor on top of the
concrete where my cousin Lalo usually keeps an old car or
motorcycle he's repairing. Of course, this isn't just any family
gathering. All these people are here to see and meet the liar of
the century, Alex de la Torre. And I'm the little pawn in this
whole game.

On the ride over, I kept fighting Alex's hands that kept
coming across the invisible line in the car I told him not to
cross. He managed a couple of kisses on my cheek, which I
wiped off like a kid does an old relative's kisses. And he kept

saying how much he was looking forward to meeting my family and being a part of their lives. I told him even if there were no more air and he held the last oxygen tank in the world, I would let myself suffocate, and therefore why would I want him to be part of my family or my life? He just flashed his bright Hollywood smile and laughed. I swear the man is insane.

"*¡Alejandro!*"

Tía Florinda and my mother whisk Alex away from me and into the crowd of screaming relatives. They act like they're teens at a Justin Timberlake concert. My family obviously doesn't know the lengths this man will go to live a lie and that he's got us all playing a silly game. From the looks of things, they don't even know he's supposedly dating me. At least *Tía* kept that part of her promise. Everyone's got their newest *People en Español* magazines out and open for Alex to autograph. There's an exclusive pictorial of his wedding to La Princesa, complete with pictures of the celebrity guests. Someone comments on how much smaller he looks in person. Another says he looks younger up close than on screen. One of my cousins asks Alex how he knows me. He lies and says he used to date one of my female friends, and we've maintained our friendship over the past year. Alex is good. Real good at coming up with lines really quickly. Just like any actor would.

Alex looks over at me and winks. He's loving this scene and all the attention he's getting. It's his element. I do have to admit he looks sexy standing there in the sunshine and charming my family. I can't believe I'm dating him. Well, used to date him and now just putting up the charade for my parents. And pretending that he's straight to the rest of these naïve members of my family who think gay people only exist in white society. Once again, I find myself back in a closet that I don't necessarily want to be in. I fought too long to ed-

ucate myself and to be proud of who I am as a gay Latino to
have this part of me pushed aside for my family's kicks. But I
can't embarrass my parents in front of the family by outing
Alex, myself and our nonexistent relationship, or telling them
this is one big farce.

I walk to the front of the house and call up Julio on my
cell. Just to check in with him.

"*Hola, Julio. ¿Qué haces?*"

"Just finished the softball stuff," Julio says. "We're heading
to Baja Fresh for lunch. What about you?"

"Living my own *novela* at *Tía* Florinda's. I hate Alex."

"*Pobrecito.*"

"It's okay," I say. "He'll probably write this one up for
Mujer: Casos de la Vida Real. It would be like him to use our
story to make money."

"It's all over after today. One party is all you promised the
folks."

"Speaking of new beginnings, Julio, I want to talk a little
about what's happening with us."

"Don't worry about it, Marco. I was drunk."

"Drunk words, sober thoughts."

"Well . . . maybe," Julio says. "But I know you don't need
the drama. And I don't want to be your rebound action."

"Well, let's talk. We're adults."

"I'll stop by your place later tonight."

"Cool. *Gracias.*"

"*Pues.* Bye."

I have one more call to make before getting back to *la familia* Vega.

"Keith?"

"Yeah?"

"What's up? Have you talked to Cesar since Arena?"

"He's left about ten messages, but I don't feel like talking to him," Keith says.

"So what are you going to do?"

"I'll think about it when I get back to L.A. I found a red-eye flight available after the club. I'm in Detroit for Sunday dinner."

"Must be nice having money to fly on a whim," I say. "Good for you. I'm with my family and Alex. After this family dinner thing is done, I'm through with him and moving on to Julio."

"Interesting," Keith says. "Gotta run. Have church tonight. See you in a couple days."

In the meantime, I'm going back to enjoy some of this free food and will make sure to pack plenty of leftovers for me to take to work this week. That's the least I can expect to get out of this party with Alex and the family.

Before I can get back to the festivities, my mom and dad sneak up behind me with hugs and smiles. As long as I'm happy, my dad says with tears brimming his eyes, I have their blessing. Then the kicker: especially if I can manage to have a life with someone as kind-hearted and full of character as Alex. They pull me into a group hug, my mom is crying, and my guilt is growing over the lies Alex and I are pulling over my family. I don't have any desire to break their hearts once again. Not today, anyway.

Chapter 14

RAFAEL

I knew Cesar was shady when he met Keith all them weeks ago at Tempo. Accepting a beer from me, a stranger, at the bar? Handing me his business card in front of Keith? Please. I may not have all the degrees and papers Keith or Marco Antonio got, but I got common sense about how the mens work. *No soy estúpida.* Even though I know Keith think I'm just an uneducated wetback slut, I think he cool sometimes and don't want to see him get played by one of my peeps. I don't want him getting a bad attitude about Mexicans. Which is why I called up Cesar's number and asked him to meet me out at Tempo tonight. To set things straight and prove what Cesar is all about.

Much to my surprise, he accepts the date and is walking in the door, dressed in his *vaquero* best—black boots and jeans, silver belt buckle with the letters C-E-S-A-R, gray-and-black checked shirt and black felt *tejana* hat. Baby got back, front and top, and I can't believe Keith would even consider letting this one go.

"I'm meeting some friends here in a few minutes," Cesar says, shouting above the live band. "¿*Qué quieres,* Rafael?"

"Bitch, you need an attitude adjustment." I hand him a brand-new beer. "¡*Salud!*"

We tap bottles and Cesar takes a long swig of his drink, almost finishing the whole thing in one swallow.

"Sorry for the attitude," Cesar says. "Just a little frustrated with the Keith situation. Have you heard from him?"

"That fool went to Michigan today. He's so dramatic. 'I just can't take it anymore. I gotta get out of here.'"

Cesar laughs at my monologue and soap-opera-like hand gesture, planting my wrist on my forehead.

"All I have is a crazy ex. I wouldn't hurt Keith deliberately."

"Right," I say. "What you doing messing around with a *Chinito* anyway? Them be some crazy, obsessive bitches."

I grab a nearby waiter and order one tequila shot and two more beers, which, thanks to happy hour, will be two shots and four beers.

"I'll pay." Cesar takes out his wallet and hands me a twenty. "Anyway, that's a stereotype. He's Mexican and Korean. Jay was a cool dude at first, but he got too possessive. When I ended it, he just couldn't handle it and he snapped."

"See what I'm saying?"

"I'm sure you've dealt with crazy people before."

"I don't stay with 'em long enough to find out," I say and laugh.

We down the last of beer number one, and the waiter brings our new order.

"¡*Salud!*"

"¡*Salud!*"

We tap shot glasses and take the shots to the head.

"Anyway, what should I do to make things right with Keith?" Cesar asks. "You're his friend. You've known him longer."

"Forget about him tonight," I say and start my new beer. "Keith ain't about to give you up. He might not give you some *culo*, if you get my drift, but he ain't going nowhere, Cesar."

"I hope you're right. Keith is the kind of guy you want to take home to your family."

"He alright, I guess."

"But you're right about him being tight as Fort Knox in the ass department. He's not giving up the goods at all."

One of my favorite songs starts. "*La Chica Sexy*," by Los Tucánes de Tijuana.

"Finish up that beer, Cesar, and *baila conmigo*."

"Sure."

Cesar is a true gentleman and leads me onto the crowded dance floor. Everyone's looking. I don't know if they're looking at me, at Cesar, or the fact that the two best looking *vatos* in Tempo are together. "*La Chica Sexy*" is a fast song, a *banda*, and we get our aerobic workout dancing in the side-to-side bunny-hopping style that works with this music. But Cesar is a real fancy dancer. He grabs my hands and takes the lead, pulling me toward him, twirling me around the floor, then does a few off-count but on-the-beat moves. I'm sweating, and Cesar hands me his handkerchief to dab my face. Another of my favorites, "*Y Como Quieres Que Te Quiera*" by Fabian Gomez, follows, and for this one Cesar leads again, my head against his muscled chest, my right hand in his left, and we shuffle forward twice, back twice, and swirl around five or six times. By the end of the thirty-minute set of songs, I am dizzy and drenched in sweat. So is Cesar. The DJ starts up a reggae-ton mix, but like the band, Cesar and I decide to take a break. He takes off his dress shirt, throws it on a bar stool, and sits down on top of it. He's got on a black tank top, and not an ounce of fat around his midsection. The sweat on his shoulders looks so damn hot. Like I wanna freaking lick it off or feel it against my skin. Keith is one stupid bitch putting Cesar on hold.

"You're good," Cesar says, and sits down on an empty bar stool by the wall. "You know how to keep up."

"I've been told." I take a healthy swallow of beer. "But of course, you'll never know how good I am."

"I'm talking about dancing, fool."

"Right, Cesar."

"*¿No me crees*? Why would I lie?" he asks and in soap-opera style opens his mouth as if surprised, nods from side to side and holds his hands out in front of him.

"Because you and I have a lot in common," I say.

"Like what?"

"We're both Mexican. We both look hella fine. And I know we've both got needs."

"Needs?"

"Good rhythm on the dance floor, good rhythm in bed."

"I don't know what you're talking about, Rafael."

"You're smart, Cesar. Figure it out."

"You're drunk."

"Another thing we have in common." I hold up my empty beer bottle. "I need another one."

"Take mine. I've had enough."

"Thank you, *papi*." I grab the bottle and slide it along his bicep. To cool him off, of course. "Mmm, nice. Any man would be crazy not to give it up to you."

"So what are you trying to say?"

"You know what I'm trying to say."

"Serious?" Cesar asks. "Nah, you need to quit."

"*¡Claro que sí!*"

"I don't believe you, Rafael."

I squeeze between his legs and lean forward, pressing my

chest against his. I pull his hat off and start kissing his left ear and licking the left side of his neck. His hands caress the back of my hair.

"Believe me now, *papi*?" I whisper in his ear.

"*Sí.*"

"So what's up, *papi*? *¿Qué quieres hacer?*"

"I think you know."

What started as just a test to prove Cesar is no good for Keith is boomeranging on me. We barely make it five steps into his townhouse, five minutes into a blow job before he releases, when Cesar says five words I don't want to hear.

"When can I see you?"

"How about Wednesday?"

We agree on a date. And we agree on one more thing before I leave his place.

"Keith doesn't have to know about this."

"He can't know about this."

Chapter 15

TOMMIE

My Tyrell got an extra thousand dollars in his account from his pops, so he taking me out to Universal City Walk for dinner and a few rides in the amusement park. It ain't often that we get the same weeknight free. Tyrell usually got some paper to write or some kinda team practice or workout, except tonight his coach is sick and told the team to enjoy the free day.

This going out on dates with dudes is new territory for me. Usually, I'll just kick it at my place or the dude's with a movie, maybe eat a little bit of Chinese takeout, and most definitely get our sex on. My Tyrell done opened up a new world to me. Don't get me wrong. The sex good with my Tyrell. But we done more things in just a few short months than I ever did while singing or touring everywhere with Renaissance Phoenix, and we supposedly was living the high life in the music industry. Maybe 'cause Tyrell so bousghie and got parents who taught him how to entertain someone the right way. Tried Jamaican food, Ethiopian food, Indian food. Listened to some ska, British punk and even a little black rock. Even been to some of those fancy UCLA parties and campus events with him, where those Afrocentric peeps and professors be talking about real smart things. I don't usually get it, but I stand there and pretend like I do. Being cultured just come natural to my Tyrell, and he take me along. No embarrassment. No issues. No trying to make me be all proper and white-boyish, like Keith act sometimes. In public, we just kick it like friends, but at night he sex me up real nice. Maybe 'cause he so young and ain't been burned yet by these crazy punks, cause they'd be all on his ass if they knew what side of the court he play on. He was raised right, with dignity, family pride and respect.

Not like Sylvia and me, where the way our family entertained was with everyone bringing over a dish, a coupla forties of beer or Boone's, a little bit of bud and red or blue lights in the living room lamps. Slammin' bones on a card table. Bid-whist game in the basement. Making sure everyone gone by three or four in the morning so we can wake up on time to make Reverend Hemmings' Sunday morning sermon. That's what I'm talking about. Back when me, Dennis, Andre, and Montell were forming our little four-part harmony singing group. Sylvia wrote our songs. We performed at talent shows, backyard parties and sometimes at church, when Keith could talk his father into letting us sing as a group at Sunday service.

But things changed. Sylvia and Dennis got hooked up with coke as soon as we got to L.A., and she stopped writing the bomb-ass songs that got Renaissance Phoenix discovered in the first place. I was fighting daily with the other group members over money, who would sing lead, who was gonna do what interview. We couldn't agree on costumes or even haircuts. Not a damn thing. Then Sylvia ends up pregnant with Dennis's baby, my niece Keesha, and the whole situation pretty fucked up now. I can't stand Sylvia. Hate Dennis's ass even more. And the best thing I got going is this relationship with Tyrell. And maybe Keith's friendship.

"If we wasn't in public now, I'd grab you and kiss you," my Tyrell whispers across candlelight at our corner table. "You never talk this much about yourself. I'm loving it."

"Must be the wine, 'cause I'm rambling too much. I hope you ain't put nothing in it like no date-rape drug or shit like that." I sniff the glass and laugh. "I'ma tell you a secret. You don't need to drug me. Tommie Jordan ready all the time."

"I know that much is true."

"So none of this bother you? About my issues? My crazy sister?"

"We all got issues. My pops always says you hang in there."

"I ain't have a good role model like that in my home. Keith's father and family always been there for me."

"Good. And you gotta be that for your niece."

"True."

My Tyrell orders another glass of wine. It's for me, he say, because he can't drink until basketball season over. I tell him just one more glass, 'cause I'm driving tonight, but I gotta hit the men's room bad.

"So speaking of parents, I wondered if you'd want to meet my mom and pop?" Tyrell asks me. "They have some political party fundraiser to attend in a few weeks."

"One of them tux and tail deals?" I ain't sure I wanna do this.

"Well, you don't have to go to the fundraiser," my Tyrell says. "But I want you at least to come to some of my games with my folks while they're here."

"I can handle a game. But how you explaining a grown-ass man hanging out with their little college boy?"

"I don't know. You're the older one. Help me figure it out."

"Well, let's both think about it while I go take a leak."

I head across the restaurant to the bathroom, when out of a booth on the right I hear a dude call, "Mmmmm, look at this fine chocolate bitch."

I know the voice. I turn my head to see who it is. It's Keith's friend Rafael. Looks like a date to me.

"Bitch, what you doing over in this part of town?" Rafael yells.

I kneel down by the table. This punk don't know a thing about being discreet or having a little class, especially being around all these white folks here. Even I know better than that.

"I'm having dinner like everyone else up in here," I say. "Shouldn't you be working tonight?"

He coughs and smiles. "I'm sick. Can't you tell? Anyway, Tommie, this is Cesar. Cesar, Tommie."

"Keith's friend?" I ask. "Nah, I don't wanna know."

"Anyway, Tommie. Don't keep your baller-shot-caller waiting."

"That's messed up, man. See y'all later."

I stand up, and Rafael whispers, "If anyone asks, you didn't see me out. Especially if your roommate asks. Cool?"

"You owe me big, Rafael."

I heard from Keith a while back that keeping secrets for Rafael ain't too cool, but I think in this case it's smart. I just don't know what Rafael doing out with Keith's boy.

When I'm walking back to my table, I notice Rafael and his date done left. My Tyrell is finishing up his cranberry juice and has a full glass of wine waiting for me.

"I hope you can take me back to UCLA in the morning,"

my Tyrell says. "It looks like I'll have to take the keys from you tonight."

"You staying over?"

"Just spot me some fresh gear in the morning and I'm staying. So have you thought about how to explain this to my folks?"

"A little. We'll talk more tonight."

"Cool."

"Oh, those fellas you were talking to stopped by on their way out." Tyrell hunches up his nose. "The little Latino was giving mad attitude to me and said for you to call him. Here's his number." Tyrell flicks the number across the table.

"That's Keith's friend Rafael," I say. "I wonder what he wants?"

"I don't know, but I don't like him. I don't get good vibes."

"Rafael's a joke, Tyrell. No need for jealousy."

Why Rafael leaving me his number is a mystery to me. But I take it, whisper to my Tyrell he ain't got nothing to worry about—that I don't do Mexicans—and get ready to head over to the amusement park side of Universal City for a few rides, games and shows before my Tyrell and I head back to Pasadena.

Chapter 16

RAFAEL

I can't have all these *jotas* sweatin' me like I'm the last boy on earth who give good head. If I could bottle my secret, I'd be a millionaire and everyone would get laid like me. Maybe it's the brown eyes, maybe it's the smile, maybe it's the body I work out and eat right to have, maybe it's just my sexy personality, but whatever it is, it's not working on Keith's roommate, Tommie. I thought for sure he'd be calling me by now, but that bookworm boyfriend of his probably never gave Tommie my number. I guess they're both too loyal to each other to fall for my "it" factor.

However, it *is* working on that kid, Enrique, and that old man, Cesar. Shit, you let a high school boy fuck you a few times and he ready to dump his little *barrio* girlfriend. Like this morning, when I dropped him off at his mom's house in East L.A., Enrique starts whining and almost crying when I tell him I don't know when I'm seeing him again. Mind you, this boy is a starter on the Garfield football team, got arms and abs of steel and look like he could gang bang with the best of them, but he's huffing and puffing like Erica Kane from *All My Children* because I tell him I gotta work two jobs to make ends meet and need to slow down our thing. Poor kid even offered to give me part of his 7–Eleven check, but I told him I can't take his little money.

Now Cesar, on the other hand, I'll take a handout from. I got one free dinner outta him the other night at Universal CityWalk. But with that freebie, I kinda had to give up the goods again. Dude think I give the best head this side of the border, and now ready to buy me all kinda shit because I take it all in and finish him off in minutes. I guess he ain't grew no stamina in his twenty-nine years, because just like the high schooler, Enrique, Cesar can come before I even get my lips wrapped all the way around the shit. But I ain't complaining. I ain't gotta fuck, and I still manage to get a few dollars out of him. Anything to help keep up with my bills. I told him he can get a quickie from me anytime, but if it's a long-term thing he wants, he'd be better off with my friend Keith. It's the least I can do for a friend.

Roneshia and I are clocking out from our Macy's shift, legally this time, and taking our asses up to Keith's condo. We're heading out to Tempo once again. It's Roneshia's first time at a gay bar, and she been dying to meet her some Keith Hemmings. She says she ain't met a brotha with legit money, so she curious. Plus she said she read some stuff about him and his family on the Internet. I ain't know Keith's family was all that large, but she told me about all these articles she seen. I tell her despite all that, he can be nice and down to earth when he not being all Judge Judy about how other people living.

Keith is waiting in front of his condo in his car when we arrive and park.

"You know if we don't get there by six-thirty, there's a huge line," Keith says. "And I don't want the people looking at me like some uppity Negro because I pay to get to the front of the line. You know that's what they think when they see me."

Damn. This bitch always gotta disturb the groove.

"Keith, there was mad traffic on the freeway, and we had to drive up the streets through Alhambra and San Marino. And you know how those Alhambra cops are with a nigga. They pulled me over supposedly because of my brake light being out, but I know it's because a black girl and brown boy were rolling through their town. Anyway, long story short, the good thing is we're ready to party," I say, and open up a Smirnoff Ice that Keith has in a small cooler in the back seat. "By the way, Keith, this my girl Roneshia. Roneshia, Keith."

"Good to meet you, Keith," Roneshia says. "I'll shake your hand when you're not driving."

"Smart move. Help yourself to a drink, Roneshia."

"This a phat ride, Keith. How much does an A6 cost?" Roneshia asks, and I try to signal to her to shut up. Keith hates questions related to his money. That's a quick way to get on his bad side. But she don't get my hint.

"You know the saying, 'if you have to ask, you can't afford it'?" Keith says.

I knew he would find a smart-ass comment for her. Keith can be like that sometimes. That's probably why his ass on the verge of thirty and with no man in the near future. Unless he counts my hand-me-down, Cesar.

"Well, I just wanted to know," Roneshia continues. "Rafael be talking about you all the time, about how you made some money investing in computer stocks or something, and that you ain't gotta work if you don't want to. And I heard about your family's church. Y'all like royalty up in Detroit. I wish I had it like that."

"Before we find out more about you, Roneshia, I'll just say I'm lucky and blessed, and my family works hard."

"You must be blessed," Roneshia says. "I hope some of it rubs off on me. I'm tired of struggling." Roneshia laughs and opens up a drink.

Keith warms up to Roneshia eventually, and he's told his entire life history from being a preacher's son in Detroit to getting his degrees from Stanford to starting his diversity business in L.A. It's the same story I've heard a million times, but it's interesting to Roneshia, who keeps asking Keith questions. I don't mind. It helps us pass time from Pasadena to Hollywood, which is good, because after three of those Smirnoffs I'm ready to get my dance on tonight. I decide to change the subject to something that might get Keith cheered up a bit.

"So how's things going with you and Cesar?" I ask.

"It's okay."

"Just okay? Have you gone out with him or talked to him since you got back from Michigan?"

"Yeah. A couple times."

"How was it?"

"Why all the questions, Rafael? As if . . ." I swear Keith's got issues. "Nothing. Forget it. I don't want to talk about Cesar now, okay?!?"

I don't know why Keith all of a sudden clamming up like he ain't got nothing to report. You'd think after the drought he been in, he'd be way more excited about this new love interest. Though I can imagine if he experienced Cesar's dick, he might feel a little shortchanged, so to speak. Oh shit, what if Tommie said something about seeing me and Cesar together? Or if Cesar opened his big mouth? Keith woulda said something before now, wouldn't he? Okay, I'ma chill with the paranoia.

Anyway, we don't have to wait too long to see why Keith ain't too talkative. Cesar standing in the line, with his tall, fine self, and got his arms around someone new—a brotha. Well, the brotha ain't new to the Latino club scene in L.A., but he obviously new in Cesar's life, the way they kissing and hugging all over each other. And I can tell it's bothering Keith. Keith snatches a hundred-dollar bill out his wallet and hands it to the valet. He don't even wait for the change, and I grab what I can. And the three of us march ourselves past the dozens of people waiting in line. None of us even come close to matching the western wear attire of the club goers this evening. Keith is urban prep, with a fresh fade cut, jeans and a black sweater-shirt. Roneshia's glammed up in her shimmery champagne-colored pantsuit. I'm sporting the newest Sean John gear shipped to the store today. We all look out of place for Tempo, but still look good. Even Keith, for a change, looking kinda fly.

"Keith, don't worry about it, baby." Roneshia puts her arms around Keith. "We will get you fixed up with some cutie tonight. Ain't no reason a brotha like you, with all your money and brains, should be single."

And I agree. There's too many good dicks out there for *any* of us to be single. So as soon as I can ditch Keith, Roneshia and their "Relationships 101" discussion, I'ma take advantage of all the single opportunities awaiting me at Tempo. I'm ready to be the designated drinker and dick hunter tonight.

Tonight's lucky winner at Tempo is a beautiful half-Puerto Rican, half-Dominican college student from West Covina, which is about twenty minutes east of where I stay. Leonardo. From the look and feel of the package in his jeans, he should more than pick up where Enrique and Cesar left off. And the stories I hope to create with Leonardo should more than entertain Keith and Roneshia next time we're out together. I just hope they realize I'm already gone from the club.

Chapter 17

KEITH

The Magic Johnson Starbucks in Ladera Heights is one of my favorite places to spend an afternoon. Right now, I'm working on my laptop, sipping on a cold caramel frappuccino and checking out the scenery. Some of the nicest looking—and richest—black men in the city live nearby and come through these doors. Today is no exception. I can't help but take a glance when some nice caramel, cappuccino or chocolate shoulders and pecs are filling out a clean, crisp tank top or T-shirt. I need to sell that condo in Pasadena and move into a house here in Ladera or Baldwin Hills or View Park, where there's plenty of brothas nearby.

I know this will probably come as a surprise to Marco, Rafael and Tommie, who seem to think that all I do is go after Latinos, but I'm going to slow down on the Latino thing for a bit. Imagined or not by my friends, when I think about it, my list of recent dates have tended to tilt toward the brown side instead of the black side. Before Cesar, there was Juan Carlos, the auto mechanic who lasted all of two weeks. Nothing to talk about. Language barrier on both sides beyond the basics. Then Michael, whose real name was Miguel, the publicist for an independent movie studio, who lasted two days. A card-carrying conservative who hated his ethnicity, hated his parents' Spanish language and hated anything related to my diversity work. You'd think we would have never met nor wanted to go out together, but three martinis and two years of loneliness can make anyone seem attractive. Then Jesús, one of Rafael's club friends, who was after one thing only, and I knew it—proving a myth or two about black men. Took us at least four or five times trying to make sure his curiosity was thoroughly satisfied. And after going through the motions of trying to keep a friends-with-benefits deal going, we figured it wasn't worth it. Okay, who am I kidding? Jesús just stopped calling. It's not like it's been a deliberate choosing of others over people like me. You tend to meet who's around you and your circle of friends—for me, kicking it with Marco Antonio and Rafael has meant that I've met mostly Latinos. It's not like Tommie has a huge entourage of available black people he hangs with. They're all down low and staying away from each other to avoid suspicion.

At Stanford when I kicked it at the Black Community Services Center, known as "The Black House," I met the one who should have been the one, Shawn Bentley, a medical student in his final year at Stanford, during a community roundtable on the anniversary of the L.A. uprisings and civil unrest. Politics, diverse opinions and busy schedules aside, I found Shawn's intelligence, sense of humor, energy and spiritual centeredness as attractive as his good looks and future income potential. I knew he was planning to start his residency that fall in Washington, D.C., where his mother and father were a dentist and pediatrician, respectively, but I let myself surrender to live theatre, beach outings, a spontaneous summer cruise to Ensenada, Mexico, homemade Jamaican food at his place, reading passages from Toni Morrison, J. California

Cooper or the Bible after dinner, listening to John Coltrane, Nancy Wilson and Cannonball Adderley in the midnight hour, and morning jogs through the dry hills of Palo Alto and Menlo Park. Anything to be near Shawn, the mature, soon-to-be-doctor who was going to make my talented tenth existence multiply tenfold. Too bad I didn't believe him when he said he didn't do long distance and that our situation was just passing time before his move across the country. Broke my heart to hear those words. That's when I wrote the letter in which I poured out my feelings for Shawn and made the mistake of leaving it at Hemmings House during holiday vacation. Led to my parents' major cross-country "don't ask, don't tell" talk about the Hemmings' image management, my life, and that they wouldn't bring this up to Stephanie, Solomon or anyone else.

But anyway, I thought, and still think sometimes, there were feelings there. But like any other young and naïve person in love, I thought I could change his mind with a cell phone I bought him (before cells were even chic), open-ended plane tickets I sent him, or spontaneous visits to D.C. to visit other friends (but secretly and stupidly hoping/assuming he'd take time out of his new medical residency to entertain me). We lost touch, and I soon discovered that when you're focused on your academics and career, like I became when I started my Stanford graduate program a year later, you don't let temporary relationships get in the way of your goal. You wait until you've reached your goal and then seek permanent relationships.

Flash forward to Cesar. This situation is going nowhere fast, just like most of my L.A. relationships, if you can call them relationships. We've been out two times since I came back into town, and both dates were more focused on other people than on the two of us. *Lord, please give me the strength to get over Cesar and to remember what a bad person he is for me. Amen.*

Date #1. The afternoon I return. Cesar asks to meet at eight-thirty at 7-*Mares*, this Mexican seafood restaurant. In East L.A. of all places. Not my favorite location to drive alone at night in my new car—not because of fearing crime, but because of fearing police. Black man, nice car, middle of East L.A.?!?! You do the math. But that's another story. Anyway, Cesar calls ten minutes before we're supposed to meet. His car died. He needs me to pick him up from Pasadena City College. Silly man knows I live in Pasadena, and we could have chosen from a million seafood and Mexican spots up there, including 7-*Mares*. I don't even know how a working professional could own a car that breaks down. Anyway, I pick him up, and we drive to East Los. He's looking good as always, even reshaped the sideburns and goatee a little bit. He's smelling delicious with his Hanae Mori cologne. He's holding my hand, making conversation, apologizing for his car situation. We get a table and order large shrimp cocktails and Dos Equis beers for two. We're talking some more, but never keeping any eye contact. Not because he's shy, or because it's a cultural non verbal I have to be aware of. Cesar can't keep his eyes off the male waiters and cooks, or the cute male patrons, or even the male mariachi singers. He's even so bold as to hand out his cheesy business card to our waiter, Eduardo, a very young, very built and very good-looking man, and offers to help him get into community college. Right in front of me. Much in the same way Cesar did to Rafael the night Cesar and I met. I'm thinking to myself, this seems a little strange. But then I'm also thinking, I have a real date, with a real man, and could get some real dick to end this real long drought. Besides, Cesar could be a keeper, and if I don't give him something in the bedroom, he might not stay around. If not this date, at least by the next one. So I'll give him the benefit of the doubt and overlook his wandering eye disease.

Date #2. The next night. I know Tommie's got a late night doing inventory at the record store. So I invite Cesar to my place for the dinner-and-movie date, also known as the dinner-and-straight-to-bed date. I remember Cesar mentioned early in our dating that he liked soul food, but hadn't had very much to know what he liked. So I cook basics: crab cake appetizers, greens, sweet potatoes, fried chicken and pound cake. I mix up some good Southern Comfort and 7-Up drinks for us. We're cozying up on the leather sofa, about to watch *Punks* on DVD, still enjoying cocktails, and as I lean in for a kiss, Cesar turns away and asks if I want to invite Rafael or any of my other friends over to watch the film with us. He says it's a good film to watch with a group. When I tell him Rafael's probably working and everyone else is busy, he says we can pause the film and just talk for a while. I'm cool pausing, and cool with talking, but not cool with what the conversation centers on—Rafael. Do I think Rafael is cute? How did we meet? How often do we hang out? Is he visiting tonight? Have I ever slept with Rafael? I ask him if he'd rather be with Rafael. He denies it, but I trust my gut. I tell him that I'm nice, but not stupid, and that he needs to leave. The date is over. He says he'll give me a call in a few days when I get over my issues. *My* issues?

And then Cesar's got the nerve to flaunt a new brotha in front of me at Tempo the other night. As if feeling up on some black has-been who couldn't even compete in the Bay Area scene when Marco Antonio and I lived up there is going to get to me. It's like every other minute I look up from talking with Roneshia, and there's Cesar and Has-Been dancing, hugging, laughing and kissing in front of me.

Roneshia even made a sign, like those judges in skating com-
petitions, except her version was a bar napkin with "2.5"
written on it in eyeliner, and she flashed it at them every time
they were in eyesight of us. So besides hanging out with
Roneshia, who's a lot of fun, Tempo was a bust for all of us
except Rafael, who hooked up with yet another stranger.

So my slowing down on the Latino dating thing is actually
just more of a slowing down on the Cesar thing. I still think
he's incredibly smart, handsome and has his life together, for
the most part. In my head, I know what's happening between
us, or more like what's not happening, has nothing to do with
Cesar's ethnicity or the whole population of gay Latinos in
L.A. It's a personality thing. Or rather a Cesar-fixated-on-
my-friend thing. But I can't help but feel like when I'm doing
my best to put myself out there, there's something ethnicity-
related below the surface that makes my personal best a moot
point. Because no matter how much personality I show, good
looks I try to maintain, money I have or cars I drive, the fact
remains that I'm black in a city where beauty reigns, and
black ain't considered beautiful anymore.

And making matters worse, my laptop dies on me. Low
battery. So I can't even do the work for Marco Antonio I've
been procrastinating on.

I drive through Leimert Park to see what'll be happening at
Lucy Florence Café or the World Stage tonight. It looks like
another evening hanging out by myself, but maybe there'll be
something fun and cultural happening. Before hitting the
café ticket window, I buy a sweet potato pie for Tommie and
Tyrell at the bakery next door. Well, I ended up buying
three—one for Tommie and Tyrell, one for me, and one for
later . . . for me.

Looks like tonight is comedy night at the Lucy Florence. The show's sold out for the next couple weeks. The ticket attendant, a light-skinned black man with a neatly trimmed thin beard tracing the edge of his face, smiles and says he might be able to work something out for me. I decide I'll just head back to Pasadena. I'm brain dead from working on this presentation for Marco.

My car looks good but a little dusty in the hot L.A. afternoon sun, so I'll probably swing by a car wash on the way home. I should also stop by Esowon Bookstore while I'm over this way to see if the new Jervey Tervalon and Percival Everett books are out yet, and then check in with Marco to see if I'm still on for facilitating the new group at his job. As I'm pulling out the parking spot, the ticket attendant runs out of Lucy Florence Café toward me. What does he possibly want?

"Sir, your pies!"

I roll down the window, and he hands me the bakery bag. He flips his USC cap to the back before he leans in, letting all my air conditioning out and ushering in his cologne.

"Thanks. I guess I have a lot on my mind."

"Hey." He flashes his Colgate smile. "If you want to come back for the show tonight, I can probably . . . no, I will definitely hook you up, bro. You got a number or something?"

"I have a card." I hand it over. "Thanks, but you don't have to go through any trouble. I'm heading home to Pasadena and probably won't be back in Leimert Park for a bit."

"My folks stay in Altadena. I'm just passing time over here in between classes."

"Good for you," I say, and ease the car back a bit. "See you . . ."

"Since you're going home, how am I going to reach you? You only gave me your work number."

"My office is at my home."

"Fo'sheezy," ticket attendant man says and looks at my card. "Keith Hemmings, diversity trainer. Cool. I'm Dante Covington. I'm taking some Pan African studies classes at USC."

We shake hands. He smiles again.

"I should go. Don't want my pies to die in all this heat."

"That's cool," Dante says. "Hey, I haven't seen you around Lucy Florence much, but you should definitely come back. I'm here almost every day."

"I'll see. It's kinda far to be making regular visits from Pasadena."

"Don't worry. I'll pick you up one day when I'm visiting my folks in Altadena. We can catch one of the poetry nights or spoken word shows here."

Is he hitting on me? Can't be. I just met him.

"Well, Dante, thanks for your help and for saving my dessert. Give me a call."

"Fo'sheezy. Tonight."

Dante smiles, stands in my spot as I'm backing away, and watches me drive down Degnan Avenue and out of sight. He's probably just some young player and flirts with everyone who stops in his workplace. It's part of his act, charming the customers, I'm sure.

I stop at the red light, just before entering the 10 Freeway, and my cell rings. It's Cesar. What does he want? *Lord, please don't let this boy sucker me in again.*

"Hey, Keith. What's up?"

"I'm driving and talking to you. Why?"

"Attitude, *morenito*. The way I like you."

"You asked what's up. I told you."

"Hey, I won't keep you then," Cesar says. "Do you want to get together this weekend?"

"As in a date, Cesar?"

"And maybe some nookie," he says and chuckles. "What do you say?"

"I don't know. Have you gotten over your Rafael crush yet?"

"How did I know you'd bring that up? Keith, I'm talking to you right now. That's gotta tell you something, *moreno*."

"That you're talking to me now, but probably just got off the phone with my friend . . . or the younger, blacker replacement."

"You mean that one you saw with me at Tempo?" Cesar asks. "He's crazy and gone like yesterday's garbage. No substitute for you."

"I'm sure you got your hands dirty in the garbage before tossing it. Anyway . . ."

"So paranoid, Keith. Look, I'll call you in a couple days to let you know the plans. It's a date, okay?"

"Alright. Cool. I need to go."

"I'm taking you to meet my sisters."

"Why? They don't even know me. It's barely been a month since we met."

"I told them all about you," Cesar says, and blows a kiss in the phone. "You're the kind of guy a guy can take home to the family."

"Yeah, because I'm not crazy, or obsessive, or a whore."

"Exactly. Well, I'll call you later."

"Cool."

"Later, *moreno. Te amo.*"

I know Cesar didn't just say he loves me. What a flirt. What a playboy move to make, when he knows I'm mad at him because of our disastrous last dates. I'll give Cesar credit, though. He's book smart and has boy smarts. He definitely knows how to play a boy good.

Still, I'm not convinced Cesar is over his fascination with Rafael. Regardless, it feels good getting a call from him. I'm smarter than this, I know, but still Cesar seems about the best possibility—the only possibility—I have for love before I'm thirty. I flip on my system, hit CD number five and forward to track three. It's Kylie Minogue's "Can't Get You Out Of My Head." I sing along as I sit in rush hour traffic.

La-la-la. La-la. La-la-la.

They're happy to get the sweet potato pie when I walk through the door. Tommie and Tyrell are cuddled on the living room sofa, watching a *Soul Food* rerun on Showtime, but when he sees the dessert in my hands, Tommie leaps across the room. He's wearing only boxer briefs, and it's obvious he's having a happy evening with his man.

"This is exactly what I been craving," Tommie says, and cuts a couple slices for himself and Tyrell. "Thanks, man."

"No problem. I hope you guys enjoy it."

"Come eat with us, Keith," Tyrell says, and gets up from under the blanket he's relaxing under. "There's room."

"No, that's okay. My laptop died, and I still have work to do for this meeting with Marco tomorrow. Any messages?" I leaf through the pile of mail on the kitchen counter.

Tommie's stuffed his mouth with pie, but answers, "*Nada*, man."

"Hmmm, not even from Cesar?"

"You gets no love from him either," Tommie says.

"Isn't that the one who was with Rafael the other night at CityWalk?" Tyrell asks.

I look up from the mail at Tyrell. "You saw Cesar with Rafael? When?"

"Tyrell's just talking shit," Tommie says, and gives Tyrell a you-better-shut-up look. "He don't know what he talking about."

"I swear Rafael said his date's name . . ."

"Drop it, Tyrell," Tommie says, and continues eating a second piece of pie. "Keith, where'd you get this?"

"A bakery near the Lucy Florence Café," I say, not quite believing Tommie, but don't want to press him now about why he's covering for Rafael. I've got work to do, anyway. "Tyrell, we'll talk later when Tommie's sick in the bathroom from too much pie."

Tyrell laughs as he hugs Tommie from behind. Tyrell pulls back his dreadlocks and mouths to me, "Rafael and Cesar, it's true," before planting small kisses on the back of Tommie's neck.

I mouth back, "Thank you," and walk back to my bedroom. I'm in no mood to finish up this presentation outline for Marco now, especially hearing that Cesar has been seeing Rafael, my so-called friend, behind my back. Then I remember the advice my grandmother used to tell my mother about all the single women at our church and Reverend Hemmings: "When it comes down to your man, you don't have a best friend." And then I wonder, if Cesar and Rafael could lie about something like this, what other lies have they, or would they, tell to me?

Chapter 18

MARCO ANTONIO

"I wish I wasn't such a fat ass," Keith tells me as he lifts a spoon full of peach cobbler to his lips. "Maybe I'd be able to get a man."

"You're far from fat, Keith."

"Thanks for being kind."

"No, thank you," I say, and take a sip of my sweet tea. "As always you're a big help. I think the young men in my group are going to enjoy your workshop."

Keith and I are finishing up our lunch at M&M's Soul Food in Pasadena. I'm not watching my calories as much since deciding to break up with Alex, so I'm eating whatever I want. Today it's barbeque chicken, green beans, mashed potatoes covered in thick gravy, and I'm having red velvet cake for dessert. I'm just glad I have a friend like Keith who loves to problem solve over a nice plate of food.

"Now, back to Alejandro. All I suggested is you might give him the benefit of the doubt," Keith says. "Gay actors have to do so-called 'straight things' to serve their images and career. ¿Comprende?"

"This isn't the 1940s when studios completely owned their actors," I say. "Plus, he's not even all that big yet."

"True."

"But the worst part is keeping this breakup from my parents. The only reason they're accepting my sexuality now is because Alex is on their friggin' *novelas*."

And it's true. Before Alex, my parents couldn't give a damn about my love life. In fact, the only one who gave me any kind of support or acknowledgement about being gay is my *abuelita*.

"Well, there's always Julio waiting in the wings. What do you think about that, Marco?"

"I don't know about rebound action," I say, and take a small bite of cake. "You'd think I'd have all the answers since I counsel people on these issues, huh?"

"You'd think, but hey, I'm a preacher's kid and I'm walking around in a moral hangover every weekend," Keith says and smiles. "But I do know that Julio is fine, and if I had the chance I'd be all over him in a heartbeat."

"Be my guest, Keith. I think Julio's open to chocolate."

We laugh and take sips of tea.

"But Julio's your territory," Keith says. "I wouldn't touch that, unlike some people we know."

Keith and Rafael are having issues again. It's like this every other week. I swear they should just sleep together and get it over with. Instead, I'm in the middle. My best friend and my former client-turned-friend.

"What happened now, Keith?"

"You and I both know that Rafael's hobby is collecting men like others collect spare change."

"And?"

"First, what did Rafael tell you?" Keith asks.

"Actually, nothing," I say. "I haven't seen Rafael much these past few days."

"You remember Cesar?"

"Sure. The professor guy? With the crazy ex-boyfriend who threw his drink all over you?"

"Yeah. But forget about the ex. Cesar assured me that's over."

"Okay. So why the problem with Rafael?"

"I never told you Rafael hit on Cesar the first night I met Cesar. While I was in the bathroom."

"Really?"

"And even though our first few dates were perfect, when I came back from Michigan, everything was different."

"Maybe because you left Cesar hanging at Arena," I say. "No explanation. No returned phone calls."

"Whatever, Marco. Whose side are you on?" Keith sips some tea. "Anyway, our past couple dates all Cesar can talk about is 'Rafael this, Rafael that.' And last night, Tommie's boyfriend told me they saw Rafael and Cesar out on a date."

"Have you talked to Rafael about this?"

"What's the point?" Keith says. "You've seen him and how he gets out of everything. First, he denies everything. Then he confesses, and plays innocent. 'Bitch, I can't help it. It's just feelings that can't be controlled.' It'll be the same if I ask him about Cesar. I don't see how you can trust him."

"That's a pretty harsh conclusion, Keith."

"I wouldn't put it past him to make a move on Alex now that you've broken up. I bet 'Whassup Bitch' copied Alex's number from your caller ID."

"Keith, that's really not fair to say."

"He was flirting with Tommie last time we were leaving for Tempo. I could sense . . . the sin in the air."

Keith rolls his eyes at me and shakes his head. I know he's upset that I'm not taking sides in the matter. It's my job as a counselor, and as a friend caught in the middle. I think Keith just overdramatizes everything.

"You're sounding paranoid," I say.

"Marco, get your head out of the clouds and look at that cheap retail queen for what he is. A home wrecker. He flaunts his youth, his body and his looks like he's better than us. Like we're all just wallpaper or something."

"You're about to turn thirty, Keith, and have too much education, money and class to be feeling threatened by Rafael."

Keith's silence tells me he's internalizing my analysis. I love it when my friends and my clients make a breakthrough.

"What if I did that to you, Marco?"

"I think you're looking at this through the wrong lens," I say. "This situation has taught you about Cesar's character, or lack of it. Maybe it's a blessing in disguise that you and Cesar haven't gotten too involved. Who knows what road he may have led you down? Besides, you're criticizing Rafael for the same things you and I did when we were naïve and twenty-two years old in Palo Alto."

"Excuse me?"

"Don't play innocent, Keith. You and I both did our fair share of bed hopping and sleeping around when we were in college. We even kept lists, remember?"

"But we never slept with each other's dates," Keith says. "We never went after someone we knew the other wanted. Real friends respect those basic rules of friendship. We carried ourselves with morals and integrity, and that's something Rafael knows nothing about."

"I think you're right on some parts," I say. "But you're wrong on many things. Rafael's had a tough life. He's just a kid. You know his family kicked him out when he was fifteen. His brothers beat him up all the time because he wasn't man enough to be a 'Dominguez man.' I'm just trying to be a role model and show him what he should aspire to be in this gay life."

"Hmmph."

"And I know he looks up to you and me," I say. "We're the only stable role models he has, and much better than the people he used to hang with on the streets."

"You're such a goody-two-shoes, Marco Antonio," Keith says and flashes me the middle finger. "It's gonna take a while for me to trust him anymore."

"Keith, you're the church boy. What about forgiveness? What about being nonjudgmental?"

"You won't let me get from under that shadow, will you?"

We laugh. Things will be cool again, I know. Probably sooner than later.

A college-age young man walks into M&Ms with two older adults who are probably his parents. The father's white, the mom's black and the young man is fine beyond belief. A definite looker for Keith, or anybody, to notice.

"Hey, Keith, don't be obvious. Check out the boy at your three o'clock."

Keith looks over and smiles. The young man notices, and when his parents sit in a booth on the opposite side of the restaurant, he walks over to our table.

"Whassup, whassup, Mr. Hemmings?"

Hmmm, he knows Keith already. Keith never told me about this boy, who looks like a younger El or Chico DeBarge.

"What's up with you, Dante?" Keith says. "I thought you were going to call."

"Just chillin'," the guy says and then holds his hand out to shake hands with me. "Whassup, I'm Dante Covington, an old friend of Mr. Hemmings here."

"Marco Antonio Vega," I say, and shake his hand. He's got nice long fingers with well-manicured nails and a heavy silver link bracelet on his wrist. "I'm Keith's best friend."

"Cool. Cool. Now I know who to go to for all his secrets," Dante smiles and looks at Keith. Dante's turning bright red, a combination of blushing and youthful innocence. "Hey, I'm just grabbing a little lunch with my folks before taking them to LAX. They're heading over to see my dad's family in London for a couple weeks."

"How nice," I say. Dante can't keep his eyes off Keith, and Keith's trying to play it cool. "Keith and I are thinking about going over there this fall."

"Let me know and I'll hook you up with some of my boys over there, fo'sheezy," Dante says.

"Thanks. But don't let us keep you from your mom and dad. We're actually having a lunch meeting," Keith says.

"Cool. Cool. I gotta bounce anyway," Dante says. "But I haven't forgot your number, Mr. Hemmings. I'll be housesitting in Altadena the next two weeks, so I'll give you a holla and maybe you can come up. Bring your boy Marco, and we'll heat up the Jacuzzi, eat their food, drink their liquor and get to know each other."

"Actions speak louder than words, Dante," Keith says.

I interrupt before Keith's attitude gets in the way of any developments. "We'll be there. You just call Keith with the time and location."

Dante nods at Keith. "Don't worry, Keith. I'm legit. Anyway, fellas, gotta get back to the folks. I'm off like a prom dress."

When Dante strolls back over to his parents, I laugh and catch Keith with a smirk on his face as well.

"So, I think he likes you, Keith. You didn't even tell me you met someone, and you're sitting here complaining about being a fat ass and about Cesar."

"Dante's an interesting kid," Keith says. "He goes to USC, supposedly."

"You little cradle robber."

"He asked for my number. But I'm not even looking for anything right now. I don't even think he's gay."

"Oh, there's no question what he is. Did you see the way Dante was looking at you?"

"Whatever."

"Well, maybe Dante can help you get over Cesar."

"Just like Julio can help you get over Alex."

Checkmate. Maybe Keith is right. Maybe giving Julio a chance is just the thing I need to make a move in the right direction.

Chapter 19

KEITH

It begins much in the way of the phone conversation I'm having with Cesar right now—my first contact with him in several days.

"So what's up, Cesar? I've been trying to reach you all day."

"You have?" he asks. He sounds surprised. "I didn't realize . . . Anyway, what do you want?"

Lord, hold my tongue from saying something really unChristian. Amen.

"You said you were going to call," I say. "It's been a week."

"I guess I lost track."

"So now you're playing hard to get, Cesar? I see how it works."

"If you say so," Cesar says, and then there's a few seconds of silence. "So, what's up?"

"Well, I thought that by leaving messages at your home, and your work, and your cell phone for the past few days, that you'd get one of them. Anyway, I guess messages get lost. I guess people forget about dates they were going to set up."

"Look, Keith, I've been busy with work and classes. I've had a butt-load of papers to grade lately and gotta make two midterm tests for my classes, because little shit-head students cheat. No offense."

"I see. That's cool."

"So anyway, what did you call for?" Cesar asks.

Hmmm, Sherlock. Why else does someone call the person they've been seeing off and on?

"I wanted to know if maybe you'd want to do something tonight? Maybe come over for a movie or go eat somewhere? Or I could watch a movie while you grade papers. Whatever we do is cool with me."

I don't want to sound like I'm begging, but I really would like to see Cesar. Maybe give him the benefit of the doubt. Start over again. For real this time.

"That sounds like fun, Keith, but . . ."

"But you're busy with work and classes and the butt-load of papers to grade. Right? I get the picture."

"Well, you're kinda right. But I'm a little under the weather, too. I'm not feeling too well today." He lets out a little cough, like the kind a person fakes to a boss over the phone. Probably a little trait he picked up from Rafael. *God, please remove any doubts and misgivings I have about this man.*

"I could come over to your place and bring you some chicken soup or something."

"Oh, that's really nice of you. You're a sweetheart, Keith."

"So . . . can I come over?"

"I don't want to get you sick. I think I'm just gonna chill out at home tonight and get some rest. Raincheck?"

"Looks like I have no choice," I say, and decide to mess with his mind a little bit. "But don't be surprised if I come by with that chicken soup later."

"You're too funny, Keith. I'm about to go to bed, though. Talk to you later."

"Okay. I guess I'll talk to you later?"

"Yeah, I'll give you a call sometime."

The phone clicks, and a dial tone buzzes in my ear. He hung up on me. Cesar hung up before I could even say good-bye. And he doesn't even call me "*moreno*" anymore.

Sometimes you just know when the person you're into isn't feeling the same way about you. It could be the way he looks at, or doesn't look at, you. It could be the increase in the amount of time it takes for him to call you back. Most of the time, you can just tell by the lack of passion or excitement in his eyes and voice when he's around you.

What I know to be true right now is that Cesar is not into me anymore. Maybe he never really was, especially from day one when he and Rafael got connected at Tempo.

It makes me sad.

And no matter what kind of efforts Cesar may make to try and show me otherwise, I know that his mind is on something else other than me. I pray it's not Rafael. The thought of them being together, of Cesar being seduced by Rafael, makes me feel sad and angry and frustrated at the same time, because it's a hopeless situation. What exactly am I supposed to do? I can't make Cesar feel anything for me that he doesn't feel already.

Then maybe I'm just too suspicious. Maybe this third Belvedere martini isn't helping either. I have a tendency to get like this—pensive, melancholy and a little imaginative—when I have a drink or three by myself. Maybe he does feel something for me, considering we've spent a few dates watching movies, walking on the beach, cooking meals to-gether, talking about ethnic literature and even holding hands. My God, how seventh grade! He hasn't even tried to go beyond holding hands or putting his arm around me since the first date at the beach cottage. What a crock! Granted, it's only been a little while since meeting Cesar, and maybe I shouldn't be expecting much. It's the right thing to go a little slow anyway, but I know even church folks like to get busy at some point.

My phone rings. I pick up right away, hoping it's Cesar calling back with a change of heart. It's not. It's my old friend from Stanford, Chris Aquino, who I haven't seen since the night I met Cesar at Tempo. Chris always has something fun planned on his weekends.

"Keith, you gotta be at my place in an hour. We're going to a real hot party up in the Ho Hills tonight. Bring whoever you want."

"Hello, Chris. I'm fine too."

"I know you're fine, and I know you're living large off your dot-com money," he says. "Count your blessings you sold before the market dropped. So anyway, you have no excuse but to come party with us tonight."

"But I was working on a project."

"I have a project for you to work on. It's called 'Project Get Some,' and you need to get your big booty over here so we can crack the case. There'll be lots of cuties."

"There's only one I want right now and he's not into me," I say.

"Well, there's plenty others who'll want a young hot black millionaire."

"Try thousandaire. But anyway, I'll go with you. You're closer to Santa Monica or Melrose?"

"Santa Monica. Fourth house from the corner. See you in a bit, Keith."

I head across the 101 Freeway to West Hollywood, where Chris lives in a small house with his partner, Jake. Their house, small and well-decorated with designer furniture and a carpet of navy and gold, is crammed with Chris and Jacob's designer-label clad friends. Chris introduces me to the group

I'll be hanging out with tonight—Daryl, Eric, Eddie, Dan, David and Howard—and we caravan up to the party in the Hollywood Hills. They seem like a fun crowd, and definitely something new for a change. I haven't hung out with a mostly white crowd in years.

We arrive at the party around midnight, and we're all a bit buzzed from the champagne we've been drinking on the way to the house. The house, which is at the top of a flight of a hundred or so stairs, looks to be made mostly of glass, and you can see everything and everyone inside. It's owned by a white fifty-something movie producer who was big in the eighties, has millions of dollars, no romantic partner and plenty of time on his hands to throw these monthly parties for young up-and-coming pretty-boys from the Midwest who hope to become the next movie superstar. I see dozens of white twenty-something actor types in the various rooms of the house. And unless they're being hidden in the back or upstairs servants' quarters, there aren't any other men of color here except for Chris and me.

Everyone is dressed in the standard party uniform of the gay community—black tight-fitting shirt, sweater or tank with black jeans or black pants. I guess nothing changes, no matter what community you're in. Except this one is definitely of the Versace, Gucci and Prada kind. No Ross "dress for less" paycheck purchases here, for sure. They also give attitude. Not necessarily any more than men of color, just with more of a natural condescending delivery, with an air of privilege and pedigree. And another difference—these boys are either painfully anorexic-looking, like they haven't eaten anything that had parents in years, or they're healthy, corn-fed Iowa types with sexy forearms, blond hair and blue eyes. Everyone has spiked hair and pasty skin covered with the glow of fake baked tans. The skinny waif boy look is so late nineties. Some say hot? Say what you want about men of color, but we definitely are packing where white boys are lacking.

One similarity—they all tell the same story: the story of themselves.

"Keith, this is Reese. Keith, meet Ben. You gotta meet Jerry. Keith, have you met Matt?"

"Wow, I haven't seen you on the audition circuit." (As if we'd ever be up for the same parts in Hollywood. Hello?!?!)

"I'm putting together a one-man show right now, and just looking for investors." (Not gonna be me!)

"I wish I had an ass like yours. Maybe I'd get some good parts then." (Maybe it's lack of talent, not lack of a rear end, that's holding you back!)

"You totally look like that Will Smith guy. Hey guys, what do you think? Couldn't he be like Will Smith's double?" (Will is a cutie, but I know this is definitely a case of the "they all look alike" syndrome.)

The next one, I tune out.

"I. I. I. Me. Me. Me. BLAH

BLAH BLAH BLAH BLAH BLAH BLAH BLAH BLAH
BLAH BLAH BLAH BLAH BLAH BLAH BLAH BLAH
BLAH BLAH BLAH BLAH BLAH BLAH BLAH BLAH
BLAH BLAH BLAH BLAH BLAH BLAH BLAH BLAH
BLAH BLAH BLAH BLAH BLAH BLAH BLAH BLAH
BLAH BLAH BLAH BLAH BLAH BLAH BLAH BLAH
BLAH BLAH BLAH BLAH BLAH BLAH BLAH BLAH
BLAH BLAH BLAH BLAH BLAH BLAH BLAH BLAH
BLAH BLAH BLAH BLAH BLAH BLAH BLAH BLAH
BLAH BLAH BLAH BLAH BLAH BLAH BLAH BLAH
BLAH BLAH BLAH BLAH BLAH BLAH BLAH BLAH
BLAH BLAH BLAH BLAH BLAH BLAH BLAH BLAH
BLAH BLAH BLAH BLAH BLAH BLAH BLAH BLAH
BLAH BLAH BLAH BLAH BLAH BLAH BLAH BLAH
BLAH BLAH BLAH BLAH BLAH BLAH BLAH BLAH
BLAH BLAH BLAH BLAH BLAH BLAH BLAH BLAH
BLAH BLAH BLAH BLAH BLAH BLAH BLAH BLAH
BLAH BLAH BLAH BLAH BLAH BLAH BLAH BLAH
BLAH BLAH BLAH BLAH BLAH BLAH BLAH BLAH
BLAH BLAH."

"Keith, you haven't heard one word I said, have you?"

"I'm sorry, Nick. My mind's been on something all night and this party's not helping."

"You wanna talk about it?"

"Are you sure you want to listen?"

"Sure," Nick says. His slate-gray eyes go well with his black curly hair. "I don't see anyone I need to talk with yet, anyway."

Yet? I'm not in the industry, so I'm not on anyone's A-list for schmoozing at this party. So I decide to tell him, probably a little too freely, about my situation with Cesar. How he's not feeling me the way I'm feeling him, and that it's got me a bit down. That I'm here at this party only because Chris invited me, but it's not my thing. That I don't really hang in circles like this. He asks what circle I am talking about. I figure since I'll never see him again anyway, I'll tell him that the circle in question is white, and that my typical social scene involves primarily people of color who are professionals actually working in their chosen fields. I guess you could even count Rafael in that circle, despite his numerous faults. I'd even choose a bad night with him over this scene. Nick grabs two cocktails from the passing waiter and hands one to me.

"You know," Nick leans toward my ear. "There's no need to settle for anything less than a perfect situation."

"You think?"

"And I'd date you in a heartbeat, but I've never been with a black or African American, whatever's the PC thing, before."

"It's not about being PC, Nick. It's just about being correct."

"I don't know. I'm from Nebraska originally. Not too many of your people in my town."

"I think I should go look for my friends. Your insight has been soooo helpful."

I turn and walk around looking for Chris or any of his friends who came to the party with us. If I have to deal with one more dumb wanna-be actor trying to show me how sensitive and open-minded he is, I'm going to puke.

Chris isn't anywhere to be found, but a few of his friends are in a corner passing around some kind of drug. Definitely not my thing, you know? So I ask for directions to the closest restroom. It's at the top of the stairs, everyone tells me. I pass through more black-shirt-clad men to get to the bathroom. I feel like I'm waiting for an eternity, when finally the bathroom door opens and a familiar face walks out.

"Cesar!?!?"

I know it's Cesar. I'd know that body, and walk, and Hanae Mori cologne anywhere. Why is he here? He's supposedly sick. And why is he such a loser that he'd turn his face and just whisk on by rather than acknowledge me? I feel my Detroit roots about to come out—the roots that come in the form of cussing someone out in public and not caring who's watching. But I'm also the Baptist minister's son, and I know that I have to have a certain way of being in public, even when I'm feeling like a fool.

It makes me mad. And I'm not letting him get away with this.

I force Chris to drive me back to his house so I can get my car. Chris doesn't want me driving in my condition— buzzed and angry about seeing Cesar—but I do so anyway, and whip through West Hollywood looking for an all-night diner. I find one open on LaBrea near Santa Monica Boulevard.

"I want chicken soup," I tell the clerk behind the counter.

"It's more like a cream of chicken tonight. You want a bowl or a cup?"

"I want the whole pot you've got back there." I throw a hundred-dollar bill on the counter. "Just put a cover on it."

"Sure, sir."

The clerk puts the canister of soup in my trunk, and I head over to Cesar's complex. The lights are out in his townhouse, and I drive around the back to see if his black pickup truck is in its space. It's not, just as I thought. He's out, still at that Hollywood Hills party. Good. I park in Cesar's space and lift the soup out of the trunk. It's heavy and sloshing around, but I handle it. It's unusually quiet for a weekend night. Luckily, no one is around or walking in and out of the complex. I reach Cesar's townhouse, number nine. And with a smooth and controlled motion, I hold onto the container and hurl the soup at his front door, making sure the thick, creamy mixture, with its chunks of vegetables and chicken and coagulated broth, oozes in the lock, covers the peephole, and sticks to the screen door.

I do this in the name of all the men and women who've been fucked over by pretty-boy players. In the name of those who have heard excuse after excuse from men who don't have the balls to tell you they've gotten tired of you, and just string you along while they get their minds together. In the name of all those good men and women who are sitting at home, alone, on a Friday or Saturday night, waiting for the phone to ring, while the person they're waiting for is out with someone else.

I leave a note: *Hope this helps you feel better.*

It usually doesn't end this way, but just for tonight it does.

It makes me feel good. Damn good.

"Whassup, whassup Mr. Hemmings? It's Dante giving you a ring-ring a little after midnight. I guess you know what I'm calling for . . . it being late and alls. Here's my celly, and you can call me whenever you get this. 626-555-3268. That's 555 D-C-O-V, as in Dante Covington, in case you forgot. Check you later."

I know I'm probably a fool right now for going from one man to another in the same night, but I know exactly what I want and need, and Dante's high on that list. I hope he doesn't think I've never played the late-night phone call thing, because this certainly isn't a new game to me. This young hip-hopper wants some Keith, and I'm more than willing to give it to him, especially after the night I've had with the Hollywood

Hills party, Cesar, and nothing quite turning out how I want. Dante's going to change that.

I'm heading up Fair Oaks Drive to the foothill of the mountain. From the address and directions, it sounds like one of the more affluent areas of Altadena. It also sounds like Dante's throwing himself a private personal party from the sounds of the rap and hip-hop playing in the background of his phone. He's probably getting high and drunk, and I'm probably the only one of his late-night phone callers who returned his call. Why else would he call me? And why am I driving up to this boy's house when I'm still buzzing from everything I've had to drink tonight?

I don't know.

But I do know Dante looks good as he's waiting out in front of his parents' ranch-style home, which sits overlooking a canyon. He's wearing an unbuttoned red, white and blue Mecca starter jacket, a white mesh T-shirt, red three-quarter pants and a blue visor on top of his curly hair. His chest looks firm and is hairless. Dante directs me up the driveway to park behind a couple of SUVs and trucks. He is smiling as he opens my door, and I step out onto the crunchy gravel driveway.

" 'Sup, 'sup, boy?" he says, and gives me a brothaman hug.

"Not much."

He bites his bottom lip and stares at me.

"What, Dante?"

"Nothing. Just checking you out, that's all. Let's go on to the house. You can leave the keys in the car if you want. It's safe up here."

"What if I want to escape, or make a quick getaway?"

"Believe me, you'll be here all weekend if I have my way," Dante says and laughs. He picks up a glass he's left on the ground by my car.

"Why should I trust you, Dante? I don't even know you."

"I got it all taken care of, fo'sheezy. I have a few friends who're staying up in the house, too, so you'll meet them. They're staying in the guest rooms. You want some of this Hennessy?"

"No, thanks. I've had enough to drink already," I say. "So these friends are who?"

"Just a couple of my boys, their girls, and other surprises."

Women? Straight men? Other surprises? What could that mean? Well, for sure it means I don't know anything about Dante, and he's obviously mistaken me for someone who is hetero. This is funny.

"Dante, I think I better go," I open my car door. "I'm buzzed and I think I probably misread what you're all about tonight."

"Come on, come on. Stay. It'll be fun."

"You don't even know me, Dante. You don't know anything about me, or else you wouldn't have invited me up here to your parents' house."

"You don't know me, but I know myself," he says, and then leans in, presses me against my car and kisses me with his soft, warm lips. His hands, cold from holding his drink glass, pull my face to his for the best kiss, the first kiss, I've had since Cesar. "You know me now?"

"I think so."

"So you staying, right right?"

"I guess . . ."

A young lady yells from the front door of the house to the driveway for Dante to hurry in for the next game—naked truth or dare.

"Get back inside, Tracy," Dante shouts back. "I'm busy."

She yells back profanities, and we hear the door slam. He looks at me, rolls his eyes, and we laugh.

"I think I'm going to pass, Dante," I say, and pull him to me again by the car. "I don't want to be a babysitter or chaperone for naked truth or dare."

"You think I'm too young, don't you? I'm all man down here," he says, and moves my hand down below his waist.

I squeeze, am impressed with his size, but tell him he's going to have to call me tomorrow or some other day if he's at all serious about getting together with me. I tell him this will be the true test of his age and maturity, and that if he passes, he will definitely be pleased with the outcome. What I really want to say is I'm pushing thirty, am buzzed beyond belief right now, and the only thing I can think about, besides Cesar's rejection, is going home and sleeping. I get in the car and back away.

But before I reach the end of the driveway, I stop and step out.

"Dante."

"What?"

"Come here."

"Oh yeah?" he asks with a smirk on his face as he jogs to me. He nods his head and presses me against the car door. "What you wanna talk about?"

"Who said anything about talking?" I trace my finger over his bottom lip. "Get in, lean back and shut up. We'll worry about talking if you call me in the morning."

He does as he's told. And as he's reclining the seat back, he's undoing his buttons and lifting up the shirt under his jacket.

"You got some Sade you can put on?" Dante says and closes his eyes in anticipation of what I'm about to do.

"Sure," I say. By coincidence, I've got *The Best of Sade* CD loaded, and I turn it on high enough for ambience, but low enough to hear Dante enjoying himself.

I look at Dante's face. He's physically the caliber of person Rafael usually gets—young, built and beautiful. A college junior at a private school, so at least he's got brains to go with the looks. Looks like he should be modeling in *VIBE* magazine or something. For once, I'm getting the prize and there's no competition with Rafael. And as for Cesar, he can kiss my . . .

"Whassup, Keith?" Dante interrupts my thoughts and nods his head, as if to hurry me up. I'm the one doing the favor. Kid needs to get a little more patient. "We ain't got but a minute before they start coming outside looking for us."

"Can't I look at you? Jeez."

"You can look all you want when we got complete privacy," Dante says and sits up to look at me. "But now, are we doing this thing or what?"

"I don't do this sort of thing every day," I say. "I'm not a slut like . . ." I want to say Rafael, but it wouldn't matter at this point anyway. I should just get down with the get down.

"I'm just excited, as you can see," Dante says. "Sorry to seem so bossy or like I'm rushing, Keith. You probably think I'm acting childish, huh?"

"Now who's talking too much?" I ask. "We'll talk. Uh, we'll see what happens tomorrow and who calls who first."

"Fo'sheezy," Dante says. He leans back in the reclined passenger seat. I feel like a teenager on prom night, or worse yet, a troll getting used by, or taking advantage of, someone who's just in his third year of college.

But I can't be a troll; I'm not ugly.

I can't be too old for Dante; he pursued me.

I can't be a slut; I'm not Rafael.

And I'm a church boy.

"Fo'sheezy," I say before leaning over the console dividing driver and passenger.

And as I take care of business, listening to Dante sucking in air and moaning "yeah," "damn" and "ahhh," I know he's feeling transported onto cloud nine and surely moving toward the edge of release. And even though thoughts of Rafael and Cesar pop through my mind, it's only a temporary distraction as I make sure I let this twenty-one-year-old know whose love is king and that he'll only want to be with someone pushing thirty from now on.

Chapter 20

TOMMIE

I found some weird shit in the garbage this morning: an empty fifth of vodka. I don't drink vodka, so Keith musta finished it by himself, alone. I know he been worried about Cesar not calling him, but hell, no man is enough to turn you into an alcoholic. I didn't hear nobody partying with Keith last night. That's a mystery to me. But then again, I was a little preoccupied. Well, a lot preoccupied.

My Tyrell came home from a road trip the basketball team made up to Berkeley. So after I picked him up at UCLA, we drove over to Beverly Hills to eat at this high-class soul food restaurant called Reign. It didn't take too long for us to make it back to my place for a little dessert—chocolate on Tyrell. Damn, it was good. Three full helpings.

By the time we woke so I could take Tyrell back to campus, Keith was already gone, and we had another short session. Against the kitchen counter. That's when I saw the empty vodka bottle. Me and Keith got some catching up to do. I don't know much, but I know drinking hard shit alone ain't cool. Keith should know that too. He certainly seems to know it all about everything and everyone else.

But can't think of that now. My mind needs to be on this

"Old Skool" promotion happening in the store now. Deniece Williams is here, and the place is jumping. Close to four dozen people are crammed inside the store waiting for an autograph. I keep hearing all these forty- and fifty-year-olds talking about how they don't make music like they used to. It's true. No live instruments. No real singing voices. No musical training. I can't believe this many twenty-something folks are here for this event. They just better buy some CDs and DVDs.

Days like this, I think about my group, Renaissance Phoenix. That early nineties music was wack, but we got paid and had fame for a hot minute. Before this promo, Deniece told me putting God and family first is her key to staying afloat in the music business, even when the sales charts no longer recognize your talent. God was the last thing on our minds in my singing group. I guess that's why we couldn't keep the group together and why we all a bunch of nobodies today.

Some crazy-looking white lady keep peeping over at me. I hope she ain't thinking about getting some of Tommie junior, cause it ain't happening. At first she was hanging around Deniece's autograph table. Now she walking over this way.

"Thomas Jordan?" she says and hands me her business card. "Nikki Rowan, segment producer with the Nostalgia Network."

"What's up, Nikki?" I glance over her card. "People who know me call me Tommie."

"Okay, Tommie it is. Good to meet you. I work on some of the 'where are they now' segments and wanted to bring my crew over to shoot some video."

"For Deniece Williams? That's cool with me, as long as it's cool with her and her assistant."

"We already got clearance from her. We wanted to make sure it's okay to get some footage of you."

"Of me?"

"Yeah. I was a big fan of Renaissance Phoenix when I was in college. You sang lead, right?"

"On the songs that was hits, I sang lead," I say, and start grinning it up. "I can't believe you recognized me. I don't look the same."

"Hell, none of us do. But you guys were so fresh before all these little white-boy groups took over the music scene."

"True dat, Nikki."

"What are you doing nowadays, Tommie?"

"I own this store and run it full time," I say. "I guess I'm indirectly still in the business."

"Such a shame you're not doing shows anymore," she says, and twirls her finger through her red curly hair. "You guys were hot. But I'm sure after doing this segment, you'll be on the road and performing like back in the day."

"I don't know about that," I say. "I ain't growing no high-top fade or putting on those Cross Color jeans no more."

"Well, I hope you at least do a segment for the Nostalgia Network. This could open up doors for your music career again, and maybe even give you a chance to pursue a solo career."

"You saying that could happen if I do a 'where are they now' story? I don't want to be one of those sorry, sad Hollywood nobodies grasping at any bit of fame they can get."

"It's possible, Tommie. You never know until you try. I know you miss the crowds and the fans."

That's true, I do. And without another thought, I sign Nikki's performance waiver. What have I got to lose but a chance at having the fame and fortune I used to have? At least it'll give my Tyrell something to be proud of where I'm concerned. I want so bad to make him feel like being with me is worth it, that I'm as good as he is.

But with every good thing going on, something bad has got to go down. As usual, it starts and ends with my lovely sister, Sylvia.

"Tommie, who the fuck do you think you are taking my girl over to Dennis's place?" Sylvia screeches while pushing her way through the crowd. Gustavo, with his old-ass-out-of-breath self, catches up to her. "Just who do you think you are?"

All the dozens of customers, Deniece and the Nostalgia Network people turn around and look back and forth at me and Sylvia like they're watching Venus and Serena on a tennis court.

"Let's take this to the back office, Sylvia. Now!" I'm surprised I'm yelling.

"Oh, hell naw, muthafucka. I'm putting you on blast right now."

"This my place of business, Sylvia. Let's go to my office."

"You mess with my business, I'm fuckin' up yours," Sylvia says. "Next time you take my baby girl over to Dennis's place without my say, I'm going after your ass. I should sue your ass right now for all the cheap shit in this store."

"I don't wanna get into this right now in front of these people."

"Why not? 'Cause you know you wrong trying to get my girl taken away from me? Well, fuck you, little bro. I want everyone to know what you trying to do to me."

"You left Keesha alone with strangers, she was scared, and she called me to pick her up. I did what any good uncle would do, Sylvia. Besides, why you just now coming to me with this? This was weeks ago."

At this moment, I realize that Sylvia been gone, probably with Gustavo, for all this time, and that Dennis probably called her out on it. Fucked up as Dennis's and my relationship is, he's Keesha's father, and that's where the girl belonged that night I got her. All three of them, Sylvia, Dennis and Gustavo, messed up as far as I'm concerned, and they putting my niece in the middle of it.

I ask everyone, as nice and calm as I can, if they mind if I reschedule the promotion event for another time. I get a few boos and hisses. But Deniece and Nikki help me out and say it's cool. They even help to calm the crowd.

Now I just gotta figure how to calm myself and figure out what I'm going to do about this situation with Sylvia, Dennis, Gustavo and my niece, 'cause Keesha is about the closest thing I'll have to my own daughter, and I ain't about to let her life get fucked up by them.

I'm sitting here in the back office of the store, just thinking, after taking Sylvia's cussing and ranting. She so fucking embarrassing, coming up in here like a damn crack addict, with mismatched brown and purple sweats, high-heeled shoes, a leather patch purse from the 1970s and black do-rag over her head. I hope she ain't on drugs again.

Anyway, I ended up closing the store early and sent the employees home so I can be by myself. Sylvia just don't get it. She older than me. She supposed to be the responsible one between the two of us. She supposed to be the role model for me to look up to. Instead, she mad at me for doing the right thing by taking my niece back to her father's place. That's where Keesha was gonna end up anyway, so it shouldn't be a big deal. It's not like Sylvia got full-time custody.

Needless to say, the Nostalgia Network taping is put off until further notice, and I can't find my Tyrell nowhere to even tell him what's up. I need to talk with someone who'll understand. Sometimes I swear I don't know what I need with a busy college boy who can't be around when I need him to be. He ain't returned none of my pages, and I left a message on his cell already. I'ma try Keith at the house to see if Tyrell been calling over there.

"Keith, whassup? It's me. Has my Tyrell called or been by?"

"No," Keith says. "He's probably at the big celebration at UCLA tonight. They made the NCAA brackets."

"I been trying to reach him for a couple hours now."

"Why? What's up?"

"It's Sylvia, man," I say. "I had a big promotion today at the store. Media. Deniece Williams. Dozens of people. And Sylvia comes by and cusses me out in front of all of them."

"No, she didn't! She's a walking Jerry Springer guest."

"I know. Remember I told you how Keesha was stuck in East L.A. with that man's family?"

"Yeah," Keith says. "The married man Sylvia's sleeping with or whatever she does with him."

"She mad because I picked Keesha up and took her back to her father's."

"That's too bad, Tommie."

"No shit, Sherlock," I say. "I can't stand Dennis. Sylvia blaming me for all the shit going wrong with her life. And I know Dennis'll be a punk-ass-bitch about letting me see my niece when I want to see her."

"You're at the store? You need anything?"

"Yeah, I closed early," I say. "I need Tyrell so I can talk to him. I think I need a lawyer, too. Just for advice."

"I can cover the attorney," Keith says. "As for Tyrell, all I can say is wait. He'll call you when he can."

"I need him now. Not later. That's the problem with these bousghie faggots. Always busy doing something except taking care of business at home." I realize I'm more mad with the

Sylvia situation than with my Tyrell, but that's just the first
thing that came out my mouth.

"Maybe you should come home and calm down. I made
smothered pork chops and fried corn."

"I will. I'm about to bounce," I say, and hear a knock at
the store gate. "Well, it looks like I have company. Your little
friend Rafael tapping on the door out front. I'll talk to you
later, Keith."

"Well, I'm sure Tyrell will call you soon. Don't forget
you're married!"

"I won't, Father Keith."

"I'm not trying to be your daddy," Keith says. "I just don't
want that slut trying to get in your pants next."

I hang up and walk to the front. Rafael smiling and jumping up and down. I lift up the gate and let him in. He swishes
past me and goes straight to my office in the back of the
store. He smell like a bad mixture of weed, beer and drug-
store cologne. I close up again so no one will think I'm open
for business.

"What you want, Rafael?"

"Nothing. Just passing time before going down to Macy's.
I saw your light on. Why you closed so early?"

"It's personal."

"Don't 'it's personal' me, bitch. I'm Rafael. I know something went down. I heard from my girl Roneshia about some
crazy bitch cussing you out like you some pimp cheating her
out her money. It's all over the mall, bitch."

"You been smoking out, huh?" I ask. " 'Cause you reek,
and if I was your supervisor, you'd be going straight home."

"To your bed." Rafael nods at me and tries to lean in to
hug me or something.

"Look, Rafael, I need you to step on out. I'm going
home."

"Alright, I'm leaving," Rafael says. "But to answer your question, no. I ain't been smoking out. Two of the mall security guards let me suck they dicks in the security van while they lit up some bud. That's all. Must be a contact high. And I had two beers."

"Too much info, Rafael. Let's go," I say, and nudge him by the arm toward the door. He reaches down for Tommie junior and starts massaging. I let him get whatever kicks he's getting off by feeling me up.

"Come on, Tommie," Rafael starts begging. "No one got to know. You can just sit back in your office and let me take care of business for you."

It actually sounds nice, and I'd like to get some special attention right now. My Tyrell is nowhere to be found, I'm mad at Sylvia and Dennis, and it wouldn't really be cheating because I'd just be standing there . . . doing nothing.

"Rafael, thanks for offering up some head action," I hear myself saying, but not completely believing it. "But I can't do this. I can't mess around on my Tyrell like that."

"You feel like you could use a good blow."

Even though Tommie junior is at full attention as Rafael loosens his grip, I know it's just a temporary state and not worth fucking up my relationship. Besides, if I'm out here taking head from everyone who makes an offer, who's to say Tyrell won't do the same? It's a trust thing.

"Thanks, but no thanks."

"Well, don't mention any of this to Keith. You know how he is."

"No worries, bro," I slap him some skin.

"You never mentioned seeing me and Cesar out, did you?"

"I didn't. My Tyrell did."

"Fuck. That's why Keith been ignoring my calls lately."

"Things were bad before Keith found out about your date with Cesar."

"Tyrell can go fuck off," Rafael yells out. "I should suck you off just to get back at Tyrell for opening his big mouth."

"Thanks, but no thanks," I say. "You a cool dude and, you know, sometimes we do crazy things. It's good."

"Well, I betta get my cool ass to Macy's before they fire a *vato*."

I'm lifting up the front gate for us when my cell rings. It's my Tyrell. Rafael notices, sighs, and stumbles down the mall corridor to his evening job. I'm thinking maybe Tommie junior ain't hard for nothing. Turns out my Tyrell wants me to come pick him up at UCLA, says he loves me and wants to spend the night together. I knew all my worries was for nothing, and just hope Rafael keep his distance for a while, cause little do he know, but I was this close to taking him up on his offer.

Chapter 21

RAFAEL

Another letter from VISA! What the fuck?!?! I just sent them their funky little payment, and they still say I'm over my limit. And what does T-Mobile want? I know I ain't gone over my minutes or been anywhere to use roaming charges, so I don't know why they want $234 from me this month. Shit! I got just twenty minutes before I have to get to my evening job at Macy's, and the last thing I need is the bill collectors sending me letters and getting me all nervous. Especially on a Friday evening. This is my *fiesta* night, and a paycheck Friday at that. When I lived in South Central for a split second, after I left the folks' place in Boyle Heights, I had a neighbor named Miss Shirley, who used to say the only thing bill collectors could raise is her credit limit or her blood pressure. I know exactly what she was talking about.

The only kind of blood pressure I want on the rise is when I'm feeling on a man. But not the one who's calling me up right now—Cesar. I wish he'd stop trying to work me. For someone who is as old as twenty-nine, Cesar sure wants to get it up and get it on a lot, even if it ain't all that. Cesar's going straight to voice mail, which means he's basically gone from my world. There's always another boy waiting in line to get a hit of Rafael, and it looks like it's Enrique, who's calling right now. He's going straight to voice mail, too, though he'd be a good quick lay before I go to work.

Twenty seconds later, my cell rings again. Gotta be Enrique again, so I pick up.

"What's your fantasy, papa?"

"This is T-Mobile collections calling for Rafael Dominguez."

Damn, another bill collector.

I hang up and turn off the phone. I change from my French Connection uniform to my Macy's clothes. I'm tired of this two-job action during the week. Driving on the 10 freeway to the west side every morning and back to Montebello at night is a pain in the ass. I thought by the time I was twenty-two or twenty-three I'd be pretty stable, money-wise. My paychecks at French Connection and Macy's are decent. But credit card bills, rent and student loan payments for a junior college degree I ain't even finish yet add up each month. I don't know how much more of working with snotty customers and stupid retail queens I can take. I wish I had an easy-ass office job like Marco Antonio, where I can just talk to people about their problems all day. Or a bunch of cash like nerdy-ass Keith got and be able to work when I wanna work. Shit, I might have to hook up with Cesar one more time and see if he can hook me up with a desk job at his college. I need to get something out of this situation with *el viejito* before it's over.

I hate working at Macy's anyway. So when Mr. Monroe calls me and Roneshia into his office to tell us we're getting terminated after tonight because of our Sunday time clock scam and also for me coming in smelling like weed a few days earlier, I don't cry or frown or even think about going postal like most fired workers would. I go straight to the phone to call Enrique, to see if he wants to hook up after work. No answer. So I take a fifteen-minute break, finish a Corona beer, finish off a mall security guard and head back to the store to finish my last night selling CK, Sean John, Eckō and other urban prep gear for this store. My bills and this job ain't on my mind right now. I really just want to get laid right now. And I see exactly who my next conquest will be.

"What can I help you find, Mr. Tommie?"

Tommie turns around with a couple of jackets in his hand. I'm checking out the length and strength of them hands and fingers, and know they'd be better off holding and doing nasty things to me.

"'Sup, Rafael? I got some Baby Phat on hold in Girls for my niece. And these." Tommie hands me two identical jackets.

"Who the other one for?" I'm sure it's for that college baller he been kicking it with. Lucky boy. I hope Tyrell appreciates a good nigga like Tommie.

"Quit dippin' and ring me up, fool," Tommie says. "Can you call someone to get my niece's clothes over here?"

I take the jackets over to the register. At this point, I'll take about any order Tommie wants to give me.

"So we still cool after what happened earlier this week?" I ask.

"The little head offer? Don't sweat it, Rafael."

"It still stands, in case you're still interested."

"All talk. All talk. Just ring me up, *vato*."

"Whatever." I smile. I know I'm slowly making progress

breaking down Tommie. It's just a matter of timing and finding the right opportunity.

Tommie's cell rings, and he answers. I finish up the sale
while he's talking. I ain't nosy, but it sounds like it's his man,
and they have no plans. Too bad. Tommie's going to be alone
tonight on a Friday night. Me too. Hmmm.

"How much, Rafael?"

"With my staff discount, it's $782.80."

"Dawg, thanks. You ain't have to do that."

Tommie hands me eight hundred-dollar bills.

"No prob, Tommie. We go back like the railroad tracks."

"You can keep the change, since times is hard for ya."
Tommie smiles and hands back a ten and five to me. Nice
seeing his smile. He's always so hard and reserved around me.
"What time you get off tonight?"

"Whenever I want, fool. I just got kicked to the curb. You
hiring?"

"I might be able to work something out," Tommie says.
"You free to talk tonight? My boy over in Pittsburgh for the
March Madness NCAA games."

"March what?"

"College basketball. March Madness. UCLA. My Tyrell."

"Sounds like my lucky day he's over there."

"Why's that?"

"I got no job, no man, and no home because Marco got a
date over," I say. "And I don't want him to know I got fired.
Not yet, anyway." I hope Tommie feeling a little sorry for me.

"We'll have to take care of that," he says. "Some of the
guys from my singing group got a gig over on Sunset. Wanna
go?"

"Well, fuck Macy's. I'm outta here."

And like that, I walk out the store and follow Tommie out to his Escalade. I don't know where we're headed tonight or what we'll get into. I just know I'm out of a job, Tommie is fucking fine and, best of all, his man's out of luck for being out of town.

Chapter 22

MARCO ANTONIO

Whoever said getting over someone you're in love with takes time was right. I'm eating, drinking and sleeping Alex. He's on my mind twenty-four-seven. I think I love him. I just can't be with him if he's going to live his life in secret, and especially if he's going to live it married to that La Princesa singer woman.

That's why I've started going out with Julio more regularly.

Julio's list of qualities is just too good to be true. He's got a new job at USC coordinating the Multicultural Student Affairs department, he's been preapproved for a mortgage—no small feat on a single income in L.A.—and we've been checking out open houses, and he volunteers his time on issues I am concerned about, such as AIDS awareness and education. He loves his family, much like me, and is very involved in their day-to-day lives. He even goes to Mass with me and the family on Sunday mornings. I couldn't ask for more in a partner. Except for one thing: sex appeal.

I don't feel anything for him sexually.

Julio feels more like a brother than a boyfriend.

It's not that Julio isn't attractive. I've always thought he was fine. Tall—much taller than most Salvadoreños I've met. Brown eyes. Long black lashes. Beautiful skin. He inherited the pretty-boy genes from some great Salvadoreño ancestor. And while most of my family and friends, including Rafael, think that a Mexican dating a Salvadoreño is the biggest sin on earth, I haven't bought into their simplistic and racist thinking. Julio's background isn't a problem for me, though it probably is for other people. He's a good person.

Yet, Alex has a pull on me. Still. Even when I'm having fun with Julio.

I keep asking myself if I am creating unnecessary drama and angst for myself. I just want everything to work out in a positive way for everyone involved.

The doorbell rings. Julio is right on time, as usual. He's holding a vase with a nice-sized bouquet of red, white and yellow roses for me. I place the flowers on the dining room table and give him a hug. I don't want to kiss him. Not in love yet. He's brought two DVDs—Pedro Almodóvar films— and a bottle of wine with him. It looks like another nice, quiet, innocent and friendly evening in with Julio. He snuggles up next to me on the same spot I shared with Alex just a couple months earlier.

"I'm so glad to be with you," Julio says and places his cheek on my chest. "*Me gustas tú.*"

I hope he can't feel my heart beating faster. Not from attraction or arousal, but from nervousness. Eventually, I'm going to disappoint Julio, much in the same way Alex disappointed me. I'm going to be added to a list of exes that gay men love to rant and rave about, much like some of my clients do when they can't let go of the past. The thought of doing that to another person, of making another person anguish like that, makes me feel like I should indeed give this a chance. I can't hurt this good man. Maybe I don't deserve him. I certainly don't appreciate what I've got.

How many times have I prayed for a good man to come into my life? And here I am getting ready to waste this opportunity, this gift, because I can't, or won't, get over an ex who obviously doesn't have any respect for me or my family.

I may not feel any sexual attraction right now, but it can grow over time. We've got a good foundation starting for a relationship.

"I'm glad to be with you too," I say. "You don't know how glad I am."

He leans in to kiss me. I close my eyes in preparation for our first kiss.

We're interrupted.

The living room window crashes wide open. Glass and two bricks land just inches from Julio and me. I run over to the window and see a rice-rocket Accord, one that's been lowered with neon under-lighting and spinning rims, speed down the street. This isn't supposed to happen in Montebello, at least not this part of the city.

Two police officers come by, write up my report and take a few digital photos of the broken window and the glass on the floor. By the time they're finished, the apartment manager is here and covering the open hole with plywood until he can do a permanent repair.

"You know, your roommate probably fucked over the wrong person," Julio says, and pulls me back to the sofa. "We're lucky it wasn't anything more dangerous than a brick."

"I'd like to think Rafael's grown up since we started living together."

"I think he's trouble," Julio says. "But he's your friend."

"Yeah, and if you're going to be part of my life, you better get used to Rafael being around."

"Let's not argue," he says, and kisses my cheek. "At least not about your roommate."

"I like this."

I'm liking sitting here in the quiet and darkness, just holding each other. No words are needed. This feels good.

Someone fumbles with the front door lock, and it flings open. Rafael and Tommie are all over each other as they stumble in, obviously drunk, and don't see us on the sofa. I hear them kissing deeply and noisily, like two people in heat for a one-night stand, and Rafael leads Tommie back to his bedroom.

"Oh, my God," I whisper to Julio. "That's Tommie, Keith's roommate."

"The one with the boyfriend playing in the NCAA finals now?"

"Yeah. I can't believe he's here with Rafael."

"That's messed up."

"I should say something, shouldn't I?"

"I think you should stay out of it. For now, anyway."

Maybe Julio's right. I don't know. The only thing I know for sure now is that what I have with Julio may not be the perfect sexually charged romance that everyone longs for, but it's high quality and has lots of potential. That's worth more than what any one-night stand, instant passion or undercover fling can bring into my life.

Chapter 23

KEITH

I'm sweating bullets. I just finished leading an intense diversity training session for the new faculty members at Pasadena City College, and it skipped my mind that Cesar would be attending. I'm sure the chicken soup incident is still in his mind, though he doesn't officially know it was me who did it. It's kinda hard keeping your cool and appearing smart, calm and collected when Cesar's keeping his eye on you the whole time. It's a mixture of anger and pity on his face. I just kept reminding myself of one thing: every cause has an effect. Cesar definitely cheated on me with my friend, but Cesar doesn't definitely know I vandalized his door. Still, it's hard facilitating meaningful discussion on heavy topics like remedial classes, white supremacy and institutional racism in college when juvenile actions by juvenile people are on your mind.

Cesar does get credit for one thing. He stood up for me when one of his faculty peers accused me of advocating quotas and allowing unqualified students in the college setting. Sometimes these so-called professionals are more closed-minded than the average "joe blow" in society, which makes this kind of work even more challenging. People with degrees sometimes think they know everything and don't need to learn any more. It's ridiculous how misquoted and misunderstood my work gets, but Cesar was there with his quick wit and intelligent comments. *Lord, why does he have to be so good-looking and smart, too? Please help me get over him.*

Cesar walks up behind me as I'm packing my handouts and laptop. I don't want to appear too eager to talk to him, even though it's all I've wanted to do this evening. I want to play it cool. I don't want to swoon in front of him or his colleagues. Most of all, I don't want him to think all is forgiven regarding him being at that Hollywood Hills party on a night he was supposed to be at home sick.

"Excuse me, Mr. Hemmings," he says as he taps me on the shoulder. "I just wanted to thank you for your work with our faculty group. We needed this."

"Thanks." I smile and acknowledge him with a handshake, as I would any other participant at my workshops. He scratches my palm with his index finger. "I hope you liked it and learned something."

"You don't have to be so formal with me, Keith. And yes, I liked the session."

"I'm formal? Didn't notice."

"Yeah, *moreno*, you are," Cesar says, and smiles at me. "We're friends, right?"

"I wouldn't exactly call us friends, Cesar."

"Come on, man. You know how this game works—it's all fun." He pouts and nods his head. Cesar knows how to use his charm, and he obviously knows gold is a good color on him. He's wearing a nice-fitting stretch dress shirt with matching gold tie. "You know you want to forgive me, right?"

"You play too much, Cesar."

He laughs. "You too, Keith. Wanna go out sometime? Like maybe for some soup?"

"What?" I look him in the eye, like a deer caught in a headlight.

"I know it was you," he says and laughs. "Let's call it even. We all fuck up sometimes."

"I don't know what you're talking about, but I'm sure you've got a lot of brokenhearted enemies out there."

"What happened with us? Remember the dancing, the beach and all the good conversation? We started out so good."

"Yeah, until you started sleeping with Rafael—my friend. Did you think that was cool or something?"

"It would be fucked up if I *had* slept with Rafael," Cesar says. "If it's any consolation, I didn't sleep with Rafael. And I'm not seeing him."

"No?"

"Of course not. You're the only one for me. You're the kind of guy . . ."

"You want to take home to your family," I say. "I've heard it before. Too bad you can't be honest about what's up with you and Rafael."

"Look, *moreno*, he came onto me. He knew you and I weren't sleeping together yet, and he just put it out there for me to take. I admit it, okay. It meant nothing. Rafael is trash, just like you always said. Wouldn't you rather have everything out in the open and someone who's honest? Who told you this anyway?"

"It doesn't matter who told me," I say. "You're so lame, Cesar. You're twenty-nine, not some nineteen-year-old kid trying to score any piece you can get."

"My bad. I'm sorry. We'll just start over."

"There's more, Cesar."

"What now, *moreno?*"

"The party? You lied."

"An old friend called me up and wanted to hang out. He dragged me."

"And what about my replacement? The one you took to Tempo? It didn't take you too long to trade me in for a younger and hipper model. Are black boys your fetish or something?"

"You're wrong for that one, Keith."

"Well, that's nothing compared to how it feels knowing you slept with my friend. And then flaunting that San Francisco has-been in front of me at Tempo was contemptible."

"Believe me, he's nothing compared to you, *moreno*," Cesar says. "I'd like to erase the board and start again. We've got potential. At least that's how I feel. No more Rafael. No one else but my *moreno* boy."

"So why should I believe you?"

"I don't know," Cesar says. "Maybe because I love you."

"You don't even get the point." I slam my briefcase shut and put on my jacket. "You can't mess around with my friend and solve it with 'I love you.' It's not that simple."

"That's it, *moreno?*"

"There's nothing more to say," I say. "I opened up to you about a lot. You know I'm not the most secure person."

"I'll give you a few days to think about what you're doing."

Though I still think Cesar has a lot of potential in terms of being a long-term catch or husband material, I realize that as long as he's under the spell of Rafael, I can't or won't compete. I wouldn't win. And even though Rafael's and my friendship is on shaky ground, I won't go that low and do unto him what he did to me. I may have had one momentary lapse of judgment by vandalizing Cesar's door, or helping to ease Dante's stress in his time of need, but I will not sink to their level any more than that.

I fix myself a Belvedere vodka martini and walk to the back of my condo to my office. On the way, I knock on Tommie's door to see if he watched Tyrell's game on television today, but surprise, he's not home yet. I'll just catch up with him later.

I turn on my desktop and hit the play button on my answering machine.

"Whassup, whassup, Mr. Hemmings? Or should I call you Keith now? We tight like that, on a first-name basis now. Yo, look, I'm hoping you'll call a brotha back. You got the digits, right, right? 555-D-C-O-V. I wanna hook up with you—not like we did in the car—but go out. For reals. I got two front-row tickets to Mary J. Blige, so call a Trojan brotha back if you wanna roll. Peace out." Delete. I wish I'd never messed around with Dante. Sex before relationship confuses things, and I'm not sure what I want from that kid.

"Keith, it's your big brother, Solomon. Call me. I have an important question to ask you. Well, I'll go ahead and ask, and you can think about it. My best man and I had a falling out, over a money situation, what else? Anyway, I know I didn't ask you before, but I want you to be my best man now. Call back when you're not busy. Probably at the church office in the day. Or my cell, 313-555-8810. Hope you're having a blessed day." Delete. Yeah, I'm blessed, but not really feeling it today, and I don't want to stand up in your wedding after you said you couldn't have a person with a questionable reputation like me in your ceremony. I'm sure he doesn't know that I know about that remark, but that's what happens when families can't keep their mouths shut about stuff they said they'd keep quiet about. Kinda like

when my parents' "don't ask, don't tell" edict, once they found out about Shawn Bentley, ended up as fodder for discussion (more like debate, there *is* a difference) between Solomon and me. Things changed between us after that. When you have three kids in a family, there's always a natural triangle, a delicate balance of friendship and rivalry, and alliances change all the time. Stephanie and I rekindled a tenuous relationship for a time, until she married and started raising her own family. She's not uncomfortable with me being around her son, Julian, but she doesn't want me necessarily teaching him or shaping his opinions on life and issues. What once was a tight Solomon/Keith brotherly bond dissolved, and now when we are in the same room it's just that. Same space. Peacefully coexisting. No debating. No drama. And now he wants me to be a best man in his wedding? What miracle came from above to change his mind? Should I even question it? What does Kool Moe Dee say: How you like me now? Maybe I should just do it and see this invitation as the olive branch, the mending of our strained relationship. Shoot, it's too late to save that message. I'll call Solomon tomorrow.

"Keith, this is Derek Lopez, Congresswoman Womack's aide in the L.A. office. We would like you to call the office as soon as possible to talk about a possible project for the congresswoman. Please call by the end of the week. 323-555-5755." Hmmm, sounds like promising work. I like the congresswoman's politics. She's progressive and tells it like it is. Save.

"Keith. Lauren Irby, CCC Investments. You know the market's mixed these days, and many of your stocks are close to the sell-order price you set. I just want your consent before selling. And you might want to consider changing some assets around. You can still live large on what you have, but unless you want to start working a real five-day-a-week job like the rest of us Stanford grads, then you should think about reallocating. Call me at the office at 626-555-4729.

Oh, and I saw Chris Aquino last night at Ita Cho restaurant, but I don't think he saw me. And remember Helen Jenkins, the president of Black Student Union when we were at Stanford? She's in L.A. now and dating some actor from one of them WB or UPN comedies—a nice brotha. Phat pockets. Anyway, talk to you like yesterday." Save. I better call her ASAP in the morning.

"Hey, moreno. It's me. I'm thinking about our talk. I'm sorry and don't know what to say. So I'll just play a song for you." It's an Enrique Iglesias song, *"Si Tú Te Vas."* If you go.

"It's me. Marco Antonio. Don't call back tonight, but we have to talk. It's very, very important, but call me at my office tomorrow morning if you can. Yeah, it'll be Saturday, but I have work to do. Julio says hi. Bye." What in the world is Marco being so secretive about? I'll find out later. Delete.

"Keith, Stephanie here. Forget Solomon's call earlier. He's tripping over stuff he shouldn't be tripping over. You just come to Detroit and enjoy the wedding like any other guest would. Marcus is still his best man. I'll talk to you later, baby brother." Delete. So much for Solomon's momentary care for his younger brother. Looks like Stephanie and Solomon have rekindled their alliance again. That figures. Being the center of attention and gossip between Stephanie and Solomon when I'm over two thousand miles away is not my idea of traditional family values.

Sometimes I look at my clique and wish I could be in their shoes when it comes to family. Well, maybe just Marco Antonio. He has it best of the group. Mr. and Mrs. Vega are not quite enlightened, but they're getting there and really making an effort to grow from where they've been. They haven't shunned Marco from the family, which is such a common occurrence, and his grandma is the biggest supporter and influence for understanding and acceptance. Tommie hasn't dealt with a thing with his family. His choice. It wouldn't surprise me if he ends up making a trip down the aisle just to keep up appearances. Rafael's got it worst. I wouldn't want to trade spots with him any day. I couldn't imagine being beat up by my siblings and basically kicked out to fend for myself. No money. No education. No resources. The fact that he survived is the only redeeming quality I see in Rafael, because I don't know if I could have done it. At least I was almost done with my first degree from Stanford, school was paid for and, if the Hemmings had decided to cut off funds, at least I had my own savings accounts to live off of.

But money aside, what I miss most is morning breakfasts with the family around the maple dining room set made for sixteen. Taking the best hot lunches, prepared by our nanny/ housekeeper Miss Johnson, to school, which made Stephanie, Solomon and me the envy of our classmates. Reading scripture and having home Bible study after dinner with Mom, Dad and my brother and sister in the den or on the backyard deck when there was nice weather. Learning the spoken and unspoken rules of being the "First Family" of the church, which has been ours for two generations. Enjoying our huge church picnics on Belle Isle Island, where hundreds of families would get together to barbeque, celebrate, worship and give thanks for our lives, health and happiness. Traveling together on our yearly summer vacations around the country and the globe, and learning to appreciate life, people and cultures outside of our box in Detroit. That ill-timed family trip to San Francisco during Gay Pride season, when I was seven or eight, got me hooked on California. Of course, instead of seeing the humor, irony or education in the situation, my parents quickly whisked us out of the Bay Area and down to our church convention in L.A. three days early.

A lot of things I miss. Some things I don't. I guess I don't have a lot to complain about. Even though my family's religious, and is the church First Family, they're not Pat Robertson religious, or running their own branch of the Traditional Values Coalition, or picketing Pride celebrations with "Burn in Hell" signs.

But whatever.

I've got at least two more martinis calling my name before I call it a night. And two decisions to make—about the wedding and about Cesar. I'm probably stupid for delaying on the Cesar situation. Here's someone who's wanting to be with me, who has most of the qualities I prayed and looked for in someone, and now I'm sitting here drinking alone, again, making Cesar wait until I make up my mind.

I probably wouldn't know true love if it knocked me in the face.

Chapter 24

TOMMIE

I fucked up this past weekend messing around with Rafael. I never should have asked him to hang with me at that club. Why I cheated on my Tyrell is a mystery to me, 'cause it ain't like we having any problems that would make me do something so stupid. I can't hide these hickeys, even with the dark skin, and I ain't gonna lie about why I wasn't answering my cell or two-way pager this weekend, so I call up Tyrell and tell him to meet me outside the student union building at UCLA so we can take a ride around and talk.

He hops in the truck and has gifts for me from Pittsburgh, including a souvenir book featuring him and the rest of the basketball team, and an autographed jersey from some of the Philadelphia 76ers who stopped by to watch his game. He tells me to pull into the parking structure, we head up to the far end of the fourth level, and when I park, he plants a minty-fresh, recently brushed tongue down my throat.

"You don't know how long I've been waiting to do this," Tyrell says as he unbuckles and unzips my jeans.

"Not in the truck," I say.

"You didn't get tinted windows for nothing," Tyrell says, and before I know it, I'm disappearing, reappearing, and tingling from Tyrell's magic mouth. He grabs my hand and forces it on the back of his neck. It's almost like he's learned something new on that recent road trip. Tommie Junior feeling as good as he did when Rafael got on him. And I have to look down just to make sure it ain't Rafael, but Tyrell and his twists who making me . . . geez . . . right . . . now. I jerk my neck back as Tommie Junior makes a slow and sensitive exit from Tyrell.

"Damn, Tyrell, that was excellent. Sorry I was so quick."

He spits in a tissue tucked in his gym bag. "Don't apologize. That's how it's meant to be done. Especially when you're feenin like you were."

"I guess. More like you were the one feenin."

"Well, let me tell you about my trip."

Tyrell tells me how much he missed me, asks if I watched the game and saw him on television, and says he wants me to drive up to San Jose in the coming week to see him play in round two of the tournament. I hear him, but thinking about how I let myself get finished off by my dude and that Rafael punk within days of each other.

"How come you're so quiet, Tommie?" Tyrell turns on the radio. It's still on the same Spanish station Rafael turned on that night. It's not what's normally banging in my ride. "What's up with the cha-cha-*olé-olé* music?"

"I told Keesha to stop playing around with my stereo," I say. Damn, I'm quick on my feet when I wanna be. "What you want to hear?"

"Your voice."

"I'm listening to you," I say. "You got more interesting stuff going on than me. The store's the same. Keith's the same. I'm still staying up in Pasadena."

"OK. Ha ha. Funny. You act like you're not excited I'm back. I can go back to Pittsburgh."

"Nah, I want you right here," I say. "Let's ride up to Mulholland Drive for a bit."

"Why there?" Tyrell asks. "People only go up there to make out or to deliver bad news. We can kick it at your place for the good stuff."

"I like the view of the city and the valley."

"So you're all Travel Channel now. That's cool."

"You're funny."

"You just better be making some bomb-ass travel plans for my birthday in a few months."

"I got something real chill planned," I say, as if we'll even be together anymore after I get this Rafael situation off my chest.

Damn. I didn't think the guilt would be this bad. We ride in silence up through the Topanga Hills until we reach a small lot, a vista point, where we can park and talk. I can't even put it out my head, thinking about Rafael sitting in the same seat my Tyrell in now. I'm just gonna be a man about it and break it down. That's about the only thing I got from my pops—be a man and take whatever is coming to you.

"Something happened this weekend." I can't even look him in the eye, and stare out the window at Universal City and the crowded 101 Freeway down below.

"I knew something was up," Tyrell says. "So out with it, man. Who was she? When's she due? I know you got a past and all. Or was it a Sylvia scene again?"

"Huh?" I shake my head.

"Just kidding around, Tommie," he says, and play-punches my right shoulder. "So whassup? Make it quick. I gotta get to practice and study hall tonight."

It's always something Tyrell's gotta go to. Maybe that's part of the reason I did what I did. Who knows?

"I hung out with Rafael this weekend . . ."

"Why Rafael? Isn't he the one who messed around with Keith's man?"

"Yeah. Right," I say, and know I should just come straight with it. "We got together after work and went over to hear some of my former band members play at this club on Sunset. We might do a greatest hits CD with some new tracks."

"Is that it?" Tyrell asks. "Just an innocent boys' night out with a punk you don't even like?"

"Damn, do I gotta spell it out?"

"I think you better tell me something," Tyrell says, and grabs my chin so that I'm looking at him now. "I'm out here busting my ass getting good grades, playing ball when I don't want to in order to fulfill this scholarship, so that I can support your broke ass one day. Not to mention risking it all by doing nasty shit in your car on campus. You owe me something. Some kind of explanation."

"Damn, Tyrell, I didn't want to get into all the details and shit. It's done, and it's not happening again."

"I don't know why it happened in the first place," Tyrell's raising his voice. "I know I'm busy with school and my ball schedule. But am I not enough? You need some trash like Rafael to get you off? I didn't even think you liked Mexicans. That's what you used to talk shit about Keith all the time. What's changed?"

"Nothing's changed," I say.

"Educated butch black man not enough for you? It's not like we're out and about in 'the scene' and have the ability to meet other people. We were lucky to have found each other, being down low and all."

"It was a stupid mistake, Tyrell."

"You needed to keep that shit in your pants," Tyrell says, and points to my zipper. "You have no discipline or class, just like your sister Sylvia."

If Tyrell not careful, and keep treading on buttons I don't like pushed, it's about to be two grown-ass black men fighting up on Mulholland Drive. And next thing you know, the police will be here, we'll be arrested, and it's all over the newspapers and the Nostalgia Network: EX-SINGING SENSATION AND RISING BALL STAR IN LOVERS' QUARREL.

But since College Baller wanna know, I'll tell him everything.

"Look, Tyrell, the shots Rafael and me took ain't help. You know I don't even do hard liquor. But Rafael got my guard down and started going down on me in the truck after the club."

"Where I just did you? And you just sat there like a retard? Couldn't say no? Or stop?"

"The muthafucka could suck the chrome off a trailer hitch, which I know you don't want to hear, but you asked."

"You're one low-class country nig— Let me stop before I say something I don't want to say."

"I told you to leave it alone, but you wanted details, Tyrell," I say. "So when Rafael invited me up to his apartment, I just couldn't say no. I was drunk anyway and needed to crash somewhere before I got a DUI or something. Anyway, it's not like I did anything, really. All I did was lay there. Rafael did everything. I don't even want nothing with Rafael. It was really just a one-time thing."

"I should have kicked Rafael's ass when he stepped to me in that restaurant at CityWalk and passed along his number," Tyrell says. "I should have known better than to think you were any different."

"Rafael means nothing to me," I say, and grab at Tyrell's hand, which he quickly snatches away. "So you can't forgive me?"

"Forgive you?" Tyrell says. "Do you see 'stupid' on my forehead? I'm not one of these intellectual types with no street sense."

"I'd forgive you."

"Big whoop. I'd never sleep around on anyone I was supposedly committed to." Tyrell turns up the radio and folds his arms. "You taking me back to campus or what?"

"I guess so," I say. "I am so sorry."

"Yeah, you *are* sorry," Tyrell says, and raises his voice. "And you ain't shit either. Just another broke-ass hood rat trying to front like you got something. Riding around in a leased Escalade. Renting a room from a childhood friend, who shouldn't even let you ride his coattails, but I guess charity work is in these days."

I ain't been insulted and called this many names since my episode with Sylvia in the record store.

I hate being told I ain't shit. It cuts to the core of what I already think about myself and my life. No, I'm nowhere near being a college graduate. No, I ain't in the music biz no more. No, I ain't got no famous family name, with connections to all these important people like Tyrell or Keith. And true, the apple must not have fallen too far between my sister Sylvia and me. But hearing all this come from my Tyrell, of all people, hurt even more. It's like he been saving up all this mental evidence since we been hanging together, and this Rafael thing is his time to release it. He my boy, and I ain't felt this way over no dude ever. Now my Tyrell won't take my apology or explanation. I never knew he had this much pent-up issues about me.

He's silent all the way back to campus. We pull up in front of the athletes residence hall and sit for a few minutes. I don't know what to say, and Tyrell won't speak his mind. Out of the blue, he hits me in my face, side of my head, my chest. I ain't been whipped by another man since my pops did when I was a little boy, but I ain't gonna hit Tyrell back. What would be the use? We can't cause a further scene for all the little college kids sitting out front the hall, and I'm in the wrong, anyway. Before Tyrell gets out the truck, he tells me to get the fuck out his life, grabs his workout bag and the gifts he brought back from Pittsburgh, tells me not to bother going to San Jose for his tournament game, and slams the door.

I really wanted that autographed jersey.

And I really want my Tyrell to march back around and tell me that he forgives me. I sit in front of the dorm for almost thirty minutes, but see no sign of Tyrell anywhere. That night with Rafael wasn't worth it after all.

Chapter 25

KEITH

My to-do list for today is full of things that are just for me. It's going to be a renew my spirit, make over my life, center myself kind of day. I'm not doing any work-related projects and will just concentrate on me and my development.

- Consultation with that counselor Marco Antonio told me about to see if talking to a professional is for me.
- Facial, manicure and haircut at Luke's or Just In Time Barbershop in Pasadena.
- Call Marco Antonio and see if he wants to do lunch, my treat, and find out what he's been wanting to talk to me about.
- Make airline arrangements to Detroit for Solomon's wedding; call parents, Stephanie and Solomon.
- Cardio and weight session at the gym in Montebello—might even hire that man Rafael hooked up with to be my trainer.
- Stop by the stationery store in Old Town for a new journal, pens and cards for Mother's Day and Father's Day.
- Call Lauren Irby back about my portfolio and about fi-

nancing a new house to buy, either in Baldwin Hills or
Ladera Heights.
• Go out dancing tonight with Marco Antonio and Julio,
  or by myself, ooze lots of confidence, and find some
  new people to add to my life.
• Don't look for a man; if he's out there, he'll find you,
  Keith.

I know the reason for this new positive attitude is my
meeting with Cesar. Standing up to him was a freeing experience. And even though I still find him irresistible, and know
in my heart Cesar and I could be a good match for each
other, I'll let him think for a while about what he's missing
when I'm not around. Like the old folks used to say: play me
once, shame on you; play me twice, shame on me. I'm not
willing to be played twice. But I can't help but care for him. I
like Cesar.

Deciding not to call Dante back is a good decision, too.
No explanation needed. He's too young, immature, and just
all over the place. One minute, he's working at this cool cultural and artistic spot, and appearing to be a mature college
student. The next, he's inviting me up for kindergarten-like
games while his mommy and daddy are away from home, and
we end up making out. I must be getting old, because I hated
it when I was in college and some together thirty-something
man called me a kid. History must be repeating itself. Dante's
got his life together for the most part—good-looking, good
sense of humor, energy, going to college, stable family and
home life it seems—and I guess if he wants to chase after me,
I'll let him. We'll see how patient he is with this game.

Besides, I've spent too much time chasing after men who
really don't give a damn about me. Cesar's just another name
to add to the list of L.A. men I've wanted, but who don't

reciprocate the feeling. Maybe he cares, who knows? I won't bother with the rest of the list, but their names would fill a couple of address books. Who knows if Dante will join the club?

Problem number one: L.A. is a bunch of tens looking for a twelve. I'm not ugly, but I'm not the same head-turner I was when I was, say, twenty-one or twenty-two. Bodies and faces change, no matter how hard you try to fight nature without resorting to surgery or steroids. I can afford the surgery, but why go through the pain and spend all that money for something you'll eventually have to touch up every few years? And besides, I'm smart. I'm definitely smarter today than I was back in my early twenties, even with my Stanford degrees. I'm smart enough to see past the smoke and mirrors that a good face and a good body represent, but are other people? Yeah, it's important, but not in the grand scheme of things. Keeping the perfect six-pack is not going to make or break most of us in the gay world, except if you're working in the entertainment industry, and most of us don't do that kind of work anyway. What's the worry? Which leads to . . .

Problem number two: L.A. is no place for an intelligent gay boy in the gay scene. Enough said. Make conversation about superficial and mundane things and you're labeled a wonderful and outgoing person. Make conversation about life and philosophy, and you're labeled a nerd or, worse yet, a friend. A friend, because your light shines with a book and not a bed. I thought Cesar was the one boy who would be able to accept me for who I am, seeing that he's a professor and all-but-dissertation in his Ph.D. program, but I guess not. Anyway, I feel like all my conversations are like "BLAH BLAH BLAH" and no one really cares about what I say or do when I'm with them, kind of like how it was at that Hollywood Hills party with all those actor wanna-bes.

Problem number three: no matter what people say, race matters in L.A. In the ethnic hierarchy of gay L.A., black and African American most often finishes last. That's unless you're one of the following: 1) light enough to pass for being mixed with something other than black, even if you're just pretending to be biracial, which raises the value of your romantic stock dramatically, since being one hundred percent black is a liability and being mixed de-emphasizes blackness; 2) thuggish enough to pass for a gangbanger or a rapper to fulfill someone's colored boy/bling bling fetish and stereotypes of black men; 3) muscular enough to pass for a professional athlete, hopefully a basketball player, because everyone wants the long legs and torso pressed against their bodies; 4) mainstreamed or assimilated enough to blend in with the majority white crowds of West Hollywood, laugh, smile and buffoon yourself and your people for their entertainment, and spout off well-rehearsed lines such as "People are people and I don't see color," when they really do, or "I grew up around white people and I don't feel comfortable in all-black settings," when they really grew up in South Central, South Bronx or Southside Chicago and know the only white people they grew up with were an occasional teacher, a mailman, or their mother's supervisor who gave them hand-me-down clothes before the new school year. I'm not about to join the Afro-Saxon clique to get a man.

If you're white and have rock-hard abs, a tribal-band tattoo around your sculpted biceps and have endured the latest implant, skin dermabrasion or fat-removal technique, you can rest assured that you can have your pick of other white boys or any other ethnicity you want for the night, if you choose. This is for no other reason than the fact that you're white and seen as desirable and normal and a potential partner for life. You don't have to think about your place, because you and most other people see you as normal, the standard. On a slow day, you can simply rest assured that your existence in the world is not questioned or ignored.

If you're Asian or Asian American, you can count on being a fetish, objectified or a fantasy even without trying. You're exotic, much like Chinese takeout in Montana, and most of the time you don't even question being called Oriental or being placed in the same category as a rug or a vase. And don't even think of pursuing or being pursued by anything other than a white boy, because you have that "model minority" theory to fulfill. You have to prove yourself to be as good as white boys, and are nothing like your men-of-color peers, who are in the same boat as you in the grand scheme of the gay world.

If you're Latino, you supposedly have the best of all worlds—light skin (let's not start with the African and indigenous roots that are often hidden, ignored or denied), people-of-color vibe (unless you call yourself "Hispanic" and are part of that compassionate conservative clique from Texas or Florida), and acceptable to most white folks' families if they *have* to accept interracial dating. Besides, being Latino is the hot trendy thing for the new millennium according to most pop culture and literary sources, so ride the ride while it's moving. And you can revel in the names associated with being a sex object—hot Latin lover, *papi chulo*, *chulo* with the nice *culo*, *tamale*, *chorizo*. If you're culturally empowered and know your history and culture, you might object. But if you're not, well you're just plain old hot, hot, hot and probably think it's all in fun. You can date black, you can do white, on a slow night maybe even go for an Asian boy, but most likely you'll go Latino unless the aforementioned guys speak a little Spanish and can do a few merengue or salsa moves on the dance floor. Besides, going Latino or white fits best with the overall historical trend of deliberately lightening up the community. Can't have those indigenous roots and looks popping up, after all.

And if you're African American or black—well, let's just summarize it with my experience in L.A.: too dark to be the tragic, yet beautiful mulatto boy, and not dark (or "homeboy") enough to be the black mandingo fantasy. Face it, I'm in the minority in this town. Except for the pockets of talented tenth in Baldwin Hills, Leimert Park, Ladera Heights or even Altadena, there are not many black men to be found in L.A. I mean when has anyone seen more than five black men together in one setting in L.A.? Especially black guys who actually like other black guys, whether it's in the friendship or more-than-friendship context. This makes for a lonely and sad dating life for me.

So, that's me. I don't want it to be this way for me. Maybe I'm too cynical. Maybe I'm just realistic. Maybe I think too much and need to enjoy myself more. Be more spontaneous. Use the charm and wit I used to let shine back in the day. And stop thinking of ethnicity and class issues and their obvious connections to who people choose or see as options to date.

After getting all this out at my counseling session, I feel better and realize there's much work to be done inside and out. The counselor gives me some homework to do for the week, but I'm thinking twice about this therapy thing. I don't know why Marco sent me to this Afro-Saxon. He doesn't seem too comfortable handling my thoughts and opinions on race, culture and dating. Maybe it's because he's black and has a white boyfriend, who's in pretty much every picture hanging in the office and on his desk. There's got to be some culturally empowered counselors of color in this city, but then again

Marco doesn't know everyone in his field. Maybe I don't need to see any kind of head doctor. I could just call home for some good old-fashioned church advice and motivation from the family. Maybe I don't need to do anything but let the Higher Power guide my steps. Besides, if my ancestors and millions of other black and brown folks could survive and endure colonization, exploitation, objectification, marginalization, and other "ations" without the help of a sit-down therapist, there's no reason I can't do the same. I'm strong, the son of a minister and have that Detroiter attitude of being able to fight back and survive. If the only problem I have is the lack of a love life, then I'm in pretty good shape.

Even though I've decided against seeing a professional therapist, I have decided to keep my appointment with a professional fitness trainer.

I'm waiting in one of the cubicle offices at the gym and trying to think of what I'm going to tell him or her when he/she asks about my fitness and health habits. I've been a regular at this gym for almost three years and going about three times a week, but have managed to gain about twenty pounds—and it's definitely not muscle. How embarrassing! But that's why I'm meeting and hiring a trainer to work with me so I can be the man I used to be. Cut. Tight. Confident. Happy.

The trainer is taking forever. I decide to check out the surroundings of the office—an open drawer, files on the desk, memos posted on the wall—you can't help but see things. There's a small yellow envelope from the Health Department tucked underneath some new fitness client contracts. I wonder what's the deal with my trainer, and nudge the contracts and papers over a little to get a better look. A small white paper falls out, with the code JP27 on one side. The other side says HIV Test—POSITIVE.

"Man, sorry for keeping you waiting in my office for so long. Seems like everyone wants my help today."

I turn around and am surprised that the trainer, whose HIV test result I've just opened and snuck back on his desk, is the same person Rafael hooked up with all those weeks ago at Arena. Jermaine. I know it's him. But he doesn't look like the person I remember him to be all those weeks ago.

And then I realize that Jermaine slept with Rafael. Rafael slept with Cesar. Cesar hasn't slept with me, but I have to know . . .

"Cesar, how are you?"

"I'm fine, *moreno*. How are you?"

I sit down at his office desk, piled high with examination blue books and a stack of term papers. I hunch my shoulders and look away.

"I'm not sure," I say.

"So you thought you'd come visit Professor Reyes' office hours." He walks behind me and massages my shoulders. "*Pobrecito, mi moreno* boy *esta triste. What's up?*"

"I don't know where to start." I lean my head toward an empty spot on the desk. "You're okay? I just want to know if you're okay."

"I'm fine."

"Sure?"

"Yeah," Cesar says. "I wish you would make up your mind about us."

He brushes his lips against the back of my neck.

"I know that's not your mouth on me, Cesar."

"I don't know what it is," he whispers against my ear. "What do you think it is?"

"A tall Mexican from Sinaloa feeling up on a smart African American from Detroit."

"You like, *moreno*?"

"Of course I do." I turn around and peck him on the mouth. "But like I said the other day, I need time."

"I gave you a week."

"Cesar, you slept with my friend."

"I told you I love you and no more Rafael."

"I'll let you know," I stand up and move away from Cesar. "I won't leave you hanging."

My cell phone beeps in my pocket. I take it out. Someone's left me a text message. "HORNY. Dante."

"*Moreno*, who's Dante?" Cesar laughs as he peeks at the phone screen.

"Dante?"

"Looks like we're in the same boat." He pulls me toward him. "I ain't trippin', Shaniqua. You betta rec-a-nize."

Cesar tickles me and makes me laugh. He's okay. I'm okay. We're even. Maybe not. I know the definite connection from Jermaine to Rafael to Cesar. Yeah, I had a fling with Dante, but Cesar and I were on hiatus from each other. Cesar had one when we were dating. Even? Maybe I'll take him back. But I still need to make sure Rafael's fling with Jermaine and with Cesar won't result in something bigger that I won't be okay with.

Chapter 26

MARCO ANTONIO

"*Mi'jo*, we got your gift," my mom yells over the phone. "It's beautiful. Your *Tía* Florinda is here, and she's jealous that I have such a wonderful son!"

"Mom, what are you talking about?"

"The new truck. Don't be silly, son. It's shiny and black and exactly what we needed, especially with all the money your dad's been putting into fixing the old van. It was parked in the driveway—"

"This is crazy. Hold on, Mom." I cup the phone mouthpiece and whisper to Julio, who's lying next to me in bed. We did it. Our first time. Finally. "My parents have a new truck in their driveway, and they think I bought it for them. It just showed up at their house."

"That's weird. Tell your mom hello for me."

"Mom, Julio says 'hello' and congratulations on the new car. But honestly, I didn't send you a truck. My own car payment is enough for me."

"Julio who?"

"You know him," I say, not really wanting to get into her issues with my dating choices. She wants me with Alex, no matter what. "Anyway, is there some kind of note or anything?"

"Just our name on a card and on the title."

"Sounds like your lucky day."

"Well, you have to come over and see it," my mom says. "You can bring your friend if you want."

"Don't sound so enthusiastic," I say. "I'll be over in about an hour to see this truck."

"Okay, we're going out on a little test drive. See you later, *mi'jo*."

I hang up, and Julio is pressing up against me again. The man is absolutely in love with me and acts like he hasn't had sex in the new millennium. But it's good being with someone who's a reliable friend, a confidante and a very capable lover. I could not ask for more, except for him to get his warm body off of mine right now. The morning sun is blazing through the closed curtains, and it feels like it's at least a hundred degrees under the covers.

"What's the matter?" Julio asks as I push him to the other side of the bed.

"Nothing. I'm just hot. And I don't want to have sex right now."

"Excuse me, Señor Vega."

"I like sex, and sex with you is good. Just not now, okay?"

"That's cool, no pressure," Julio says, and gets this pensive thought on his face. "So, what do you think about possibly moving in together?"

It's been just a couple of weeks since we really started seeing each other as more than friends.

"I hadn't thought of it."

"Well, you know I'm house shopping now—you've been with me—and I thought it might be good for both of us.

Starting a new relationship, my new job, getting a house together, doing things the right way."

"Wow, this is big," I say. "I can't say yes. But I'm not saying
no, either. What's the rush?"

"I love you, Marco."

I don't know what to say, so I kiss him instead. He can't
say he loves me this soon. Not love. We've just made the tran-
sition from friends to more-than-friends. It's weird. I want to
change the subject.

"So, you want to go to my folks' house?"

He sighs. "Sure. Why not?"

"And then maybe we can go catch a matinee at the
Laemmle's Theatre in Pasadena and meet Keith for lunch."

"Sure, that sounds like fun," Julio says, and brings my
hand to his lips. "You're not avoiding the talk about living together, are you?"

"No, Julio. I'm not."

"Are you even interested in the possibility?"

"The possibility . . . yeah," I say, and get out of bed. "You
want to join me for a shower before going to see my parents?"

"Of course."

"Let me get the water just right," I say, and head toward
the bathroom. The doorbell rings, and I yell from the bathroom for Julio to answer it.

"No problem."

I'm still thinking about Julio's proposal. It's so soon. I'm
an independent man. I don't need to live with my partner for
us to be official. I like having my own place. I like him having
his. Julio has really put me on the spot, and it's just too soon
to be thinking about taking this relationship any further.

"Marco, babe, you've got a delivery," Julio yells, and walks
into the bathroom. "Take a look."

"Oh, my God! It's huge!"

In Julio's hands is a large arrangement of calla lilies in a beautiful crystal vase.

"Read the card," Julio says and pulls the note out of the attached envelope. "Who are they from?"

"Let's see," I read the card. "'To my inspiration. Just signed a three-year contract with *The Bold and the Beautiful*.'" The rest—I don't read the rest. I know it will hurt Julio. *You're the reason I live and create. I love you always, Alex.*

"So he just wants to brag that he's working on a soap opera, huh?" Julio asks. "You want me to put these in the trash for you?"

I don't, because the flowers are from Alex. And I realize the new truck parked at my parents' house must be from Alex, too. I don't want him to have feelings for me anymore. This is so hard.

"We'll take care of the flowers later," I say, and playfully pull down Julio's boxers. "But let me take care of you first . . . in here."

Chapter 27

RAFAEL

I'm too popular and usually don't need to hit the clubs alone. But I'm itching to get some new dick tonight and am going to Club Chico, down the street from our place in Monte-bello. Alone. I'm guaranteed to get some *cholo*-gangsta love from someone there, especially since I'm dressed the part in my creased Dickies and my fresh clean wife-beater T-shirt. Who's going to resist this fine face, fine body and versatility of looks I can pull off? Who else can go from hard-core *cholo*, to pretty-boy *fresa*, to urban prep, to street-thug gangsta in a in a matter of days, and still get the men?

Anyway, it's time for someone new. Cesar's tired and kicked to the curb. Tommie's heart is with the college boy, and he don't want nothing more to do with me after our one-nighter. It was just a fling, not something to get all serious about, but I swear he was pulling major guilt trip on me the next morn-ing. Blamed it all on me. Oh well, I got what I wanted, though I'd love to get another chance at Tommie's body.

The parking lot at Chico got lots of Accords, Jettas and Civics as usual, so that means good working men gonna be up in the house. A couple of my friends from Bienestar Human

Services and *Casa Raza* are hanging by the front door, smoking and trying to get the bouncer to let they tired underage asses in. I ain't 'bout to be bothered with them tonight. It's major hookup action time, and I don't need the kids messing up my play or competing with me for the mens.

On my way up to the door, I hear the usual "He look good" and "*¿Qué pasa papi?*" shout-outs I always get when I'm at the clubs. It's too early to work the men outside, because there's more fish to fry inside. Besides, the outdoor boys are ugly and not worth my time. So I pay my cover, go inside and do my usual routine when I'm alone at Chico: make my lap around the club starting at the right side of the pool table and back to the bathroom, check myself out in the mirror, then finish around the left side of the pool table and stop at the bar. I order a tequila shot and a Tecate beer chaser. With that, Rafael Dominguez is in business.

I find an empty spot along the wall and decide to park myself there. I'm bobbing my head to some Nelly, feeling out the place and looking around. A couple of *cholos* I had a three-way with almost a year ago are sitting at the small table to my left, and both nod at me. They must remember how good that night was last summer. Unfortunately, I'm not doing recycled goods tonight, but will flirt long enough with the thicker one of the two and get a free drink out of it. He's cute, wearing Mecca jeans and sweatshirt, and got the shaved-head look I like. I look over his way and nod.

"'Sup, *jefe*?" I say. "*¿Quieres bailar?*"

"Yeah," he says putting his wet, thick lips against the rim of my ear. I think he drunk already, which means I got an open credit line at the bar.

Before leading me out to the crowded dance floor, Thick Boy, whose name I remember is Ramiro, stops at the bar and puts up two fingers to the bartender—as in ordering two more of whatever he's been drinking all night. The bartender, who's another old fling of mine, nods at me and smiles a wide, toothy grin, like he wants to get with me again. He hands Ramiro two drinks and tells him it's on the house. Just like I like it. Bartender winks at me. Just add Bartender and Ramiro to the list of recycled goods I don't want anymore.

Ramiro pulls me to the side of the bar, toasts and plants his full indigenous lips on my neck. He grabs my free hand and puts it in the open zipper of his jeans. I guess he think one drink entitles him to a repeat episode of some Rafael loving, but I don't play like that. I jerk my hand away and tell him I'm just trying to take it easy tonight, but apparently Ramiro has had one too many drinks and wants me to be his baby tonight. He looks at me like he ready to bring it on right here in the bar, and shoves me back hard. I fall into Bartender, who's got a stack of empty and half-full glasses in his hands, and we both tumble down to the nasty, wet floor behind the bar.

Two security guards swarm over to our area and wrestle Ramiro out of the club. Everyone's peeking over at the bartender and me on the floor, and a woman screams that there's blood on our shirts. Two other bartenders help us up and start clearing away the broken bottles and glasses.

"Come back to the office, Rafael," Bartender says.

The office, also known as the dressing room for the male strippers, is where me and Bartender messed around a few months earlier. Now it's a makeshift *General Hospital*, and Bartender brings out a small first aid kit to fix our cuts and scrapes. He got it worse than me.

"Let me get you first, Rafael." He opens up a small alcohol swab. "Take off your shirt."

He wipes down two small cuts on my lower back and says I'm lucky that I'm not going to need stitches. It stings like a mug. I'm gonna have to find another shirt, he says, because I can't be walking around with blood on my clothes. Through all this, he repeats my name like he remembers it.

"Sorry to keep you away from your tips and customers."

"Hey, I can't afford to get sued by injured customers." He goes to a rack with costumes—shirts, bikinis and bow ties. "You a small or medium, Rafael?"

"I ain't planning on staying. Just give me back my old shirt."

"When I saw you with drunk Ramiro, I tried to give you that look."

"What look?" I ask.

"The why-you-wanna-hook-up-with-that-loser look."

"Shiiiiiit, I just wanted a free drink."

"I work here. You and I fucked. You could have asked me if you were that desperate for a drink. You young cats think everyone offering a free drink is cool or something."

"Whatever. Fuck you. I don't even remember your name."

"Damn. Had that many, Rafael?"

"Whatever."

"Jose. That's my name. I'm glad I made an impression."

"Well, I'm sure we both have left impressions on half of the men out there." I motion to where the dance floor and bar are outside the office. We laugh.

"We're young. We're adults. Why not share our bodies with other people?" Jose says.

Now it's all coming back to me. The night Jose and I were together, here in this same room, all he wanted to do was talk. He didn't want to have sex, explore each other's bodies or anything. Of course, after his long lecture on philosophy, I taught him a little about my philosophy on men. Jose still wanted to talk, even after we were done with the deed. Most men just want to come—and go. At the time, I went.

"I wish my boys felt like that and didn't judge me so much. They're all a bunch of fucking saints and angels."

"Here," Jose throws me a black sheer T-shirt. "I know it's a little tacky, but you're leaving soon anyway, so no one will see you in it."

"What about Magic Juan? Won't he need this shirt for his little show tonight?"

Jose giggles. "Magic Juan called in sick. No strippers tonight at Chico."

"*Pobrecito.* All his fans will be disappointed."

"Well, I better get myself cleaned up and back out to the bar."

"Need any help? I mean, I caused a scene out there."

"Wanna be a dancer tonight?" Jose asks.

"I ain't no sissy-ass stripper. I was talking about helping clean up your bruises."

"Those sissy-ass strippers, as you call them, pull in a lot of business for us." Jose looks himself over in the mirror, his front and back, and puts on a clean V-neck T-shirt. "And most of the dancers take home a couple hundred dollars a night— if they're good—and they get free drinks." Jose play-socks me on my shoulder and smiles. It's a nice smile and lights up his face. "I know you like to get your drink on, Rafael."

"Thanks for the news flash, Jose," I say.

"Now, I'm not going to flatter you much or stroke your ego," he says. "But you know you look good. Look at that six-pack, your tight waist, those cut arms. You working that shirt, man."

"Tell me something I don't know, Jose. ¡*Dios mío!*"

"And you got a little bitchy and flirty attitude that turns

people on to you. I've seen you work the crowd. You worked me that one night around last Christmas, remember."

"I worked you? I thought it was the other way around, fool."

"You're blushing." Jose grabs my hands and kisses my forehead. "So you dancing for me tonight or what? I got business to take care of out there."

"Yeah. Sure. Why not? But I need a Long Island or some other strong drink to loosen me up."

"Whatever you want. I'll get your drink and then have the DJ announce the debut of our newest dancer."

"Thanks."

"No, thank *you*, Rafael," Jose says. "You're saving the night. And I'll make sure you get home safely, just in case Ramiro or his friend decide to cause any more trouble."

When Jose leaves the back office, I start to think about the extra money I'll make tonight, and how this will help me pay off my cell phone bill and all the other bills that's bound to pile up since losing my Macy's job. That's if Jose is telling the truth and the customers like my dancing. I've always had a way with men, but usually in the bedroom. This'll be different.

I just hope that this doesn't get back to anyone I know. Especially Marco Antonio, or even Keith, for that matter. If my phone was working, I'd call Roneshia's ass down here to see me dance. It's just a one-night job, a favor for Jose helping me out from that fight, and that's that. No need for dramatics. No need to be ashamed. Just a couple hours dancing on a pool table in the middle of a bar.

Jose brings me the Long Island Ice Tea I ordered and tells me the DJ is ready to introduce me. I gulp it down quick, like it's a shot, and am starting to feel warm and ready for whatever the night brings. What have I got to be worried about anyway? The boys love me. I'm young and beautiful and have a body. I hear the DJ announce that the Magic Juan show is cancelled, but that it's being replaced by what he calls "A Night in Rafa's Room." Cheesy, but whatever.

He's got my song on—Beyonce and Sean Paul's "Baby Boy"—and I make my way to the pool table, which also works as the stage at Chico. The buzz I got from the drink is making me lose myself in the bright lights, the swirling glitter balls, the dark dance floor below me and the crowd around me. The energy of the men and the club take over. My body—hips, ass, back and legs—moves in ways that I never even thought possible. I am the striptease. I make eyes at the shy boys and the confident ones, too, who surprise me with numerous dollars, drinks and phone numbers. I'm loving this more than I ever thought I would.

"You were the shit, boy," Jose greets me in the office after my performance ends and the bar closes. "Look at all the money you made." He grabs a handful of bills from my G-string, at least fifty or sixty dollars.

"I was good? Really?" I ask, wanting my ego stroked a little more. I press him against the wall. "How good was I?"

Jose grabs my hands, leans in slowly and kisses my forehead. My forehead!

"You're a good kid, Rafael. And you dance like a pro. Much better that Magic Juan."

"I ain't a kid . . . I'm twenty-two years old."

"I have a son almost your age. You're definitely a kid," Jose says. "Anyway, I'm wondering if you want to do this again? Like next Friday?"

"What's in it for me?" I ask, and press against Jose one more time, anything to get a rise out of him. I plant small baby kisses on his neck. "How old are you anyway, *papacito*?"

"Don't worry about my age, kid. Anyway, I'm thinking

you'll get some drinks . . . mmmm, that feels good . . . hourly salary and lots of tips."

"What else?" I move my hands lower, below his belt.

"I'm thinking promotions—flyers, photos, ads."

"Ads?" I nibble his neck again. "Promotions?" I nibble.

"Like in *QV* magazine or *Adelante*. I see it so clearly. 'Rafa's Room at Club Chico.'"

"Sounds good. Hmmm, wanna come to Rafa's room tonight?"

He pats my cheeks and laughs. No one laughs at me. They laugh with me, but not at me.

"I knew you were a creative boy, Rafael."

He walks back out into the bar area, and I follow. It's empty except for the bar staff mopping and clearing away glasses from the tables. I watch him take care of his closing duties and wonder why he's resisting my obvious seductions and come-ons. I love and hate this.

"Hey, Jose, what if we talk more about this proposition tonight at my place? I got more questions."

"I'm listening," Jose says. "We can talk here."

"No. Come over," I say.

"Five more seconds and you're out the door."

"Well, how old are you, Jose?"

"You'll find out in time," he says and hugs me. "And I am not telling you about my son, either. He's a high school version of me, and I don't want you trading me in."

"Well, come back to my place tonight, and you won't have to worry about losing me."

He walks to me and kisses my forehead again. "No funny business, okay? We're talking and that's it. Nothing else."

"Sure, whatever you say, Jose." And I mean that—whatever. Once I get them home, it's definitely on, no matter how much they resist.

"I'm serious," he says, and grins. "Besides, I must not have been that good the last time we hooked up. You didn't even remember my name."

"Hey, I meet a lot of peeps. I got lots of fans in L.A."

"Well, don't pull any of that playing with the covers, touching your feet to my feet, asking if I'm still awake tonight in bed. Cool? No games?"

We'll see about that. I know Jose's itching to get with me again, with his old-ass self. I don't know why he playing all innocent and pure with me. It ain't like these old men get hit on like they used to in their youth. Especially by someone young and fine like me. I'm about to be his rising star, in bed and in business, so Jose better get hip to the way I'm playing this game. No one ever turns down Rafael Dominguez, especially when I put my mind to getting them.

It's dark and quiet in the apartment when Jose and I arrive. Good. It means Marco Antonio ain't here or asleep, so me and Jose got some privacy. ¡Qué bueno! Exactly what I need, because I plan to turn him out every way I can in the next few hours. He thinks he's just going to play nice and innocent, but this *hombre* don't play like that.

The memo pad got lots of messages for me. Great. Marco's staying at Julio the Salvadoreño's place. Tommie—twice. Shit, what does he want? That was just a one-time thing, I thought. Cesar—once. Once too many. He's so 1995. Gone and forgotten. Enrique—three times. He's definitely gone and forgotten. Roneshia—talking about her new job at The Gap. And what's this? Keith?

"Hmmm, I wonder what Keith wants?" I ask, and crumple up the note. "That's my little party-pooper friend. Anyway, I'll just call them all back tomorrow. I got bigger

and better things to think about now," I say, and rub Jose's
arms.

"Rafa, can I have some water or some Kool-Aid?"

"Sure. Whatever you want." I pour a glass of water from
the dispenser. "Anything else?"

"No, *gracias*. Just some sleep."

I grab Jose and take him back to my bedroom.

"Welcome to Rafa's room." I take off Jose's T-shirt and
push him down on the bed. He's tight for an older man.
"What's your pleasure tonight, *papi*?"

"I told you, we're just talking and falling asleep," he says.

"Why do you insist on being a challenge? Just give in to
your desires. You know you want me."

"You won't quit, will you Rafael? Okay, so then I'll fuck
you and leave like the rest of them. Is that what you want?"

"Men don't leave me. I leave them." I point a finger at
him. "Besides, you want me to be your star dancer at Chico."

"This is L.A., Rafael. I can find someone with rhythm, a
good body and a pretty face any day." He turns me over on
my back and rolls on top of me, keeping himself in a pushup
position so we're face-to-face. "I want to get to know you,
but *really* know you. Not with all the sex and seduction."

"Why are you doing this? Can't hang, *viejito*? How old are
you anyway, Jose?"

"I'm thirty-six."

"Oh, shit. I thought you were twenty-four, maybe
twenty-five tops."

"I told you I have a son almost your age, remember?" Jose
asks. "I've been around the block, and in the club scene, since
you were watching *El Chesperito*. Just drop the pretense and
be real, Rafael."

I am not being clocked in my own apartment. All I

wanted was to seal the dancing deal and then have a few rounds in the sack with Jose. This fool trying to get deep on me. Must be the way Keith manages to ruin all his potential dates. Must be an old gay man thing. I huff and sigh.

"Hello . . . Rafael . . . ¿*Qué pasa?*"

"Nothing," I say. "I don't know if I want you to stay here tonight."

"Why? Because I won't give *chiquito* what he wants?" he says in a high-pitched baby-talk voice that annoys the hell out of me. Who does he think he is? Why am I putting up with Jose?

"Okay. Fine. Let's talk business then." I reach over and flip on the lamp by my bed. We both squint. "What's up with the 'Rafa's Room' night?"

"Me and my partner were thinking you could start out on Fridays and Sundays dancing. We'll pay you a couple hundred a week just for dancing, and you can keep the tips. We keep the name 'Rafa's Room,' and if for any reason we end our agreement or contract, you can't dance at any other bar in L.A. for three months. It's a noncompete clause."

"Stupid, how will you know if I'm dancing at another club? What if this doesn't work out? What if I become bigger than Club Chico? What if I want to stop?"

"You'll find me to be a good boss," Jose says, and kisses me on the freakin' forehead again. "And even a good lover, if you can just be yourself."

"I don't know if I can deal with this. One time you say, 'no sex.' Now you're wanting to be my lover. Make up your mind, Jose."

"My mind was made up when you and I hooked up all those months ago. You just didn't know it yet."

"You're confusing. I don't get you."

"You're young and beautiful. Isn't that what you say about yourself all the time? It's understandable that I'm confusing you. Beauty and brains don't mix."

He laughs. I play-punch him on his biceps.

"Let's just go to bed, Rafael. I'm tired and have to get to the gym by noon."

I flick off the lamp. "I'm doing you a favor letting you stay here tonight. It's only because you're tired, and I'm tired of fighting with you."

"Then don't fight," he says, and moves to the opposite side of the bed. I see he's turned his back to me. "Just go with the current."

"You ain't cuddling me at least?" I ask.

"Good night, Rafael."

"You're such a . . . ooooh. I don't even want to get started."

"Thanks for sparing me the drama, kid." He laughs. "You'd think you'd want to get some sleep, too. Don't you work at the mall on Saturdays?"

"You keeping tabs on me?"

"Shhhhhh. Good night."

I want to kick his brown ass out of my bed, out of my apartment. I can't believe I wasted my night on this *pendejo* who won't even give me a taste of his body. There was plenty of fools at Chico who would have slapped me some meat tonight. I huff again and turn my back to Jose's and stare at the wall. I can't sleep knowing this fine-ass man is in my bed and he won't have me.

Jose ain't a fool, though. He turns over and wraps his big arms and legs around me. He spoons me. Kisses the back of my neck. Wishes me sweet dreams and good night. It's a start.

Chapter 28

KEITH

It should be so easy. The right thing is to tell Rafael I think he slept with someone who's HIV positive. Tell him what I found out about Jermaine. After all, Rafael is a fellow human being, and despite all the numerous faults I think he has, he deserves to know what I suspect could be going on. I'd want to know if a former sex partner tested positive for any kind of sexually transmitted disease, so certainly I'd expect a notification about HIV. Why'd that dumb jock trainer have to leave his personal papers all out in the open like that? Then I wouldn't know anything, and I wouldn't have this burden.

Still, I've sat on this information for almost a week. Part of me is delaying saying anything because the whole situation with Rafael and Cesar still sits in my mind. In a weird way, I like having control over this information and being able to decide when or where to share it, but I'd never let Marco or Rafael know this.

I take another long sip of a vodka and cranberry juice cocktail, my second in the past fifteen minutes, and enjoy my drink in the darkness of the living room. I decide to call home, even though it's past my parents' bedtime—they have an early morning at church. But I have to talk to someone who'll help put this in perspective.

"Hi, Mom. Are you awake?"

"Yeah, wide awake, my child," Mother says. "Stephanie stopped in for a small checkup and had the twins an hour ago, a boy and a girl. Your dad and I are on our way to the hospital."

"Wow, tell them congratulations. It's nice to get a phone call about it."

"Son, you're always so busy with your work and whatever else you do out in L.A. We didn't want to bother you."

"Anyway, I'm not wanting to fight."

"So why are you calling so late?" Mother asks. "Shouldn't you be out barhopping or whatever people like you do?"

"I'm going on hiatus for a while from the bars, I think," I say. "Anyway, I just wanted some advice on a situation. But you're going to see Stephanie. I can call back tomorrow afternoon after you all get home from church. How are things there?"

"Can't complain. Membership is up. Tithes are up, too, even with the recession. We finished building the school."

"Nice."

"Maybe you should go see one of your father's colleagues out there," Mother says. "You sound like you need some spiritual guidance. There are good churches out there."

"Thanks, Mother. I'll keep that in mind."

"Probably been a while since you've been around decent church folks, son. You know Quincy asks about you all the time."

"He's not my type, Mother," I say.

"But he's a church man. And he's the star at Channel Four News."

"Good for him. Well, send my regards to Stephanie and her babies."

"I will. Oh, son, have you bought your ticket yet to come home for your brother's wedding?"

"Yes, I'll be there next month." And just when I think the conversation is over, Mother brings up more issues.

"Good. How are Tommie and that poor excuse of a sister of his doing? I told Solomon under no condition was he to invite Sylvia, even if he and Lisa are little Keesha's godparents."

"I don't think she'll be showing up anywhere but the Las Vegas casinos anytime soon," I say.

"Those Jordans, I swear. I hope you still hold the title to that record store Tommie's running. Make sure he pays you off before you turn it over to him."

"Okay, Mom. Talk to you tomorrow after church. Say hi to Steph for me."

"Bye, son."

I need another drink. Because it was like a "thanks, but no thanks" conversation, with the folks as usual.

Rafael hasn't been the nicest person. Put the Cesar situation aside, and there's still an array of his indiscretions and transgressions against me and his other friends:

• making digs about my age and my weight any chance he gets;
• telling Marco Antonio and other people we meet in the clubs what a dork and old maid I am because . . . I read and have intelligence;
• flaunting his perfect little V-shaped, no-fat body;
• freeloading constantly off Marco Antonio's and my generosity;
• stealing Cesar from under my nose at Tempo;

- using the "N" word repeatedly and without any thought to the word's history or use in society;
- and, finally, the other major character flaws—no class, no education and no future in a career besides retail work.

Days like this, I totally feel like I am my father's son. Third child of a prominent Baptist minister from Detroit. Full of judgment, scorn and condescending attitude. I really am everything I told myself I didn't want to become. I've brought everything I wanted to flee in Detroit with me to L.A.

I take another long sip of my drink and pick up the phone to call Rafael. I have to tell him everything. Two rings later, the T-Mobile operator is telling me Rafael's cell number is out of service. Hmm . . . just like him not to pay his bills on time. I'll look up his work number at Macy's when I'm done in the bathroom.

While I'm walking into the bathroom, Tommie's phone rings in his room. Two open doors—the bathroom and Tommie's room—means you hear things on the answering machine.

"*What up, you fucking coward?*" slowly yells a deep and angry voice. "*Can't even pick up your cell phone, but you can't avoid the home phone for long . . . This shit is fucked up, Tommie . . . I couldn't even concentrate on making my shots, and now we're out of the running for the NCAA championship 'cause I'm fucked up thinking about you cheating on me. I thought I was your boy? This shit makes me wanna throw up every time I think about how I let you be my first. What kind of bullshit excuse is 'He was there. I didn't do anything. He did all the work'? Fuck you, Tommie Jordan, and your fucked-up little music career and your fucked-up life. I hope you're happy with some little fuckup who's down on your level, 'cause when I graduate from UCLA and make it to the pros, you'll*

*hate the day you fucked up what we had. Don't call me anymore
with your bullshit, Tommie!"*

Loud hang-up and dial tone. Damn, I didn't know
Tommie and Tyrell were having problems. I thought they
were still the perfect Mr. Black America couple in L.A.

I flush and go finish up my drink. Tommie's phone rings
again. I rush back to his door to listen. This is almost as good
as *The Young and the Restless.*

"It's me again," Tyrell starts. *"Don't forget, I got boys. My family's got connections, and they'll take care of you and that little bitch
Rafael. Don't let me find Rafael first."* Hang up. Dial tone.

Rafael and Tommie?

I know I didn't hear that right.

I feel my insides churning. That, along with my breathing
picking up pace and turning to hyperventilation, forces me to
the toilet, where I vomit, cry, dry heave and vomit some
more. And no matter how tight I hold onto the rim of the
bowl, I can't stop the room from spinning and my head from
exploding with thoughts of Rafael and Tommie, Rafael and
Cesar, Rafael and the rest of the damn world.

Why am I so consumed with Rafael? Why am I so mad
with envy and hate and concern for my friends? I grab a
towel and bury my face in it. I sob some more. I don't know
if it's for me or if it's for all the people who may be hurt by
Rafael's infidelities—Tommie, Tyrell, Cesar, that high school
boy . . . The list could take up several pages. But who's count-
ing?

I hear Tommie fumbling with the front door lock. I get
up and look at myself in the bathroom mirror. My eyes are
bloodshot and rimmed with leftover tears, which I try to dry
off before going back to the living room. Tommie and I need
to have a talk.

"You're home."

"You drunk or something?" Tommie asks. "Smell like a damn liquor store up in here, Keith."

"Don't worry about what I've been drinking," I say, and walk near where Tommie's standing. I'd be in his face if I were a few inches taller. "Is it true? Did you sleep with Rafael?"

"First of all, don't step to me like that in my house, Keith," Tommie says. "You drunk. I had a bad muthafuckin' day today. That's not a good combination."

"You're not denying it? And it's my house, by the way. I hold the deed."

"Keith, you ain't my parent," he says. "You can try it with Marco Antonio or your other faggoty friends, but not with me."

Wherever Tommie moves, I move in front of him. I bang my fists hard on his chest.

"You stupid fool, Tommie. You dumb, stupid, black fool. How could you do this to Tyrell? How could you have sex with that slut? I can't believe you did it."

"Look, I don't know what to say, but I don't have to answer to you."

"My God, you're just like the rest of them. Can't keep your pants on when it comes to Rafael. How could you be so stupid, Tommie?"

"I ain't like the rest of them."

"Don't you tell me you're not like the rest of them, because you are," I shout. "You had a good thing with a nice college-educated black man, which is a very rare thing to find these days, and you throw it all away for that whore, Rafael, who's seduced practically everyone in L.A. Are you that weak? Are you that hard up for sex?"

"I fucked up, Keith," he yells back, and sits down at the dining room table. "I heard all this from Tyrell already."

"Maybe we're all destined to be a statistic one way or another," I say. "I drink every now and then."

"If every now and then is once an hour."

"But you cheated on the best thing to happen to you in years . . . for as long as I've known you, Tommie." I wipe the sweat falling down my face. "But what I'm angry about is you slept with Rafael of all people. Couldn't you have found a hooker on Santa Monica? I pray to God you used a condom. You did, didn't you? Tell me . . ."

Tommie looks at me and hangs his head down again, shaking it slowly side to side.

"God, Tommie, you're a fool." I slap him across the back of his head. "I found out that Rafael hooked up with someone a few months ago who might have HIV."

"HIV?" He looks up at me again. "You lying?"

"I have no reason to lie."

"And Rafael knows this?"

"I haven't told him," I say.

"You haven't told him?" Tommie asks. "And you're trying to get all moral on me, Keith?"

"Don't worry about Rafael. I'll talk to him when I'm ready."

"I can't believe you ain't told him this yet."

I wipe my face again and grab my cocktail glass, empty it in the sink and fill it with water from the fridge door. I don't feel like talking anymore and just want to sit and think for a while.

"You need to worry about your own damn health, and trying to repair whatever is left of you and Tyrell, rather than thinking about Rafael. He can look after himself like he always does," I say.

"You ain't planning on telling Rafael, are you?"

I roll my eyes and smirk, look Tommie up and down and sigh while he's talking to me.

"You always put yourself up on a pedestal like you're some kind of god," Tommie says. "You been doing it since we was kids. But the fact you gotta *think* about talking to Rafael about this HIV thing say you ain't no better than the rest of us. And you wonder why you're by yourself and never have anyone."

I watch Tommie get up and leave. He slams the door.

"You better not be going to Rafael!"

"Don't worry about where I'm going!" Tommie yells from the courtyard.

I finish the water and think about what he's just said. Maybe I am just like the rest of them. The fact that I think I might not be, that I think I may stand above most people, means I have serious issues to get over and get through.

And, as usual, I find myself alone, bitter and thinking about my lonely life on yet another cold night.

Chapter 29

MARCO ANTONIO

The gifts continue. After my parents found the new truck in their driveway, other gifts started showing up at their house. My mom received new kitchen appliances. My dad, a completely modernized set of tools. Then came gifts of Hilfiger, Baby Phat and Phat Farm for Chloe and Ryan. For me, some things I wanted for my office and apartment, but can't quite afford for myself. Some nice original artwork from Latino artists—Alma Lopez and Antonio Rael—and two VIP tickets for the sold-out Luis Miguel concert in Las Vegas, including airfare vouchers and a reservation for me and a guest, non-specified, to stay in a suite at the Bellagio. Even a five-figure donation to *Casa Raza*.

Are my family members grateful? Yes.

Am I? No.

Is it getting under my skin? Yes.

I don't want Mom, Dad, Chloe or Ryan to like Alex. I don't want to be drawn back into him, which this buying spree is obviously meant to do. Everyone just pretends like Julio doesn't even exist, that he's not my new partner and that things are going like normal with Alex. It's not like *Tía* Florinda doesn't watch enough Spanish tabloid television; she should know he's married to the up-and-coming pop diva of the Latin and U.S. music worlds. It's not like my parents don't see the look in my eyes or on Julio's face when they're fawning over every new gift and gadget Alex has given to them or to Chloe and Ryan. Why does Alex have to do this?

When I caught Keith for a brief moment on his cell, his advice to me was to return everything. By keeping the gifts, I'm giving Alex the message that I want him in my life, and it could drive a wedge between Julio and me. He knows, and I know, that Julio is probably just putting up a strong front with Alex's interference. If Julio's bothered, I wouldn't know. He hasn't said or done anything to show otherwise. I know what's right, but just needed to hear it from Keith. Keith, on the other hand, is angry with me that I kept the news about Tommie and Rafael's fling a secret from him. He says we'll talk about it after I settle this Alex situation later today.

So I'm sitting outside Alex's Silver Lake house. His red convertible is in the driveway. All I need to do is knock on the door, tell him he has to stop sending me and my family these expensive presents, and get back to Julio. It's all about Julio and me now.

Alex springs out the front door, wearing only madras pants and flip-flop sandals, flaunting his firm chest and stomach for the world to see. He's carrying a bag of trash to the curbside bin. He sees me waiting in my car, and his face lights up. I hate to admit it. I'm a little excited to see Alex, too.

"What are you doing out here?" he asks. "Stalking me, *mi'jo?*"

"I just got here. I was coming to see you, Alejandro. We need to talk."

"Well, come on in. I was about to catch a bite to eat. I've got some Thai food. Unless you want to stay out here?"

I set the parking brake and get out of my car. Alex shuts the door after me and pats me on the butt. I swat his hand away. "That's not yours to touch anymore, Alex."

He ignores me and chuckles. "You feeling tight back there, babe. Still working out, I see."

"I'm not your babe, Alex. Anyway, I'm not staying long. I've got stuff to do at home." He still knows how to make me smile, even when I don't want to.

"Like what, *mi'jo*? You can't spend a little time with little old me? After all, I'm just a boy, looking for another boy to love and be loved back in return." He makes this sad puppy dog look with his face and wraps his arms around my waist. I have to remind myself that Alex is an actor and will say and do most anything to make a scene go his way. Besides, that line sounds just like something Julia Roberts said in the movie *Notting Hill*. Does he think I'm that stupid?

"What's up with you, Alex?" I say. "Why are you so touchy-feely? You're still married, right?"

"You know the deal. I'm not in it for love, that's for sure. I haven't seen her in like a month, anyway." He takes off the wedding band and sets it on a shelf above his stove. "Anyway, eat something. This is too much food for one person. And I gotta watch what I eat now that I'm the new Latin lover on *The Bold and the Beautiful*."

"Congratulations. I know you wanted the regular work and money."

"All I want is someone to share it with." He stares at me. "But anyway, I hear you're taken. I thought you were more picky than to mess with a Salvadoreño."

"And so what?" I say. "I swear us *Mexicanos* are getting

more closed-minded like white people every day, just because we're the majority in L.A."

"It was a joke, babe."

"You see I'm laughing," I say. "So, anyway, who says I'm taken?"

"I have friends. *Chisme* gets around." He's put a heaping plate of *pad thai* in front of me. "Eat. *¿Quieres vino?*"

"Sure, why not?" I smile and take a forkful of food. "I'm curious. Who's your spy? Why are you checking up on me?"

He hands me a glass of white wine. A Sonoma Valley winery.

"Next subject, babe."

"Don't 'babe' me. I'm not your babe anymore. Anyway, I wanted to talk to you about the gifts you've been sending to my folks and to me."

"I know—they're nice things. You're welcome. There's more coming."

"Why? Stop. You can't do this. We can't keep them."

"Babe—"

"I told you I'm not your babe."

"Okay, Marco Antonio. I needed to get your attention somehow, and the gifts were the only way I knew how. I still need you in my life, even if you say you can't have me while I'm married. It's in name only, anyway."

"I'm in a new relationship now."

"Look, what do you want? You want me to come out of the closet? I'll do it. You want me to divorce my wife? I'll do it. You want me to bring you to all the cast parties and functions as my man? I'll do it. Tell me what you want. I'll do it. I just want to be with you."

I sit back and put the wineglass to my mouth, like I'm going to take a nice long sip, but I know if I start drinking I'll get really loose lips and start to tell Alex how much I really, really want to be with him. I just don't know.

"Are you acting, Alex?" I ask. "I can't tell when you're serious or playing."

He leans across the table and kisses me. It fits perfectly. Feels like warm butter mixed with maple syrup. Warm. Delicious. Full of craving and wanting more. I remember how it used to be when we were together. It was nice. We fit.

"Did that feel like acting?" he asks.

"It felt really nice."

"Want more?"

Do I want more? Heck, yes, I want more. I want to feel the passion and excitement of spending every day with Alex. I want to drown him with kisses each morning and bathe him in hugs each night before going to bed.

"Of course I do, Alex. I just have to think about it."

"Don't think too hard on it, babe. I can only hold out for so long."

"So what's that supposed to mean?" I ask.

"I'm leaving it up to you," Alex says. "Whatever you want us to be, we'll be."

"And you have no say in this?"

"You know how I feel. I just don't think you know how you feel." He raises his hands up in surrender.

"Fine. Give me a week or so and—" I stop because I hear fumbling at the outside kitchen door. "You expecting company?"

"Oh, shit." Alex rushes over to the door and tries to push it shut. It's forced open by a tall, very actor-looking white man who walks into the kitchen. He's carrying some DVDs in one hand and a small overnight bag in the other.

"Sorry I'm early, Alex. We finished filming early today because the lead got sick, so I decided to come over now instead of later."

"Paul, this is Marco Antonio. Marco, Paul."

Paul rakes me over with his eyes and says, "Who's this? And why is he eating my dinner?" before kissing Alex on the cheek and proceeding his flat ass through the kitchen and up the stairs to where Alex's bedroom is.

"What the hell?" I ask, and push my plate away. It falls to the floor. I don't usually cuss. I'm on my way out of here. Alex is not about to make a fool of me again.

"It's a long story and not at all what you think, babe."

"Whatever, Alex. This is not even worth my energy."

"Babe, don't go," he whispers. "Please?" He grabs his wedding band off the shelf and tries to force it on my finger.

"What are you doing? Are you crazy?"

"Crazy in love."

"I'm out of here," I say. "This is the last time you'll be making an ass out of you or me."

I rush past him, through the living room and out the front door. He's following me, in fast pursuit.

"He's my co-star on the soap. He's playing my lover. There's more to this than you see."

"The only thing I see is a sorry, sad excuse of a liar, and you don't know who you are or what you want."

I slam the car door and rev up. As I'm racing down the curvy hills of Silver Lake, my mind runs through scenes of the times Alex and I have spent together. It hasn't always been good, but the memories are still there and make me cry. He knows how to suck me in and suck me dry every time. This time I know it's over. I cry.

My cell phone rings just as I'm rounding the last curve before I hit Sunset. It's Julio calling. Probably wondering when I'll be over to his place. Sooner than he expects. I'm ready to commit, to move in with Julio and do whatever else he wants to make a life with each other. As I reach over to pick up the phone, I hear a screech, feel a jolt, my car lifts into the air and a spray of glass and metal swirls around me as my car lands hard against a parked car at the bottom of the hill.

Chapter 30

KEITH

The car accident could have done more damage to Marco than the broken arm and body bruises he got. He's lucky to be alive, and his family and I are very glad Marco will be fine. I don't know what I'd do if my best friend were no longer around. We've been through everything together for most of our adult lives—Stanford undergrad and grad school, enduring the suspicious looks and curiosities of people wondering why or how a black guy and a Latino guy could be such good friends. We've endured coming out, the spontaneous move to L.A. from the Bay Area, living in his family's garage apartment while looking for our own places, growing older into our twenties and now almost thirty, not to mention the long list of dates that turned into nothing. I can't imagine anyone taking his place in my life. I couldn't have asked for a better friend.

Mr. and Mrs. Vega stood vigil by Marco's bed all night and this morning, praying over him to wake and for the doctor to give a report to us. Once Marco was alert and knew what was going on, he told me what happened with Alex and asked me to go by his apartment to get a few changes of clothes for him. You'd think having his heart broken by Alex once again and being in a car crash would put a damper on the vanity.

But I guess once a gay boy always a gay boy.

Which is why I'm not surprised to walk into Marco and Rafael's apartment and see Rafael doing what he's most skilled at—being a whore. This time, it's in the middle of the afternoon and in the middle of the living room floor. As if he owns the apartment.

"What the hell are you doing?" I ask Rafael as I slam the front door behind me. "You need to take that to your room, Mr. Slut. Don't you have any respect? What if Marco were to come home?"

Rafael raises his head up from the zipper of yet another stranger and wipes off his mouth. The man, who looks awfully familiar, quickly fastens his jeans and moans, "What the fuck!"

"My God, Keith, what are you doing here?" Rafael asks.

I tell him about Marco's accident and that he wants me to bring some clothes to the hospital.

"Well, why didn't he call me?"

"He did call, and so did his mother and father. All night. Obviously you were too preoccupied to pick up the phone, and your cell is out of order."

"Oh. I got in late," Rafael says. We stare each other down for a few seconds. "Uh, this is Jose, my new boss at Chico. Jose, you remember me mentioning my good friend Keith?"

Jose gets up from the floor and shakes my hand. He excuses himself and goes to Rafael's room.

"What are you doing working at Chico?" I ask.

"I'm a dancer there on the weekends now."

"How classy, Rafael," I say. "Sleeping your way to the middle."

"Better than having to sleep by yourself, *verdad*?"

"I don't want to interrupt your fling, so I'll just get Marco's things and go."

"Well, what hospital is he at?"

"What does it matter to you anyway?" I yell at Rafael. "You've obviously got more important things to attend to, like your impressive career in exotic dance. Shake it like a salt shaker, huh?"

"You're talking crazy," Rafael says. "Get Marco's shit and get the fuck out if you can't be normal."

"Like I have to take orders from an uneducated retail queen like you," I say. "The last thing I expected to walk in on is you rolling around like a cat in heat. Can't you do anything else with your time but chase men? Don't you have your little mall job to get to?"

"So the attitude ain't about me not being there for Marco last night. It's about Cesar, right?"

"This isn't about Cesar, Rafael." Though part of it really is.

"I know you know what happened," Rafael says. "That's why you and Cesar can't get it together. You think he wants me. So sad."

"I told Marco back when he took you in off the streets that you were trash," I say. "And you've proven me right time after time. It's too bad Marco and the rest of them can't see you for what you are. But they'll all know soon enough what bad news you are."

"Whatever, Keith. You're just jealous that you never had a chance with Cesar, or anyone else for that matter, and you're taking it out on me. It's not my fault nobody wants you. Take a look in the mirror. You're getting old. You're gaining weight. You don't even act like a brotha."

"And so what are you saying?"

"Take it for what it's worth, Keith," Rafael says. "Besides,

Cesar does want you. He's always talking about how you're the kind he'd take home to his family. But bitch, you don't take care of your man when it really counts—in bed."

"Let's see. We'll call this 'Lessons in Seduction 101' by Professor Rafael Dominguez, the expert on how to seduce a man and freeload off a man, but who can't keep a man for longer than one night."

"They always come back begging for more."

"Rafael, it's no secret that you go through men like a hooker on a Saturday night," I say. "Everybody knows who and what you are, and pretty soon you are going to pay the consequences."

Rafael rolls his eyes. "Look, Keith. Slow your roll. I don't appreciate your put-downs and threats. We can take it outside if you want."

"But don't you do it best indoors and on your back? Or half naked on a go-go box with your underwear showing? Well, that's of little importance anyway. Your days are num-bered, and all of L.A. will be better off when you're gone."

"Fuck you trying to act all better than everyone else when you know it's your issues with yourself that make you hate me," Rafael says. "Do you expect for me to be like a minister or something?"

"That's funny. There'd be snowstorms in hell before you were even close to being a minister."

"Well?"

"Rafael, if I were you I'd take my sorry butt and get out of town before all the innocent victims come after you. Let's see . . . there's the Club Chico boy in your bedroom now, and then Cesar, and then Tommie and Tyrell, and you know Tyrell didn't even need to be brought into this sickness. The high schooler, Enrique. Need we go on with the list? You're just a ticking time bomb, destroying everything you come in contact with."

"I hope you're through and will have the decency to tell me what hospital Marco's at. I would like to see my room- mate. He's my friend, too."

"Yeah, I'll tell you," I say. "And while you're visiting, you can just walk down the hallway and get yourself an HIV test, because I found out your fitness trainer trick is HIV positive, and if I know you the way I do, I know you didn't use any protection with him or with any of the others."

"Keith, you're pathetic. Why you gotta make up lies like that?"

"I'm not the one who knowingly sleeps with married men or men with partners. If you're questioning my integrity versus yours, I would win every day. A long time ago, you said something like the only difference between you and me is beauty and brains. Remember that? You laughed it off at the time, but it wasn't funny. It's the biggest insult you've ever made, comparing you and me. The difference between you and me is not just beauty and brains. It's dignity. It's respect. It's education. It's morals. And you'll never have anything close to those qualities, because to you life is just one big bedroom. One more man to conquer. One more bed to lie in. One more cock to play with. But those days are over, Rafael. It's last call for alcohol. Lights out. Last dance. Now if you'll excuse me, Marco's asked me to do him a favor."

"Are you through?" he asks, and rolls his eyes at me. "Because if you are, I have a man waiting in my bedroom for me. I know it's been a while since you've touched one, but maybe you can put yourself in my shoes—I know you really want to—and just leave me the fuck alone."

Rafael slams his bedroom door behind him. I slam Marco

Antonio's door behind me. What a bitch—ignoring everything I told him about Jermaine's health so he can have one
more roll in the hay. Serves him right if he does end up a statistic. He's destined for failure, so my help won't do him any
good.

I thought I was anal retentive, but Marco's room is set up like
a department store. It should take no time at all finding the
clothes he wants me to take back to the hospital. All his
T-shirts and underwear are folded neatly in one drawer. Socks
sorted by color in another. Rows of jeans, khakis, slacks and
button-down shirts hanging neatly inside the closet. His hair
and face products are lined up exactly in the order he told me
they'd be. My goodness.

As I pick up a duffle bag from the closet floor, I notice a
row of photo albums on the bottom shelf of his bookcase.
One is labeled "The Stanford Years" on the spine, and I pull it
out. Talk about time flying. There are pictures of Marco and
me playing hetero (before we knew about each other) at fra-
ternity rush parties in our freshman year. What was I thinking
wearing that texturizer and green contact lenses? As if that
weren't a big fat clue as to my sexuality issues and my lack of
fashion sense at the time. My God, pictures from the first
time we drove up to San Francisco from Palo Alto and
walked around the Castro District. We told everyone it was
for a sociology class and that we wanted firsthand interviews
and research for our papers. Of course, we knew what we
were really there for. This is so cool—pictures from the year
we worked in the residence halls as R.A.'s. That was one of
the best times of my undergraduate years. And I totally forgot
about that trip Marco, Chris Aquino and I took to Guadalajara
our junior year for spring break. We were so popular with the

boys down there. I can't believe he has pictures from my twenty-first birthday party at The Café in San Francisco. That was a crazy night, and we all got so drunk. Oh, no, he got a picture of me puking over the balcony. I think I'll remove this one from the book—we don't need this kind of evidence lying around. Hmmph, there's a picture of the man who should have been "the one," Shawn Bentley, one of a handful of black medical school students at Stanford. If only he'd wanted to do long-distance while doing his residency in D.C. . . . OK, I don't want to go there right now . . . Next page . . . Look at this, graduation day for our undergrad degrees. I remember it was the first time my family had spent any significant time with people other than black people. It was funny hearing them trying to pronounce Mr. and Mrs. Vega's first names. And there's little ignorant me posing with Tommie at my graduation, holding several hundred-dollar bills in front of my face like it's a fan or something. Look here, Marco even has pictures of me hanging with the computer nerds who got me interested in investing in their start-up dot-coms. Grad school graduations and parties . . . the first nights hanging out in L.A. at Catch One and Arena . . . the Madonna CD release party at Catch One . . . Club Papi over at Circus, hanging outside on the patio with our favorite party girls, Miss Martin, Lola, and Ozzie dressed up like Jenni Rivera . . . the house party we went to in L.A. where we first met Rafael and discovered the bad state his life was in . . . If only Marco wasn't trying to be a candidate for sainthood, we'd never have Rafael in our lives. Oh, well.

Looking at these pictures from my past opens up my eyes to who I used to be. What happened to the fun-loving Keith Hemmings? The one who used to laugh. Play. Joke around. The one who took home a stack of phone numbers each weekend and had at least two dates to look forward to the next? What happened to the Keith who used to see everyone and everything as basically good? Who saw everyone as a potential friend and who talked to everyone like they were my closest friends, like life was a permanent college freshman year? Who had no walls or pretenses built up? Who didn't worry about other people's behavior? Or how others would react to mine?

Sometimes I surprise myself when I hear the thoughts and words that come into my head about other people now. I've become so judgmental. Mostly about Rafael's actions. Who am I to stand in judgment, when I did some of the same kinds of things when I was his age? Well, maybe not to the same extent. But I never used to be like this—bitter. I used to be so happy, accepting of others, open and free-spirited. Certainly not like the minister's son everyone expected me to be. Close, but not a carbon copy. Certainly not like my sister Stephanie or brother Solomon, who do everything by the book and for the sake of our father's and church's image.

And another thing looking at Marco's photo album makes me think about. Even though I'm not the young, fresh ingénue I used to be, I can still take care of myself like I am one. I need to lose these twenty pounds I've picked up the past couple of years. I need to be serious about it this time. That means no diet pills or fad plans, just plain old exercise and good food choices. I need to treat myself to a professional massage and facial at least once or twice a month, and even though I dress very nice, I could use a wardrobe update. Enough of dressing classic and traditional all the time, Keith, you can splurge on something new and trendy if you want. Also, I've been stingy about spending a few hundred dollars on whitening my teeth, even though money isn't really an issue. Heck, I spend that much on liquor and going out to clubs every month, so why not on something a little more permanent for me? And speaking of drinking, I know I need to wean myself off the bottle. That's why I'm twenty pounds heavier and why I'm always thinking so much about what other people do and don't do in their lives. Drinking gets me depressed. It's always fun in the beginning, trying to reach the buzz, but when it goes beyond that point, I'm a walking psych patient—pensive, down and not happy—when I should be energetic and outgoing while clubbing and dancing. And this club thing needs to be reconsidered too. I like going out, that's for sure. But am I going out only to find a man? To meet somebody? Or to have fun with my friends? It's supposed to be about having fun, and not about feeling inadequate or comparing myself or competing with someone else for a boyfriend. Pleasure. Excitement. High spirits. It's time to put my life back in order. For real this time. It's time for a new era and bringing the joy back into my life. That means making it work with Cesar, or moving on. That means helping Marco recover from his accident. Finding a way to bring Tommie and Tyrell back together—they're both good people and deserve to be together. Maybe giving that young man, Dante, a chance to show me what a man he can be. He's a nice kid, you know? And it means helping Rafael get through what's probably going to be the scariest time of his young twenty-two-year-old life. I was scared to death of my first HIV test, back when I was young and naïve about what was risky and what wasn't.

I can be the bigger person and use my life to uplift Rafael's. But I've also got to uplift my own as well. That's a commitment worth honoring and keeping.

Chapter 31

MARCO ANTONIO

If I'd known being in the hospital would turn me into a mini-celebrity, I'd have car accidents more often. The other counselors from my job were here earlier today, *Tía* Florinda and her dysfunctional family set up a makeshift altar on the other side of the room (as if my injuries were life threatening!), and my mom, dad and *abuela* have left an assortment of my favorite foods next to my bed. I'm glad I sent Keith away to pick up some clothes, because these hospital greens are not my style of pants. I have a lot to be grateful for. That I'm alive and survived that accident is a miracle. That I've got some time alone from everyone fawning and gawking over me is a godsend.

When Julio was here earlier, he broke down as I told him why I was in Silver Lake before the accident. He tried to stay strong and keep a straight face. But I could see the hurt in his eyes as I tried to explain that I was ready to commit to our future, that Alex was nothing to me anymore, and I was stupid for being so mentally torn between the two of them for so long. That it takes an idiot not to see the gifts in front of them. But what really upset him was when the nurse brought in a large vase of white roses from Alex, who obviously doesn't know what the phrase "it's over" means. I swear he sends more elaborate flower bouquets than one of his soap opera characters. Do I have to hit him over the head? No amount of gifts to my family or me will change the fact that I'm done with Alex. No amount of fame from his *novelas* and soaps will change that. It's not going to happen for Alex and me. I don't need the flash and glitter that Alex's Hollywood lifestyle brings. I don't need the limos, guest lists and freebies. I want the down-home stable man. Julio is my future.

Now if only I could convince Julio that I'm real. That I want the commitment, the house, the picket fence and the matching Volvos in the driveway. And I want him to know that no matter how hard Alex tries, I won't be getting back together with him any time in the future. But I also want Julio to be a man and get secure about us. Or what we could have. I'd be very happy and comfortable with our life together as college-educated working professionals and our close-to-perfect middle class Latino lives in Montebello or Downey or La Puente. Our families could come over on weekends for barbeques and pool parties. Keith and Rafael could keep us entertained and in touch with the ups and downs of single life at our weeknight dinner parties. And one day, Julio and I will bring home our own little boy and two girls from the adoption agency and raise our perfect little family together.

I'm through with the delays and excuses and want to commit to him. Forever. I wish Julio would come to his senses and believe me. There's only one way to do it. I'm going to show him tonight that he's the only man I want to be with.

"Mi'jo, donde necesitas las flores?" my mother asks as she, Keith and *Tía* Florinda transform my bland hospital room into floral paradise.

"*Allá, cerca de la ventana*, Mama." I point with my good arm to a spot near the small window of my room. "Go help her, Keith."

This is short notice, I know, but I managed to get my family, Julio's friends and a few of my friends to commit their Saturday night to my event—my commitment ceremony with Julio. I know it's not common for gay Latinos to participate in something that's more common in mainstream gay life, but this is something I want to do to show Julio that I'm serious when I say I want to spend my life with him. It's more of a symbolic union than anything else, but that's significant to me because it will show all the people around Julio and me that we're serious about this. I wish I hadn't wasted so much time waiting on Alex.

Speaking of Alex, my family isn't too thrilled about me letting him go. Even after I told them about the whole charade—the wife, the lies, the staying together just to make them happy. Even after I shared that Alex and I had had a major fight minutes before my car accident. They're blinded by stardom. They think Julio and I are going to struggle, in terms of money and in terms of how society will react to two everyday Latinos making a life together. I tried to explain that we're both smart, educated, have safe careers and that we can take on whatever prejudices or issues other people have. The biggest struggle, I let them know, is going to be keeping other gay people out of our relationship. There's so much envy and unhappiness out in the gay community, and I know there will be friends, acquaintances and strangers who'll try to test us and tear us down. I've seen it so many times. I'm glad I'm a counselor and can handle it. Most people just give up on relationships because of other people's interference, but I know Julio and I are stronger than that.

Keith, *Tía* Florinda and my mom ask me what I think

about their decorating job. It's amazing, and I can't wait for
Julio to see all the work I've put into this night. I ask them to
leave me for a few minutes so I can get my thoughts together
for the ceremony.

I reach for my journal and continue writing. Now, it's
some words for my commitment vows. I want to talk about
how sometimes the person we're meant to be with is in our
life already, under our nose, and we don't have to search very
far. How Julio's been the most patient, kind, respectful and
generous best friend someone could have. I have always wanted
my partner in life to be my best friend. How he knows me so
well, and has seen me at my weakest moments as well as my
strongest. How he's always made me happy, and I've taken
that for granted, but won't when we're together permanently.
How when I'm down, he says just the right words to support
me and pick me up. And how, most of all, he's everything I've
prayed for in a partner: funny, smart, *muy guapo*—very handsome—honest, full of integrity and honor, and is proud of his
heritage. And for all the good things he has done and brought
into my life, I will always be eternally grateful.

My goodness, I sound like a character on one of Alex's
novelas who's talking to himself on his wedding morning. But
this is how I feel. And in less than an hour, Julio will know
how I feel.

A delivery man brings a bottle of champagne to my bed-
side table. There's a card attached, and I don't really want to
read it before the ceremony, however, knowing it's from
Keith makes me read it anyway.

Turns out it's not from Keith. It's from Julio.

Dear Marco Antonio,
*   I hope this note finds you in good spirits and on a*
speedy recovery from your accident and your injuries. I'm

happy you were not hurt too badly and know that you will soon get back to a normal life. Unfortunately, I don't think I can be a part of that life. I know you're not over your ex, Alex, and honestly I don't think you ever will be. I can't compete with what he represents to you. So I'm moving on with my life. I've decided to take a leave of absence from the USC job and have accepted the assignment with the Peace Corps that I've been delaying for the past year. I'm flying down to Chiapas, Mexico, tonight. I know it's short notice, but this opportunity just came up. It's a good time to get away. Sometimes you've got to take a chance with the things you've been afraid of committing to. So enjoy this champagne with your friends and raise a toast to truth, and how living it in your life frees you up to be happy!

Love always,
Julio

How can he end a breakup letter by writing "love always" when he obviously doesn't? I reread it at least a hundred times looking for some clue that maybe this is a forgery or a joke, and that maybe Julio will come prancing through my hospital door with all our friends and family and yell, "Surprise!" and that I'm on some sort of hidden camera show. But it's not a joke. Everyone I invited for our supposed commitment ceremony obviously knows it's not happening, because they're not frolicking in and out of my room every five minutes to check up on me like they were earlier in the day. I call Julio's home number, and it rings and rings with no answer, and his cell goes directly to voice mail. He's not even taking my call. I can't believe Julio is leaving town like this. What an embarrassment. I don't know if I should laugh at the craziness of me sitting in a hospital room that looks like a Hawaiian garden, or if I should cry at the fact that within a twenty-four-hour period I have left one loser and gotten dumped by another. And let's not even think about the kick *Tía* Florinda will get out of this. I'm sure she'll think this is better than an episode of *Salomé*, except I don't want to be seen as a long-suffering heroine who's been dumped at the altar.

Once I'm released from here, I'm going to follow Rafael's simple, yet somewhat eloquent advice that he always shares with Keith and me: Build a bridge and get over it! Because I'm a good catch, and before long I know both Alex and Julio will be distant memories once I plan a commitment ceremony with the real man I finally settle down with.

Chapter 32

TOMMIE

I don't know what's worse—messing around on my Tyrell like I did, or having to tell him that we gotta get a damn HIV test? I shoulda known better than hanging out with Rafael like I did. Keith always warned me that Rafael is bad news, but I guess I let curiosity get the best of me. I ain't gon' lie, it was a damn good night with the little Mexican, from what I remember. We had too many shots of that tequila shit—shit I don't normally touch—and I introduced him to several of my old musician friends. We had a lotta fun kicking it, and one thing led to another. I just don't know if it was worth it. Because now I gotta think about my health and shit, and wonder if I'm the next one to check outta here because of a stupid-ass night of fucking around with Rafael.

If it's one thing I know is true: faggots is trouble. No, I ain't talking about the kinda men like me or like my Tyrell who keep the shit on the down low and off the street. I'm talking about those tight-pants-wearing, rainbow-flag-waving, pencil-thin-eyebrow-arching-types who keep "the sauce" flowing through the community like they do. 'Cause I know it ain't us straight-acting hard brothas who passing the HIV around. If it wasn't for brothas like us, those faggots would have no kinda real men with some sense of masculinity to fuck around with. I need to just go on and get myself a girl and some kids, like my boy Jermaine up and did. He gets busy at home and can kick it every once in a while with some dude if he wants. And no one have to know about it. Not that I think it's right to mess around on your wife or anything. I'm learning just how much it hurts the one you love when you cheat. It's even worse when there's a chance STDs have been introduced into the equation.

I'm sure I ain't HIV–positive. I take care of myself. I ain't been losing weight or having any of them night sweats, like I heard HIV people get. My only sex partner in recent months been my Tyrell, well, except for Rafael. I gotta take care of my Tyrell and my niece Keesha, if I do have it. That's a whole 'nother story.

I ring up Tyrell. As if he'll actually pick up. It's been three weeks since I told Tyrell about the HIV twist. Well, left him a message, since he wouldn't take any of my calls after I told him I cheated.

"What do you want, Tommie?"

It's a miracle. Tyrell answers.

"Hey. I was wondering if we could talk?" I say.

"What do you think we're doing now?" he says.

"I mean on the serious tip. Can I pick you up from your dorm or something?"

"I don't think that's a good idea now. My father's in town, and in fact you just missed him. He went down the hall to the bathroom. He wants to kill you."

"Why? You told him?"

"Damn, Tommie, try using your brain for a minute. Who else am I going to tell? It's not like I can just go and tell coach or a teammate, 'Hey, I have a male lover, and he cheated on me, and where can I go get tested for diseases and shit?' My pops knows everything and I'm up here defending your ass to him. Don't ask me why. Call me stupid."

"You got tested? How come you ain't call me? What happened?"

"The usual. Blood drawn, urine sample, that fucking swab up my—"

"I get the picture, Tyrell."

"Anyway, everything is cool for now. I'm clean. No diseases. No thanks to you, Tommie. My pops told me to just get tested for everything since we don't know where you've been playing around."

"Thank God you're okay now." There are small miracles.

"I gotta go back in a few months, though, for another HIV test since you let me go down and finish you off right after you fucked with Rafael."

"You gotta bring that up, huh?" I say. "You're alright for now, though? That means I must be alright, right?"

"Listen, Tommie, I'll give you the name of my father's doctor friend who can get your results the same day, and he'll keep it between you and him. But you and I have to keep getting tested for at least a year to be sure we're in the clear."

"Well, I ain't done this before with anyone, Tyrell," I say. "You can tell your pops that much."

"Yeah. Right. Anyway, you need to get tested. Today, if you can. I don't know why you're putting it off. When did you find out about Rafael's situation? March? It's late April now."

"Yeah. Right. Okay."

I write down the information about the doctor, who's a good friend of Tyrell's father. The office is in Baldwin Hills. I guess it pays to have connections who will keep all this confidential.

"We have a lot to talk about," Tyrell says. "Everything's messed up. This never should have happened."

"That's why I kept calling," I say. "I miss you."

"I know. I'm the best thing to come into your life."

"So you forgive me?" I ask. "It won't happen again. I promise."

"Tommie, please," he says, and pauses. "I'm not talking about getting back together with you. Not right now. It's not as easy as saying, 'Sorry, I fucked up. Forgive me.' I'm smarter than that."

"So what then? Don't play games with me."

"I don't know, Tommie. I don't want to talk about us. Let's change the subject."

"To what?"

"I don't know," Tyrell says. "The agent my dad got me has been trying to work a few pro deals. I probably won't be a starter, but I can be a millionaire bench warmer for a little while."

"Damn, that's tight."

"We should talk, Tommie. But my dad's coming in the door. I'll call when he's gone."

"When can I see you?"

"I'll have to let you know."

I'm hearing a dial tone, but know that it's not because of my Tyrell hanging up on me in anger. Things sound promising. Like he ain't closed the door on us seeing each other again. And if he end up doing the basketball thing on a permanent tip, then we set for life. I can pay off the loan for the store to Keith. I'd move to wherever my Tyrell end up playing. I'd put my own little recording studio together in our place and make some demos. Maybe find some new young talent to get together for a singing career. And I'd do the one thing I been meaning to do for a while—make sure Keesha's in a safe and secure home. But that's all assuming my Tyrell takes me back and wants me to be part of his future.

Keith been gone for a few weeks—the first two he was at a spa and rehab place up in Ojai, and now in Detroit for Solomon's wedding—and I really don't feel like going over to the record store to check in with the staff. The reliable college student staff is coming back to work for their summer break anyway, and they know how to handle business for me. I can't stand this being alone shit. Not at a time like this. I think I'll give my boy Jermaine a call to see what he been up to. Maybe we can go shoot some hoops or just catch up with each other. Someone picks up on the first ring, and it sounds like it's a party or something going on in the background.

"Jermaine there?" I ask.

"Is this some kind of sick joke?" a hysterical woman screams at me. "Jermaine died earlier this week and his funeral was today."

"What? Serious? What happened?"

"Here, Quiana." The woman who answered the phone hands it over to Jermaine's wife.

"Who this?"

"Tommie Jordan. I'm one of Jermaine's boys. Did something happen to him?"

"Hmmmph, probably one of *those* boys, right?" his wife asks. "Yeah, that muthafucker dead. If you kicked it with him that way, you better get yourself an AIDS test."

She slams the phone down and hangs up. I can't believe Jermaine's gone. Just like that. It's not like we hung out that much since he went down low and married his babies' mama, but for him to be gone . . . He not that much older than me. This AIDS shit is hitting too close to home.

I put on a clean T-shirt and shorts and head out the door to get my test. If it can happen to Jermaine—and he ain't kicked it with dudes in a few years as far as I know—it can definitely happen to me. Forget all the other stuff I been thinking about. The only thing I wanna know is do I have it or not?

Chapter 33

RAFAEL

Jose still kicking it with me even though he knows I'm going through this testing shit and all. Maybe it's that he in his thirties or something that makes him stay all patient and shit with me. He even promoting the hell out of my Friday and Sunday night gigs at Chico's. I seen a one-page ad in a couple of those gay party magazines—COME SPEND THE NIGHT IN RAFA'S ROOM! My official debut is in a few days, after I get my test results. Jose sitting over there in my dining room balancing the books and writing out checks for the bar staff. I just got off the phone with Marco Antonio, who been staying over his folks' house since he got out of the hospital.

These past four weeks been really crazy. Keith checked into one of those fancy places rich people go to get off drugs and alcohol, and then called me to apologize for being such a bitch to me. I told the bitch to hurry up and get the fuck back to L.A. and out the boring-ass Midwest so we can have a drink—a cranberry juice, virgin daiquiri or something. Marco's Salvadoreño boy left him to do free work—work for no money, ain't that a trip?—with those Indians down in Chiapas. My girl Roneshia is a manager now for The Gap and just got engaged to her on-again, off-again boyfriend, though we'll see how long that'll last. Crazy.

Even crazier, I think I'm falling for Jose. Real feelings. It's different than anything I've felt for someone. And it's not just because he's putting up the money to finance my dancing at his club, which was the first question Marco Antonio asked me when I told him how I felt about Jose. It's got to be something real, because we're not having sex, well, not real sex, which is what most guys want from me or anyone they're with. Each time Jose and I talk, I want to hang onto his every word. I never want to leave his house, and I look forward to each day when I get to see him. I want to make sure I'm a success so that he's even more successful in his business. I'm even willing to give up clubbing and the scene to make sure Jose knows I'm totally into him. It matters to me what and how he thinks about me.

I hope it's none of that deep psychological shit like I'm looking for love from this man who reminds me of my older brothers, Manny and Memo, or the father I never knew. Ewww, that's sick, but I can imagine Marco Antonio coming up with something crazy like that if I sat down for a real counseling session with him. I really don't care why I'm falling for Jose. All I know is Jose has lit a spark in me that no one else had been able to. He could be my first boyfriend ever.

To be honest, I never really cared what anyone thought of me. I did what and who I needed to in order to get through the day. And I never really felt anything for anybody but myself, especially after leaving home at fifteen and needing to survive on my own. It's just been one one-night stand after another, and there was never a need to know any of them beyond what we hooked up for. I'm sure most of them wanted something more from me; I got a duffle bag full of phone numbers to prove it. But I'm gonna take a pass on the past and dump that bag of numbers after this whole testing process is over. I'm just holding on for an ego boost. It's all about Jose and Rafael now.

I don't usually do all this inside thinking—reflecting, Keith calls it—about life. I just live my life and do what comes naturally. Usually. Now I'm thinking more about what I've done and who I've done it with. I miss Keith and all his lessons and wisdom, and can't wait to hang out and just pick up where we left off before Cesar came between us. It's some silly shit, letting a man come between friends, and it's my fault for making moves on Cesar when I knew he liked Keith in the beginning. And after Keith apologized to me, I apologized to him for all the crazy shit I said and done to him, including sleeping with Cesar behind his back. Blame it on youth, or maybe even a little bit of jealousy, I don't know. But I know I hurt Keith with all my selfish behavior and little remarks. We still like each other, even with all the fighting. Opposites make good friends, I guess. He's flying back today and is meeting me over at the clinic in Hollywood to be with me when I get my results.

I did have to tell Cesar about me getting tested and that he should do the same. He was upset, wondering if this was one more thing to come between him and Keith. I went to the gym in Montebello to find that trainer, Jermaine, but all they would tell me is he don't work there anymore and sorry. Well, I tried. Enrique lost it, and was about to jump me with his football-player body, until the security guard at 7-Eleven got in between us and prevented an even bigger scene. The others since Jermaine . . . I wouldn't know the first place to start looking. I found out Tommie's HIV test was negative, which is definitely a good sign. It means I probably didn't pass anything along to him, even though we didn't really do a whole lot in bed. He also passed a message through Keith for me to stay away from him and Tyrell, which is next to impossible, since Keith is my friend and lives with Tommie. Whatever. Issues. They ain't got to worry about me trying to get up on Tommie anymore. I'm through with brothas, and besides I got Jose now, who's looking good with his wife-beater and gym shorts on.

I can't wait for us to be able to give each other something besides hand jobs when I get my test results back. In a little over an hour, I'll know what's up. I swear if my results are good, I'll be a good little Rafael. I'll be faithful and honest and a saint if I have to.

The main thing this waiting period got me thinking about is all the free ass and blow jobs I've given away all these years. And for what? I'm still living paycheck to paycheck. These men ain't really added much to my life. None of them want to keep me around longer than it takes to get them off. They just come and go. Exchanging numbers is just a courtesy, nothing else implied. I been doing this shit for ten years, since I was like twelve, and my list is up to around six hundred or so men. Don't laugh—I decided to make a list. Something to help me pass the week waiting for my results. It seem like every few minutes—I could be taking a shower or working at the mall—another sex scene flashback enters my mind, and I add the name, or at least the description, to the list. Or I can be driving on the 60 Freeway or down Whittier Boulevard and look over into the next car and see someone I've fucked around with. And I don't know whether to laugh or cry at the fact that when I went to Target yesterday to buy some air freshener and the new Thalia CD, I counted at least four employees I've been with at one point or another over the years. I ain't complaining. I had a good time with all of them. And I know they all enjoyed me.

But when I look over and see Jose, none of those old tricks matter. He's older, yeah, but has been probably the best thing to come in my life. He's just so calm and patient. The best part is that we just clicked. After I stopped trying so hard to make him like me, he told me he's always liked me. Even after the first time we fucked around in the back room of his club and I went about my own business and ignored him, he said he knew there was something about me that made me special. I've never heard that in my life: that I'm special. Not even from my family. Which is another thing we got in common. We both grew up in the *barrio* and with no money. His family is still together, while mine is all over the place—jail and the streets mostly. He said I should be proud of who I am and what I've accomplished so far. I never had anyone point out my accomplishments. We both proud to be *Mexicano*. Jose is too good to be true.

I go and sit on Jose's lap and give him a big kiss on his cheek and then slowly lick his neck.

"Don't start something you can't finish, little boy."

"That sounds like a challenge, *viejito*."

"You're on."

I kneel in front of Jose, pull up his T-shirt and plant small kisses from his navel to the top of his shorts. His little moans turn me on, and I whip him out and stroke him in the firm and rhythmic way he likes. For him to be in his middle thirties, he sure can come quickly and forcefully, which he's just done all over my hand and his stomach. He says I make him feel like he's a teenager again.

"Was that good, *papi*?" I ask as I reach up for a napkin to clean us off.

"Damn, you don't need to ask. *Muy bueno*." He pulls me to him and kisses me hard on my lips.

"*¿Qué pasa?*" I ask.

"Nothing. Thanks for that little job you gave me. And I wanted to let you know I'm here for you no matter what happens."

"For reals? You not just saying that?"

"Rafa, I have no reason to lie. I know what I feel."

"Well, damn, I don't know what to say. I guess I have feelings for you, too."

Jose hugs me and holds me for a few minutes. And in those moments I'm in his arms, I wish I could just freeze time to ensure this ain't a temporary situation and he's true to his word.

I hate clinics. They look so sterile and cold and yet artificially happy at the same time. All those damn bilingual cartoon posters hanging on the walls about AIDS, *SIDA* and other sexually transmitted diseases ain't doing nothing for all us sitting around the waiting room table. None of the magazines scattered on the table been updated since Bill Clinton was in office, and this cheesy elevator music playing in the background ain't uplifting nobody here. If they really want to make this place come to life, they should put on some Monica Naranjo or Alejandra Guzmán. But then again, it's probably club music along with a little bit of alcohol that got most of us in this waiting room in the first place, so maybe that's not the best idea.

There's so many familiar faces here. Funny, this is the one place I don't see someone I slept with. Maybe that's a good sign. But I do see this boy Carlito who used to run with my party crew back in the day. Bitch done got fat and giving me attitude, getting up and moving to the opposite side of the room. Finally, Keith arrives and the queeny receptionist, some guy named Roy, flicks his fingers in the direction of the waiting room where I am.

"You nervous?" Keith asks.

"Hell naw, bitch. Come on and sit down." As Keith sits and leafs through the magazines, I ask, "How was rehab? And Detroit? Meet anyone?"

"I'm fine. My brother's wedding was beautiful. And no, I didn't meet anyone—in Detroit or the spa. I talked to Dante a little bit while I was gone. I talked to Cesar, too. We might see each other in a few days." Keith tosses the magazine back on the table.

"I can't believe you ain't back with him. It's about time. Stop all this wishy-washy shit about Cesar. Toss the old magazines, bitch, because you got too many issues."

"Good advice, Rafael," Keith says. "But I don't know if he's the kind of partner I pray to have."

"I ain't too much into church, but I know forgiveness is part of the formula."

"True. But let's worry about you right now. I can't believe you're not even a little nervous. I would be."

"I ain't that much of a slut. Damn."

"No, I don't mean it that way," he says. "Though you have been with your fair share of men. I'd be nervous if I were waiting for HIV results. Period. The stats are not too good for black and brown men these days."

"Thanks a lot, Keith, just what I need right now."

"I'm sorry." Keith puts an arm over my shoulders. "You'll be fine. Tommie was fine. So was Cesar."

"That's true," I say. "Jose says the same thing, that I'll be okay."

"You guys are still talking? That's kind of a record for you, especially since you're not sleeping with him."

"He's not complaining, believe me."

"Well, anyway, that's good. At least you have something to look forward to after this whole ordeal is over. At least you have someone."

"True."

"Hey, did you know that fitness trainer you hooked up with was an old friend of Tommie? And he died."

"What? You serious?" I ask.

"Yeah, it was true about him having it after all."

"Damn. But he looked fine when we met. We didn't even use nothing, but I made him pull out before he came each time. Maybe it worked."

"Hmmph, maybe. Well, I prayed for you."

"I prayed for me, too, Keith. I even told God I'd never do sex outside of a relationship again if He made my HIV test negative."

"Bargaining with God . . . probably not the best thing to do. But understandable. I won't tell anyone. We're going to turn your life around. I'll help."

"I just hope I can do it."

"You can, Rafael. And I'm going to help you."

I look over at the queeny receptionist and raise my hands. "What's the holdup, Roy?"

Just then I hear a woman's voice call, "MM80."

"That's me. Wish me luck, Keith."

"You'll be fine."

I follow the nurse into a small office down the hall. She tells me the doctor will be with me in a few minutes. I know it's not good news. Just my guess; just a feeling. Why else would a nurse bring me back to a doctor's private office? A nice-looking doctor at that, judging from the pictures of him hanging around the office. I'm through with brothas, but doctor-man got it going on. I wonder how big Stanford is, and if he knew

Keith or Marco Antonio, 'cause his big-ass medical certificate, or whatever it's called, is right above his desk. He appears to fit exactly what Keith would want in someone. But nothing compares to the real thing, and when he walk in, it's almost like he has to hunch under the door frame to get into his office because he's so tall.

"MM80? I'm Dr. Shawn Bentley. *¿Hablas español o inglés?*"

"English is fine."

"Good to meet you." He shakes my hands with fingers that have got to be a good five inches long. Keith would definitely dig this brotha. Good teeth. Good hair. Tostada brown skin. Full lips. Clean shaven. Broad chest and shoulders underneath a white fitted dress shirt.

"Well, maybe under different circumstances."

"True. This isn't the best reason to have to come to the clinic."

"I know, doctor."

"You know the stats on men of color are getting more and more devastating each day with each new study. Three out of four young gay black and Latino men don't know their HIV status. And it's only going to get worse as these kids come out of the closet at earlier ages."

"I know."

"Kids are coming out in middle school and high school, and no one's mentoring them, so they just go out and have unprotected sex with the first man who shows them a little attention. It's interesting. And sad."

"True."

"You've been with a lot of people," he says, and pulls out my initial intake form. "You need to chill. It's not worth it, having sex with everyone who says yes. It's like pointing a loaded gun at your head. Or down your throat, in your case."

"Believe me, I've thought about it. This has been the longest wait of my life."

"So, I have some good news and some bad news for you."

"What's wrong, doctor?"

"Well, the good news is your HIV test is negative."

"Oh, my God. Thank you!"

"But you tested positive for syphilis."

"What?"

"More and more young people, well, gay men in general, are getting it and don't even know they have it. It's a difficult STD to self-detect. We're going to give you a shot of a strong dose of antibiotics, and then give you a prescription to take at home. You'll need to finish the medicine, and no unprotected sex at all until you finish your meds. But you really shouldn't let it get to the point of no protection anyway, unless you've communicated with your partner that it's okay to not use anything."

"But someone I slept with just died of HIV. I just found out. Am I going to be okay?"

"Well, contact doesn't always cause or mean transmission, but you'll need to continue getting tested at least two, preferably three more times just to be sure. That's barring no unprotected sex during the testing time frame. Can you handle that?"

"Definitely."

"So do you have any questions?"

"Well, one. Maybe two. I've been giving my man hand jobs lately just to be safe. I'm not going to give him anything by doing that, am I? And two, my friend who came with me would be perfect for you. Are you gay? And do you wanna meet him? He's in the waiting area."

"You can't give him what you have from a hand job," the doctor says, and then gets a smile on his face. "And two, I can't really mix my personal and professional life. So I can't hook up with your friend. But I have to take you over to the nurse for your antibiotics and meds, and I can conveniently run into him on our way there. Cool?"

"Cool."

"Anything else?"

"Nothing, doc. Thanks for everything."

He shakes my hand and leads me out of the office so I can get my meds from the nurse. On the way, I see Keith flipping through another magazine, and I call his name. Doc stops walking, and he and Keith look at each other as if they've seen a ghost.

"You're friends with Keith?" Doc asks.

"Shawn Bentley?" Keith asks. "Oh, my God."

I don't know what the hell is going on here, but I feel it's something that won't be resolved in the little bit of time it takes to get my shot from the nurse.

Chapter 34

TOMMIE

"So you picking up the dinner tab?" I ask Tyrell, and laugh.

"You're the one working, Tommie."

"But you the one about to sign the multimillion dollar contract with the NBA."

"But you're the one about to get paid when your greatest hits CD comes out and you start promoting."

My Tyrell agreed to meet with me finally after all these weeks of not being together. We're over at Reign in Beverly Hills again and got a nice table upstairs with a little bit of privacy. His family is flying in tomorrow for the week's graduation celebrations at UCLA, so this is our only time to meet up alone for a few days. I can't believe he cut off his twists, 'cause now he look just like any other brotha in L.A. with a short 'fro, which I don't really care for. It was his hair that first turned me on, but I guess I can't have everything my way. I'm thanking God every day my Tyrell said he would finally go out to dinner. Of course, he said part of the deal was me bringing him my test results in writing, because he couldn't tell if I was telling the truth over the phone. I guess my word ain't enough right now, but considering what I done, I guess it's a normal thing to wanna be sure of.

I don't blame him, I guess. I hear about black women all
the time going through some shit with they men and have to
build back trust in baby steps, except of course my Tyrell is all
man and dealing with the same thing. This dinner tonight I
think is part of some small steps to getting what we had back.

"Give me the check, college graduate," I say.

"Look at it as an investment," Tyrell says. "Dinner today
for me . . . a Jaguar for your next birthday. That's a nice exchange."

"You making it sound like we got a future."

"I can't say for sure," my Tyrell say, and start to chuckle.
"But I know the pool of brothas is shallow now."

"You been going out testing the waters?" I ask. 'Cause if
my Tyrell has, I wanna find the punk and bust him in the
face.

"I just had lunch with this professor on campus, a real
cool brotha like us, who been breaking it down for me what
the scene is like. He's been teaching me a lot."

"Who is this professor? And what he say about me?"

"Please, don't be jealous. It's not like that," Tyrell says, and
pats my hand a little. "Dr. Vernon teaches a black fiction class,
and he turned me on to James Baldwin and E. Lynn Harris
books in class. You heard of them, I know?"

"Naw. You got some of their stuff?" I ask.

"Well, you need to read more." My Tyrell shakes his head
back and forth. "Anyway, Dr. Vernon called me to his office
and said he had a feeling I was going through something,
which was true, with you sleeping with Rafael. And he was
like, 'Look, you're young, black, talented, about to make bank
from playing ball, and you need to try and make a foundation
now with someone who's been there when you were nothing. Because there's a lot of tired folks out there with nothing

going on for them who want to get leeched onto a rising star.' So I thought about it."

"I think I need to meet this Dr. Vernon. He sound smart."

"He is smart. Anyway, he was like, 'I don't want to see you with no one but a black man, because black men, gay or straight, are spreading their sperm everywhere but in the black community in California. No black men are even trying to raise black families anymore, and you need to think about how your choices are contributing to or taking from the community, whether you choose to be out or not.' I'm not about to come out if I make it in the NBA, but I guess what I'm saying is you and I have a connection that I want to try to work on."

"For real?" I ask.

"For real," my Tyrell says. "But we're going to have to make a plan. What are you doing with your music and your career? I want you to start working on your speech and diction, not for me, but so you don't look like one of the bling bling fools on BET, MTV, or the Nostalgia Network. Keeping it real doesn't mean keeping it third grade."

"Funny and true."

"And we have to think about your niece, Keesha, and how we are going to raise her, what schools to put her in. And then we have to think about my whole career. I know I'm not starting out my NBA career in L.A., so are you moving with me? Or are we doing the long-distance thing? And if so, are you going to keep your horny ass at home and away from trash like Rafael? It's going to take a long time for me to forget about that, no matter how many apologies I get from you. Also, your crack-addict sister will not be all in our business trying to sell us out to the tabloids. I'll be generous with you, and you can send her something now and then, but there will be limits to our generosity. And you and I need a financial agreement signed, just in case . . . you know."

"Sounds like college man done figured it all out. Do I have a say?" I ask, feeling like this is *The Tyrell Kincaid Show* or something and I'm the sidekick along for the ride.

"Of course you do," Tyrell says. "If we make this work, we'll be equals. I just don't want to be a fool, and so I'm putting everything out on the table now so we both know where we stand."

"Well, Sylvia been laying low lately. And Dennis seems to be doing fine with Keesha for now. I really don't want to push the issue now, because she might have to find out about us."

"True. It's just something to think about, because I don't want this to come back to haunt us. I can't deal with surprises or scandals when my career takes off."

Most brothas I know woulda stepped out already and not dealt with the kind of demands my Tyrell's making. I know how we can be—someone tries to back us into a corner for a commitment, or hold us accountable, and it scares us. But I know if I do step, my Tyrell would be gone for good and wouldn't look back. Probably find someone intelligent like that Dr. Vernon or Keith or some basketball groupie to be with. What's a smart boy like him want in me, anyway? But all these plans sound promising and like we can really have something together. Sounds like we can have something really good. In my mind, it seems right.

"So, Tommie, what do you think about what I've just said?"

"It makes sense. I like it. All that money your daddy spent

on your college paid off. I don't know what else to say. But it sound all businesslike. Do you have any feelings?"

"If I didn't love you, I wouldn't be sitting here telling you what I'd like our life to be like."

"I love you too, man." And without any hesitation, I grab his hand across the table. In public. And nobody in the restaurant gives us any weird looks, says anything strange or rolls their eyes. And my Tyrell don't flinch his hand back either. "I think I can live with that."

The waitress comes back to the table with the bill and my credit card. Damn, I hope my payment registered and there ain't a problem with my American Express. Then she tells me, with a smile on her face, that the bill been taken care of by a third party by the name of Keith Hemmings, and that I don't have to pay a thing. That Keith is sure full of surprises. The waitress winks at me and my Tyrell, as if she know the deal with us and she cool with it. Seems like this hiding I been doing all these years don't really matter, because the only person tripping is me.

"So, you know what I've been missing?" Tyrell asks.

"I don't know. Tell me."

"Remember how you used to love my twists draping across your stomach while I—"

"Aww, man, don't get me worked up now. Plus you cut off your hair, so there's nothing to play with while you're down there."

"Wanna jet back to your place?"

"So does this mean what I think?"

"Take a guess, Tommie. But we're using protection."

I guess this mean that me and Tyrell are back together and got a future ahead of us. This is definitely the beginning of something good, and I am glad it's finally coming together. I load in a preview copy of the *Renaissance Phoenix Greatest Hits* CD in the player. I forward to one of my favorites, a cut called "Serenade to You," which was a big hit for the group when my Tyrell was probably just a kid in elementary school. But tonight, I'm using it to set the mood for our version of adult night school on the drive home.

Chapter 35

KEITH

Six months later. Instead of spending another birthday and New Year's night out at yet another club scene, I've brought the club scene, and my party, home to my new house in Ladera Heights. Even with the economy being in a weird state, L.A.'s real estate market is red hot, and I was able to make a good profit from selling the Pasadena condo. My stock portfolio, on the other hand, is taking a beating, and despite all the political heads trying to magic-wand us out of a recession, I have to do something I haven't had to do in a long time—find a real job. The income from my investments is not enough, so I've taken on the job Marco's ex, but not really ex, Julio, left at USC coordinating cultural programs and events at the university, at least on an interim basis until he returns from his volunteer work in Chiapas, Mexico, at the end of the school year.

I've wanted to throw this kind of party for the longest time, but never did because I thought I didn't have enough friends or acquaintances in L.A. who'd come. Problem solved. Between Marco Antonio, Rafael and me, we have enough exes, broken dates and almost boyfriends to fill up my new place and make it look like a happening party. It's part thirtieth-birthday celebration for Marco Antonio and me, part art opening—that's how he's categorizing *A Night in Rafa's Room*—for Rafael, and part New Year's celebration for all of us. This is our way of celebrating the new possibilities and changes we're making for the upcoming year. It's been an interesting year, and hopefully the next will be better.

The house and backyard look like a New Orleans Bourbon Street festival, thanks to the event coordinators I hired to plan the party and entertainment. There is a mock casino set up in the three-car garage, where dozens of friends can gamble fake money and not lose a cent. A dance floor is set up in the backyard, complete with my friend DJ Sal spinning the different styles of music my friends will like—some house and electronic for the younger club kids, oldies for the *cholos*, a good amount of hip-hop and R&B for the urban preps, and *narcocorridos* and *norteñas* for the *vaquero* crowd. Male go-go dancers, all from Rafael and Jose's dancer/stripper troupe, are stationed at various cages and mini-stages around the front and back of the house and handing out elaborate beads and chocolates to the partygoers. And to make sure my guests can fully enjoy all the beverages and libations of the New Orleans party, drivers are sitting by outside ready to take people home. Or if they wish, they can simply lounge in one of the upstairs guest bedrooms overnight.

I haven't had this much fun in years, and it's certainly because of the new things happening for us.

Rafael and Jose are happy together, and they're making it work, even with the fourteen-year age difference and several more months of safe-sex celibacy ahead of them. Rafael moved out of Marco Antonio's place and in with Jose. I told Rafael it's not smart moving in with someone after only a few weeks, but it's his life and he's still got a little of that I-do-what-I-want attitude lingering. Rafael is still getting tested for HIV since the Jermaine situation, but so far the news is encouraging, and we think he's going to be fine. Just one more test to go and he's out of the woods. Their club—I'm helping Rafael buy out Jose's partner at Club Chico—is more popular than ever, and Rafael is turning out to be a sought-out and popular dancer. A music video director spotted him one night and cast him in a video for La Princesa's first English language song, "Young, Built and Beautiful." Quite fitting, don't you think, considering Rafael's sky-high opinion of himself? Rafael quit the retail industry and now makes a living with his own talents. Thank God it's a talent he can't get arrested for. One thing this ordeal did was bring Rafael a little closer to his family, who still live in project-like housing in Boyle Heights. When he thought he was going to die, he decided to reach out to his family, even though they're not at all cool with his sexuality. And Rafael and I are sticking to our truce. It's helping us rebuild our friendship. He's promised not to let another man come between us, and I've promised to let go of the jealousy over all the attention he gets. Of course, it's not easy to forget how Rafael can be, or used to be, but we're going to forgive and try to move on. I'm really going to try and help that kid.

Marco Antonio is still my best friend. He's still single, but e-mails with Julio when he gets a chance—apparently there are not many computers or phones in Chiapas for Julio to write back regularly. I think they'll get back together once Julio returns to L.A. That'll be a good thing, because Alex is still trying to get into Marco's pants, and Marco still has a soft spot when it comes to Alex. I guess Alex thinks being a regular on *The Bold and the Beautiful* will change Marco's mind. I don't think so. Luckily, my friend is smart and not so desperate that he'll go back to Alex. But just to make sure he stays focused on the right thing, I asked Marco Antonio to move into the smaller house in the back of my property, once Rafael decided to move in with Jose. So Marco and I are like roommates, and we have privacy in our own houses. And I can keep an eye on things to ensure Julio and Marco Antonio will have no interference from Alex.

Tommie is another story altogether. He's big time. Major big time. Not only is he still hitched with Tyrell, who's been drafted to play on an NBA team, but he and Renaissance Phoenix are rehearsing for a reunion tour around the country, playing small clubs and doing shows with other late-eighties and early-nineties R&B boy groups. He's got his music career back, even if it's on a limited, C-list basis. He tells me he plans to do the singing and touring thing while Tyrell's playing ball from October through June, so that they can enjoy the summers together as a couple. Tyrell bought a nice home in a gated community in Malibu, and rents places in New York City and Houston for the two of them to meet up in while on the road. They're loving the living-together thing. Tommie's still closeted, as is Tyrell, but I always ask Tyrell for scoop on the boys in the NBA. He says there are some players on the down low who'd surprise me. Some players know it, but they don't talk about it. They just concentrate on the game and work toward that championship ring. One good thing about Tommie's singing group getting back together is it's brought his sister Sylvia and our friend Dennis closer, and they've cleaned up the drugs and can take care of Keesha better. I told him the moment it looks like there are problems, they should send Keesha to me and I'll look after her.

As for me . . . well, what can I say? In some ways, my life is the same script with different characters. I still go out, not as regularly as before I stopped drinking, and I host more gatherings at my house with Cesar. We're dating on a trial basis. It started again when his campus, Pasadena City College, hired me to do an ongoing series of diversity workshops for faculty, staff and students. Cesar somehow got himself appointed chair of campus diversity, and it forced us to work together. It was his passion for social issues, his culture and appreciation of others that attracted me to him all those months ago at Tempo. I knew he couldn't have had time to be dating anyone with all the long hours we spent researching the campus climate on diversity, and one night while eating Chinese takeout, we talked and decided to make a go of it. And made love in his office. Then at my place. And then at his. With protection, of course. He swore he's over Rafael, and I believe him, especially since Rafael and Jose are together now. I know most people wouldn't be able to forgive an affair involving their partner and a good friend. I haven't forgotten. But I'm not going to live in the past on this issue. Am I being stupid? We'll see what happens. I pray on it and tell Cesar he should to do the same, so that we're staying focused on us. The best part—I've met Cesar's family. *La familia* Reyes approves of me, except for Cesar's twin sister that I never knew he had. Despite that, it seems they love me more than the legal spouses of his brothers and sisters. I think they've figured out that by now we're more than just professional colleagues which is how Cesar introduced me to them.

And now I can put the others behind, including the man who I thought was the love of my life at Stanford, Shawn Bentley, whom I now call affectionately "Doc." He's in my life, but as a good friend. Too many years went by without any contact, and though we tried to see what it would be like trying to date, we realized it can't work. Too gone, too long. I'm cool with it, though. If it wasn't for going to his place for dinner one night, I never would have found this house. Thanks to Doc, I'm on a healthy eating plan, which is helping me lose lots of fat and keep lean muscle. Doc is also helping me keep the motivation up on being sober, since I don't want to go to those meetings. My hopes of dating Dante went out the window when I started the interim job at USC and discovered he's been employed as a student assistant for my office for two years. Can't date a student. But we have started a friendship outside of work, and he and I talk about his whole process of sexuality.

My family is doing well, too. I went home to Detroit for Solomon's wedding in the summer, which was interesting to say the least, since I was invited to attend, but not be in the wedding. The good old Hemmings family "Image Management" always comes into play when I'm in town. I went anyway, because I love my brother, and also because I wanted to see my sister's new twins—the girl, Kendall, and the boy, Taylor. I think it's kinda funny that my normally gender-sensitive and homophobic family has fallen in love with such androgynous names for the new grandkids. There is hope.

My friend Chris Aquino brings me over another full virgin Hurricane drink, which is basically fruit punch, and thanks me for throwing this New Orleans birthday and New Year's bash. We go out to the dance floor and meet up with Cesar, Marco Antonio, Rafael, Jose and all our friends and exes. This is a picture of L.A. we don't get to see on the news nor do we experience much—people of various cultures and ethnicities truly enjoying and valuing the company of each other and leaving all the baggage at home. This is a picture of gay L.A. we don't see—men of color who like other men of color, and without drama.

When the midnight hour closes in, my boys—Cesar, Marco Antonio, Rafael, Jose and Chris—circle around me, and we raise our glasses to toast the birthday boys, the New Year and our wish for continued friendship, prosperity and nothing but good times ahead. We make a pledge to make no more New Year's resolutions. Obviously, if I'd kept mine, I wouldn't be standing here with Cesar.

"Here's to Keith and the end of the ten-year drought!"

"Here's to Cesar for ending it."

"Here's to Marco Antonio and Keith for making it to age thirty and proving you can still have a life after the twenties are over."

"Here's to Rafael for still being a cute twenty-something. Just wait 'til the metabolism slows down in a few years!"

"Amen!"

Cesar hugs me from behind and kisses the top of my head. "Happy birthday and Happy New Year. I love you, *moreno*."

"Same to you, Cesar."

¡Salud!